A SECRET TO DIE FOR

BALDWIN'S SHORE
BOOK 4

ELISE NOBLE

Published by Undercover Publishing Limited

v2

ISBN: 978-1-912888-72-6

Edited by Nikki Mentges, NAM Editorial

Cover design by Abigail Sins

www.undercover-publishing.com

www.elise-noble.com

Three things cannot be long hidden: the sun, the moon, and the truth.

— *BUDDHA*

Sing like no one is listening.
Love like you've never been hurt.
Dance like nobody's watching,
and live like it's heaven on earth.

— *ANONYMOUS*

1

SARA

Once upon a time, someone had gifted me a T-shirt with the slogan "Sorry I'm late, I didn't want to come," and that was exactly how I felt about going to Casa de Salsa tonight. I hadn't worn the shirt, though. That would have been rude, and these folks were my friends. No matter how much I wanted to crawl into bed with a good book and a pint of chocolate chip ice cream, I'd smile and dance for hours rather than admit it.

I was good at that—hiding my feelings, I mean. Although I was good at dancing too, something that nobody in Baldwin's Shore, the town that I lived in but had never truly called home, knew about. I'd been keeping secrets since I was a little girl. Mom had taught me well.

"The music sounds amazing," Paulo squealed from beside me in the back seat as we cruised along the street outside the bar, looking for a parking spot. "Just wait until you see what these hips can do."

"Yeah, I'll wait," Blue said. "I can wait forever."

From what I'd seen so far, snark seemed to be Blue Carver's default operating mode. She was a newcomer in town, a smart, abrasive private investigator who was like a dog with a bone when she sank her teeth into a mystery. The rest of my family hated her with a passion, which was enough reason to like her, although she didn't seem too fond of me. I honestly couldn't blame her. The Baldwin surname was a curse.

"Oh, don't be such a sourpuss." Paulo rooted through his giant purse. "Look, I brought castanets for everyone."

Darla glanced around from the driver's seat. Since she was teetotal, she'd offered us a ride to Coos Bay tonight, and the fact that she'd been waiting outside the gates at the Baldwin estate earlier was the main reason I hadn't chickened out of coming.

"Aren't castanets for flamenco dancing, hun?" she asked.

"Uh... Are you sure?"

Blue snorted.

Up ahead, a station wagon turned on its blinker and pulled out into traffic.

"Oh, thank goodness," Darla muttered, then set about reversing into the space. It took her three tries, which was six fewer tries than it would have taken me. However much I detested driving, I disliked parallel parking more.

"Nearly there. How far are we from the kerb?"

Blue cracked her door open to check. "We're good."

As soon as Darla turned off the engine, Paulo leapt out of the car, his sequinned black pants sparkling under the streetlights. Those pants were my worst nightmare. Between them and the see-through shirt unbuttoned halfway down his chest, everyone would be staring at him. Although maybe that wouldn't be such a bad thing? At least they wouldn't be staring at me. I much preferred to fade into the shadows, out of sight, out of mind.

Would there be a crowd in the bar tonight? Hopefully, there'd be a crowd.

I hadn't danced for years, not since I left Virginia. When I was young, I'd taken ballroom and Latin classes and loved them, but those classes had come to an abrupt end along with the rest of life as I knew it three weeks before my tenth birthday. Ever since then, I'd been trying to piece my future back together, but each time I fit a few broken shards into place, more fell out.

Case in point? I'd finally made some friends in my not-so-hometown, but this afternoon, my twin cousins had fired me from the company I practically ran for them.

And I still didn't understand why these people were suddenly being so nice to me. Why Brooke and Romi had started taking me out for coffee, why Paulo had made me a bracelet last week, or why Addy kept inviting me to parties I never attended. Even Blue was reasonably civil, and although I'd known Darla for years—she'd helped to care for my grandfather before he passed away—we'd never been super close.

If Brooke hadn't been involved, I might have suspected I was the butt of a cruel joke. An elaborate April Fools' prank, perhaps, although April first was still over a month away.

But Brooke didn't have a nasty bone in her body. Kindness was her superpower. After what my family had done to her boyfriend's, she had every reason to avoid me, but last month, in a heart-to-heart over tacos at La Cantina, she'd promised that nobody held my appalling luck in the genetic lottery against me. *You can choose your friends, but you can't choose your family*, she'd said, and boy, was that the truth. I'd had zero say in where I ended up after my parents died.

Paulo sashayed along the street ahead of us, his ass twinkling. Fun was his middle name. Blue looked more... resigned. Behind me, Darla dropped her car key and cursed under her breath—not proper cursing, just "heck"—and her muumuu billowed out as she bent to root around in the gutter.

No, I definitely didn't want to be here. But sitting at home would be worse, even though I'd moved into the pool house at the beginning of the year. The building itself was beautiful—a single-storey guest suite fronted by Grecian columns that looked out over clear blue water—but no amount of elegant architecture could squelch the fact that the whole estate was bathed in bad vibes. Officially, the place was called The Lookout, but locals just called it the "Baldwin place," and it always felt as if the ghosts of everyone my ancestors had wronged were hanging around, watching me. And maybe somebody else was too.

"C'mon, slowpoke." Paulo grabbed my hand and pulled me into Casa de Salsa. "We're late."

Only by five minutes because Darla had gotten stuck behind a semi for miles. Overtaking wasn't her thing. But the others were already waiting at a table in the corner— Brooke and Luca, Romi, Aaron, and Addy. I'd gone to school with all of them, although I was the youngest by a year.

Brooke crushed me in a hug, and Addy followed suit. Romi acted a little more reserved—I still got a hug, but she always felt so delicate. As if she might break if I squeezed too hard. Aaron kissed me on the cheek, polite as always, and Luca gave me a brotherly pat on the shoulder. I almost cried. They acted more like family than my own family—my new friends were sometimes pushy, occasionally overwhelming, always supportive. But they could vanish in an instant. I wouldn't let myself grow too used to their company.

"The beginner class starts in half an hour," Addy announced. "I've ordered mojitos for everyone."

Darla raised a hand.

"Everyone except Darla. You get a nojito."

"You're sure it doesn't contain alcohol?"

Addy ran a finger down the menu. "It's club soda, sugar, lime juice, and mint. Plus the server's gonna bring a whole bunch of tapas dishes after the class."

This time, Romi held up a hand, but Addy answered before she could speak.

"Yes, there are plenty of vegan options."

Casa de Salsa was a cavernous riot of colour and noise in the midst of an identity crisis. According to the website, the bar's owner was a former salsa champion, but the band on stage was playing samba music, and the walls were painted with sugar skulls. A banner above the bar read *Let your feet take you to a new place*, which could have been Cuba or Brazil or Mexico or even Spain, seeing as our server was wearing a ruffled flamenco skirt. And the table itself was shaped like Venezuela. Brooke, Romi, and Addy were sitting on an orange velvet banquette near Caracas while the rest of us got repurposed beer kegs to perch on.

"How was California?" Blue asked Romi.

"Freezing. They wanted me to walk out of the ocean in a bikini, and by the end of the shoot, I was shivering under one of those foil blankets they give to marathon runners while I googled the symptoms of hypothermia."

"And?"

"And what?"

"And did you have hypothermia?" Blue rolled her eyes. "Is your brain still frozen?"

"Probably."

"Probably your brain's still frozen? Or probably you had hypothermia?"

"Both. I asked the creative director if there was anyone with medical training on set, and he told me to stop being so melodramatic. Cue more rumours about me being difficult to work with."

Romi Mendez was a bona fide supermodel. She'd always been slender, but when she hit thirteen, she'd suddenly shot up several inches and begun turning heads. Now, she flew all over the world to walk on runways and star in ad campaigns. She'd stayed away from Baldwin's Shore for years, and I assumed she'd flown the coop for good, that she'd decided she was too good for the tiny town and become a New York gal. But last year, she'd hooked up with Aaron—who'd graduated law school and returned to Oregon a year and a half ago—and moved into his apartment. And I realised that apart from the fantastic outfits she wore now, she hadn't changed much at all.

"There are pictures already," Paulo told her. "Your left boob's TikTok account went viral today." He checked his phone. "Eighty-seven thousand views, sixteen thousand likes, and it's still climbing."

Romi buried her head in her hands. "If I ever consider

putting on swimwear again, somebody handcuff me to a radiator."

Aaron gave her a side hug. "You mean in a professional capacity, right? What about vacations? I mean, I still want to stare at your boobs."

A low growl rumbled in Luca's throat. "That's my sister you're talking about."

"Shit. Sorry, buddy. But, you know…"

"Why does your left boob have a TikTok account?" Blue asked.

"A fan started it."

"What about the right boob?"

"I've always been too afraid to ask. I mean, I've measured them a hundred times, and they're basically the same size and shape." She puffed out her chest. "Am I missing something?"

No, but the man at the next table was. His mouth. He was staring so hard, he poured his drink down his chin.

"They're both perfect," Aaron assured Romi, and Luca clenched his fists.

"Can we quit talking about my sister's boobs?" he grumbled.

"Take a chill pill," Paulo told him. "Can't you see Romi needs reassurance? Sweetie, you're boobilicious, and I'm allowed to say that because I prefer dicks."

Brooke tried to kick him under the table, but she missed and caught my shin instead. I let out an involuntary yelp, and she clapped both hands over her mouth.

"Sorry! I'm so sorry."

"It's okay, really."

I took a long swallow of my mojito and nearly poked my eye out with a cocktail umbrella, but I managed to avoid spluttering when rum burned my throat. Whoever mixed these drinks sure had been generous with the liquor.

"So," Brooke asked brightly. "Who's gonna join the beginner class? Has anyone apart from Addy actually tried salsa dancing before?"

Everyone else shook their heads, and I tentatively raised a hand.

"You took a salsa class?" Brooke looked surprised, and so did the others, which was quite understandable, considering I barely left the house for anything except work. I'd pushed myself out of my comfort zone and started painting lessons at Darla's craft store last year, but I still felt uncomfortable in social situations.

"A couple of classes, years ago," I clarified. "Before I moved to Baldwin's Shore."

"Oh, right." An awkward silence fell. "So, uh..."

I should have said no.

"I'll take the beginner class."

Brooke's relief was palpable. "Great. That's great. You could dance with Paulo, or a guy Addy knows from the intermediate class offered to help out. That'll only leave us one man left to find, and—"

Darla cut in. "Don't you worry about me, hun. I'll just sit here and enjoy the music."

"You don't want to dance?"

"No, no, I have two left feet." She held up her nojito. "I'm happy watching."

"I guess that solves one problem. Sara? Who do you want to dance with?"

The answer was easy. Paulo might have been a walking disco ball, but he was sweet and he was safe. Maybe Addy's friend was lovely too, but I couldn't take the chance that he wasn't. I preferred to keep strangers at arm's length. And besides, Paulo would drive Blue crazy. She threatened to chop off his body parts on a regular basis, and although she hadn't followed through yet, the night was still young.

"I'll dance with Paulo."

He beamed at me. "We're gonna set the dance floor on fire, doll."

That's what I was afraid of.

2

SARA

"*N*ow we'll put together everything we've learned for the next track. If you forget the steps, don't forget to watch Lorena and Joaquin on the stage."

After nearly an hour of dancing, the only thing burning was my toes. Paulo knew how to move his hips, I'd give him that, but his feet were a whole other story. The teacher said go left, Paulo went right. The teacher said go right, and Paulo went left. He joked that next time, he'd bring a pair of gloves with L and R written on them—probably in glitter glue—so he wouldn't forget which way was which. Next time? If there was a next time, I'd be wearing steel toecaps, and I'd definitely opt to dance with Addy's friend. He looked about forty, and twice I'd seen Blue move his hand off her ass, but at least he hadn't managed to crush any of her metatarsals yet.

"Feel the beat," the teacher instructed. "Let the music speak to your soul. Ready? One, two, three... Five, six, seven..."

Ouch.

"Sorry," Paulo said as he stepped on my foot and

bumped into the lady next to us. "I messed up the start again."

"You want me to lead?"

"No, I've got this." He really didn't. "I love this song. It's just so happy. Do you think the original version is on Spotify?"

"Probably? I'm going to cross your lead, okay?"

"So I should…?"

"Turn clockwise. No, no, *clockwise*. The other way."

Thank the stars above that I'd worn ankle boots instead of open-toed sandals. I mean, I'd considered wearing something a bit more "dance shoe," but I figured that would only lead to questions I didn't want to answer. I was the girl who favoured black pants, a white shirt, and sensible footwear. Tonight was no exception. In life's performance, I was a stagehand, and that suited me just fine.

Once, I'd dreamed of being the leading lady.

But then everything had changed.

By the time we made it back to the table, I needed to soak my feet in the pitcher of margaritas that Addy had just ordered, preferably with extra ice. Although drinking the entire jugful was also tempting. Usually, I edged toward the Darla end of the scale when it came to alcohol consumption, but I had nothing to get up for tomorrow morning, so why not stay in bed with a hangover? I drained the glass and gave myself brain freeze.

"Salsa is harder than I thought," Brooke said, leaning against Luca. "Sara, you're good. Are you sure you only took a couple of classes?"

Okay, so I'd actually taken gold at the national junior Latin dance championship in my age category—under ten; I'd been so young—but that was all in the past. I didn't dance anymore. Dancing hurt, and I didn't just mean my toes. My heart ached for what I'd lost. My parents, the hobby I'd loved, my fragile self-confidence. For the longest time, I thought I'd lost my dance partner too, but five years ago, Marcin had been competing in Portland, and I'd driven up there on impulse just to watch. He'd spotted me in the crowd, missed a turn, and nearly dropped his partner. Guilt had sent me running out the door, but he'd caught up with me in the parking lot. There had been plenty of tears that night. Plenty of hugs too. We'd stayed in touch, but only over WhatsApp because Marcin and his boyfriend ran a dance school in Gdańsk now.

"The classes were a long, long time ago," I told Brooke. "But I guess a few bits came back to me."

Addy topped off my glass. "Have you ever tried burlesque?"

I spluttered margarita. "No! Of course not. Isn't that basically stripping?"

"Nuh-uh. It's more about body positivity and feathers. There's an ex-Vegas showgirl who moved to North Bend, and she's running classes. You know, workshops for bachelorette parties and that kind of thing."

"Bachelorette parties? Who's getting married?"

"Nobody yet, but I bet she'd do a regular party if we asked. We could use Aaron's apartment. It's plenty big enough."

Aaron and Romi's apartment occupied the first floor of a former car dealership. "Big" was an understatement. "Cavernous" was more like it. Brooke and Luca lived on the second floor, but their apartment was smaller thanks to a roof terrace that took up a third of the space.

"Do I get a say in this?" Aaron asked.

"Nope."

Luca shook his head, grinning. "Buddy, that's the wrong question. What we need to know is whether we can watch?"

"Absolutely not," Addy told him. "So, who's in?"

"Can I come?" Paulo bounced on his keg-stool. "I'm excellent with feathers."

"It depends if you're in town. Aren't you and Darla heading to Virginia soon?"

"On Wednesday evening." Four days from now. "Maybe we could do the workshop when I come back?"

"Romi, when's your next modelling job?"

"I'm flying to Paris for Fashion Week tomorrow."

"You're only in the US for two days? One day in California and one day here?"

"The swimwear company offered more money than the designers at Milan Fashion Week, and I wanted to see you guys. Oh, and Aaron," she added seemingly as an afterthought, but she was grinning. "I'll fly back right after the final show, I promise."

"Okay, Sara, what does your schedule look like? Don't you have the masked ball thing coming up?"

I'd hoped to avoid talking about that tonight, but I couldn't lie, could I? They'd find out the truth sooner or later. Probably sooner. Gossip travelled faster than a bullet in Baldwin's Shore, and just lately, the bullets had been travelling pretty freaking quickly as well.

"I'm not organising the ball anymore."

"It got cancelled?"

"No." I took a deep breath and swallowed Paulo's mojito. "No, I got fired."

Puzzled looks.

"Fired? From your own company?" Brooke asked. "Is this a joke?"

"LKB Events belongs to Lillian and Kayleigh."

When I graduated high school armed with a grand idea and a dream of working in the events industry, my résumé hadn't been good enough to land a role at any reputable business—why did every entry-level position require a college degree and ten years of experience?—and I hadn't had the connections or the funds to get a new venture off the ground alone. But my twin cousins had both of those things. While I'd spent my teenage years studying, they'd been partying, plus they'd received a reasonable-sized inheritance from their grandfather on their mom's side. LKB was born. They liked my ideas, and I figured I could work for them for a couple of years and then use the knowledge I gained to get a better job.

But then Grandpa had thrown a wrench in the works, and staying with LKB had seemed like the best option at the time. The twins had promised we'd run the company as a three-way split, and in those days, I'd been young and—okay—naive enough to trust them. Blood was thicker than water, my uncle always said. But then they'd stabbed me in the back.

To be fair, I couldn't have gotten LKB off the ground without Kayleigh and Lillian's help—they'd provided the initial capital, and our first dozen bookings had come from their friends. But in the years that followed, they'd styled themselves as "brand ambassadors," which basically meant they chatted to guests while I liaised with clients, booked venues, negotiated with staff and suppliers, created project plans, monitored finances, and dealt with any hiccups.

"Are you serious?" Addy asked. "But you do all the work? Why would they fire you?"

"We had some creative differences."

"You mean you created, and they didn't?"

A giggle escaped—that was the alcohol's influence.

"They have no idea how much effort goes into running an event."

But they were about to find out. The masked ball at the Peninsula Resort was their baby now. They could either step up and do some work or drop the ball entirely—both literally and figuratively. I was the organised one. The first thing I did every morning was update my to-do list, and I never went anywhere without my trusty bullet journal.

"Will they close the company? Or try to run things themselves?" Brooke asked.

Who knew? Only time would tell.

"The next few events will go ahead with no problems—I already planned those down to the last trash pickup. The masked ball in two weeks' time will be their first big challenge. I'd love to be a fly on the wall when Lillian realises she forgot to include a gluten-free option on the Banquet Event Order, or that the AV team doesn't have enough power strips because Kayleigh has no idea those are supplied by us or the hotel and not by the contractor."

Would they remember to hire additional valets for parking? That had been at the top of my to-do list for Monday morning. Brilliant Blooms was expecting final confirmation of the floral arrangements too—the client wanted a flower arch for photographs. Photographs... The photographer was another last-minute addition, and finding one had been another item on Monday's list. The Peninsula did have its own small events team, but they were more used to organising corporate retreats than a potential clown show like Hadley Carpenter's twenty-fifth birthday party. She wanted a ball, and since she was even more spoiled than my cousins, her daddy was paying for a ball.

Blue shrugged. "So go be a fly on the wall."

"I can't just walk in there."

"Why not? All the guests will be wearing masks, won't they?"

"Well, I don't have an invite."

"From what you've said, nobody's gonna be checking those anyway."

Was it possible? No, no, of course I couldn't go.

"I don't have anything to wear."

My wardrobe was elegant only in its simplicity. If I bought ten pairs of black pants and ten white shirts, I didn't need to worry about what to put on in the mornings, plus it gave me the added advantage of being mistaken for a server. Nobody ever gave them a second glance. Evening wear meant leggings, cute T-shirts, and sweaters chosen for warmth rather than style.

Paulo slung an arm around my shoulders. "Sweet cheeks, you think we can't fix you up with an outfit in two weeks? What do you need? A ballgown? A Venetian mask?"

"Uh, maybe? It's not a masquerade ball as such, more of a costume party. Anything goes, as long as you're wearing a mask. I heard a bunch of the men are planning to dress up as superheroes."

Kayleigh and Lillian were planning to wear Mardi Gras outfits. They'd already bought matching ruffled corset dresses, spike heels, and jewelled masks, plus decided on a colour scheme for their make-up. Their hair, spray tan, and nail appointments were booked, and a driver would take them to the hotel so they could both indulge their love of cocktails. As far as I was aware, they'd given zero thought to the actual event arrangements, even though I'd copied them in on all the emails discussing the logistics and sent them a draft checklist.

"We can do a costume. Darla and I still have half a week

before we leave for Virginia, and Romi must have some fancy shoes. What size are your feet?"

"Uh, a seven."

"Romi's an eight, but we can pad the toes."

Romi got on board with the idea, unfortunately. "I have plenty of samples, and sometimes designers send the wrong sizes. I can definitely find shoes."

"Brie might have a dress?" Brooke suggested. "She had to rent a whole other room for the overflow from her closet."

"I can't wear one of Brie's dresses," I protested.

"Why not? You're about the same size."

"Because...because..."

Because Brie was an actual freaking princess. Somehow, she'd landed up in Baldwin's Shore and fallen in love with a guy I went to school with. When Brie wasn't attending to her royal duties in Scandinavia, she lived with Colt and his daughter in the Royal Suite at the Peninsula while they waited for construction work on their dream home to finish. The two of them had bought the old paper mill on the outskirts of town, and judging by the number of trucks that drove in and out, they were building a whole new palace. Brie and Colt's happy ending was proof that fairy tales really did come true.

"Then that's settled," Paulo announced. "We'll take care of the costume, and you can go watch Kayleigh and Lillian fall flat on their ugly faces. I bet they'll give you your job back within a month. No way can they manage without you."

"But would you want to work with them again?" Brooke asked.

"I...I don't know," I said honestly.

In truth, I was still shocked that they'd fired me. But I also understood why they'd done it, and it wasn't just about the fact that they wanted us to offer a wedding planning service and I hated dealing with bridezillas. No, the problems went back further, all the way to our grandpa's death. To the day his will had been read. To the conditions he'd set for inheritance.

Aaron spoke up. "If you return to your old job, you should put safeguards in place. Ask for stock options or negotiate a golden parachute."

"I'm not sure they'd agree to that."

"Then you could start your own business. You have the contacts."

That was true, but I still didn't have the capital. Not enough to start from scratch. The three of us had agreed to reinvest most of the profits to grow the business with a view to selling before Grandpa's deadline. Now if there was anything left of the company in two years, Kayleigh and Lillian would get every last cent. And I'd tried to safeguard myself, I *had*. I'd made my cousins sign an agreement to say that as long as LKB met certain financial targets, I'd receive a hefty bonus in the final year before the target date; I'd just never dreamed that they'd terminate my employment before the bonus clause kicked in. What a freaking mess. I should have known they'd screw me over. Treachery was coded into their DNA.

"I need a few days to think things through."

"That's a sensible—"

"But you're going to the ball, right?" Paulo interrupted.

"I'm still not sure that's a good idea."

Darla took a sip of her nojito. "A little schadenfreude can be a wonderful thing, hun."

"Almost as delicious as this margarita," Addy said. "Hey, it's time for my class. Just promise you'll go to the party."

"Okay, okay, I'll go. But I have to leave by midnight."

"Why?"

"Because that's when everyone takes their masks off."

I'd designed the invitations myself, thick navy-blue card stock with *Masks Off at Midnight* embossed on the front in gold. I'd need to get the heck out of there before the big reveal.

"This is gonna be great. Can you take photos of the terrible twins doing manual labour? Like, maybe serving drinks or something? Or valet parking cars?"

I was regretting my decision already.

"I'm not going to draw any attention to myself."

That's what I said, but like so many aspects of my life, nothing went according to plan.

3

SARA

"**W**hatever happens, you look amazing." Brooke glanced across from the driver's seat of her Toyota compact. She'd offered to drive me because I didn't want to risk my car being spotted at the Peninsula. "I'd kill for those shoes."

So much for staying under the radar. Paulo had found inspiration in my midnight cut-off and created a mood board that took up one whole wall in the break room at the Craft Cabin. The theme? Cinder-freaking-rella. Brie had donated a powder-blue ballgown that must have cost a fortune, Darla had altered it to fit me, and Romi had dug out a blonde wig, blue contact lenses, and a pair of designer shoes. Paulo had stuck over three thousand tiny crystals on the shoes—no kidding, he'd counted—and added so many feathers to my Venetian mask that I felt as if I'd escaped from a zoo. Forget salsa; I'd be doing a mating dance with a parrot.

"Everyone's gonna stare." And quite possibly be blinded by my pumps too.

"But nobody will ever recognise you; that's the important thing."

Okay, I had to concede Brooke was right on that point. Heck, I barely recognised myself. Addy had spent nearly two hours doing my make-up and pinning my fake hair into an elaborate updo. My skin was flawless, my cheeks were a delicate shade of pink, and my lips shimmered when the light hit them. Brooke had manicured my nails, and she'd even painted my toes red to match, although nobody could see them. And the jewellery... Nobody would tell me where the necklace and earrings had come from, but I had to give them back to Brooke at the end of the night. The sparkles might even be from genuine sapphires.

"As long as I keep the mask on and leave before midnight."

"I'll be outside at eleven thirty, and if you need me there any earlier, just send a message. How's the organising going? Did Kayleigh and Lillian mess up yet?"

"They suddenly realised that people had dietary requirements, but it was too late for the catering team to order more food, so the twins had to run to the big grocery store in Coos Bay this afternoon." A giggle burst out at the thought of the two of them pushing a shopping cart. Usually, they got groceries delivered, or Uncle EJ made the trip, but today, Kayleigh and Lillian had been forced to interact with the rest of us mortals. "Finding what they needed took ages because they had no idea where to look, and they ran out of time to do their make-up."

"I wish I'd been there to see it," Brooke said.

"Me too."

"You missed the drama?"

"I haven't set foot in the main house since they fired me, but Parker told me they headed out late, barefaced and bickering."

My cousin Parker was the only member of the family I still spoke to, probably because a third of them were enjoying room and board courtesy of the great state of Oregon. Easton the Third and Aunt Marianna were both horrible people. And ever since his wife and youngest son went to jail, Uncle EJ had been avoiding me. Parker said Marianna was fond of bad-mouthing me from behind bars, that she blamed me in part for her predicament, but as usual, she was lying. It wasn't that I hadn't tried to bring her down, but ultimately, she'd been responsible for her own fate.

"Parker isn't fond of the twins?" Brooke asked.

"I don't think so."

"I don't really understand him."

"Neither do I."

I'd lived with Parker for over sixteen years, and I still had no idea what made him tick. On the surface, my eldest cousin was cold, pragmatic, and a master at self-preservation, but perhaps he had a heart lurking somewhere deep inside? Parker had never joined in with the others when they belittled me, and after Kayleigh and Lillian had done their worst last month, he'd shown up at the pool house late in the evening to tell me that he'd cover my share of the utilities until I found a new job. But I hated the thought of being beholden to Parker. Nothing he gave was a gift.

We drove along Main Street, heading for the Peninsula. The hotel was a new addition to Baldwin's Shore, and it wasn't popular among most of the locals. The owner, Nico Belinsky, was an outsider, a wealthy Russian who'd somehow ended up in our little corner of paradise. Yes, he'd invested a bunch of money and boosted both employment and tourism in the area, but he'd also built his resort on a popular local beauty spot that the previous owner had allowed the public to use for decades.

Brooke made a right turn. "How many people will be at the event tonight?"

"The guest list had three hundred names, but they won't all show up. They never do. Maybe two hundred and fifty will come?"

"How does one person know that many people?"

"I don't think Hadley Carpenter does. There are a bunch of plus-ones, and some of the guests are friends of her parents. Her father does something in politics, and politicians always invite a gazillion people to their events because it's not what you know; it's who you know."

"At least you'll be able to hide in the crowd."

"I'm planning to hang out by the buffet table. Hadley ordered five-star food, and Parker said that Kayleigh and Lillian are on some weird raw vegetable diet this week, so they're not gonna eat teriyaki chicken skewers or crumbed Camembert bites."

Not until midnight, anyway. The two of them would starve all day on their perpetual quest for thinness, and then they'd sneak into the kitchen late in the evening and gorge on carbs. The next morning, I'd have to listen to them complaining about muffin top and belly pooch, and

Kayleigh had tossed out three bathroom scales in the past year because they always had some kind of imaginary fault. One time, I'd suggested she give me a hand because running around at events sure did burn off the calories, and she'd looked at me like I was crazy.

Tonight, she'd undoubtedly be whining about blisters.

A moment later, Brooke pulled up in the shadows just inside the entrance to the Peninsula. I'd have to walk the rest of the way down the driveway, but there were lights at regular intervals, so thankfully I wouldn't break an ankle.

"I'll wait right here for you," Brooke said. "Have a good time. Hope the twins get a large dose of karma."

On impulse, I reached over and gave her a hug. I'd never been a hugger, not with anyone but my mom, but when Brooke returned the gesture, I got a lump in my throat. This "friends" thing was weird. It was like having to learn a whole new language.

A couple of cars slowed to drive past as I walked to the hotel, but nobody stopped me or questioned why I was there. And, as predicted, the twins had forgotten to ask a member of staff to check invitations at the door. I just breezed past, desperately trying to look as if I belonged. And I sort of did. The costumes were spectacular—no last-minute cobbled-together outfits here. I dodged a Queen of Hearts and a sexy devil on my way to the ballroom, but before I got there, I heard a sound that warmed my heart. Karma had arrived early.

"How was I supposed to know you needed a forty-inch-high table?" Kayleigh asked, presumably speaking to the DJ since that had been one of his demands.

"Because I listed it in the rider."

Which was saved in the shared drive for the event. Had Kayleigh bothered to read it? No, of course she hadn't.

"Why didn't you bring your own table?"

"Because I flew here from New York, and the deal was that you either provided an appropriate DJ desk or paid the excess baggage fees. You said you'd provide the desk."

"I definitely didn't."

"Well, somebody at your company did."

The forty-inch DJ desk was in the barn at The Lookout, the one I'd converted to store our equipment. As far as I knew, Kayleigh had never set foot in there.

"Can't you use a regular table? We have plenty of those."

"No, I can't. Either you find me what you promised, or you can handle the music yourself."

I smothered a smile as Frankie Flux strode past me, his eyes hidden behind a pair of mirrored sunglasses. He was a tall guy with a shock of hot-pink hair, and he'd probably need to visit a chiropractor if he tried to play his set on a dinner table the way Kayleigh wanted him to. Still, that was her problem tonight. How would she handle it?

I soon found out.

My phone buzzed with a message, the first time she'd been in touch in two weeks.

KAYLEIGH

Where do I get a forty-inch DJ table?

No "please," no "I'm sorry we fired you," just a question. More of a demand, really. A part of me itched to reply because I hated to see the company I'd created suffer, but if I helped Kayleigh tonight, she'd never learn her lesson. I tucked the phone back into the beaded purse Brooke had lent me and carried on to the ballroom. Let the chips fall where they may.

The band that would entertain the guests for the first two hours was already on stage, playing a Bruno Mars cover.

The quartet was made up of local guys—well, they came from Portland—and I'd hired them to play events in the past. They'd take a break halfway through their set for the birthday girl's father to make his speech, and Hadley's best friend wanted to say a few words too, then dinner would be served in the room next door.

The flower arch was set up in one corner of the ballroom, so at least the twins had managed to get one thing right. A photographer was standing in front, snapping away as groups of girls pouted for the camera. Wait... He wasn't a professional photographer. That was Lillian's friend Cody, and the only thing he was good at was keg stands. Nearly every picture on his social media was blurry. I let out a groan before I could stop myself.

"Bad day?" a voice asked from behind. "Or isn't this your kind of music?"

I turned to find Prince Charming watching me from behind a blue velvet mask. Were his blond hair and blue eyes real? The hair was slicked back with a side part, as if he'd stepped out of either the 1940s or Wall Street. Or Hollywood—he sure did have a movie-star smile. But the smile soon slipped, and he ran his tongue over his teeth.

Crap, I'm staring.

"You don't have anything stuck in your teeth," I blurted.

This is why I stay behind the scenes.

"That's good to hear."

"So, uh, I just need to..."

...to get the hell out of here. Hiding in the bathroom until Brooke came to pick me up seemed like a great idea, and the bathrooms at the Peninsula were better than average. They came with sewing kits, shoe-shine sponges, and perfume samples, plus there was a rest area with a couch. I already regretted coming tonight. There had never been any

question over whether the twins would screw up, so why oh why had I given in to the temptation to witness their mistakes in person?

You know why, Saralisa. Because every day for the past sixteen years, they criticised everything you said and everything you did.

And I was angry. At first after they fired me, I'd been in shock, but little by little, the numbness was turning to fury. The twins had ruined any chance I had of receiving my share of our inheritance, and worse, I couldn't even find another job in this county. Only one events company was hiring, and when I'd given the manager my name, she'd tutted a little and then said that she'd heard I was difficult to work with. Three guesses who'd told her that lie.

Hadley Carpenter strode toward me—at least, I assumed it was Hadley Carpenter. Her features were hidden behind a sugar skull mask and a flower crown that matched the arch in the ballroom, but she was wearing a purple sash with *It's My Birthday!* written across it in ornate gold script. A pink Power Ranger in high-heeled pumps followed in her wake.

"Why isn't the video montage playing?" Hadley asked her sidekick. "Tiffany and Skyler spent hours putting it together, and I gave specific instructions that it should be projected onto the wall above the band."

"I asked one of the organisers, and she said they were having trouble with the laptop."

Trouble with the laptop? More like they forgot to bring it.

"Why didn't someone tell me earlier? *I* could have brought a laptop."

"Kayleigh promised she'd handle it. She said her assistant quit and left her in the lurch, so she's rushed off her feet."

Her assistant had *quit*? The simmering anger turned into a five-alarm fire. Why were those shrews trying so hard to ruin my life when I'd done nothing but help them from the day I arrived in Baldwin's Shore? In elementary school, I'd given them the cookies from my lunch; in middle school, I'd customised their clothing and braided their hair; and in high school, I'd been responsible for completing their assignments, although their GPAs still hadn't been much to write home about because they never listened in class. And this was how they repaid me? By lying?

Screw them.

I lowered my voice conspiratorially. "I heard that the reason Kayleigh's assistant quit is because Kayleigh spent more time in the bar than in the office."

The Power Ranger spun around. "Really? Are you sure?"

"I mean, it's just a rumour, but I heard it from my bestie's sister, and she's right, like, ninety-five percent of the time."

"Oh my gosh."

"Five bucks says Kayleigh starts on the free cocktails before ten p.m." I smiled sweetly. "If you speak with Ingrid at the reception desk, I'm sure she'll find you a laptop to use for the video thing."

"Wow, thanks."

I hurried into the bathroom before they could ask who I was and why I'd crashed the party, and as I locked myself in a bathroom stall, a tiny smile tugged at the corners of my lips. Revenge was sweet, and I was just getting started.

4
____

SARA

"The Mardi Gras girl is hot," gym-phobic Batman said, then waved at the bartender. "Two more beers over here, buddy, plus a straw for Deadpool."

Deadpool had modified his mask to allow him to drink, but eating was going to be a problem. What was he planning to do? Wait until midnight and then hoover up the leftovers? I checked my watch—ten to eight. Still at least five hours of the party to go, and the twins were looking delightfully harried. Every time they tried to grab a beverage or stop to chat with one of the guests, somebody asked them a logistical question. Or complained about something. Or wanted directions to the bathroom.

But somehow, Lillian still managed to look good as she went down in flames.

Deadpool turned to watch her speed-walk toward the kitchen—she needed to check the food was on time—and gave a muffled whistle.

"I'd let her breathe hot and heavy over me any time."

"I heard she's wearing three pairs of Spanx," I told him. "It's a miracle she can breathe at all."

Batman snorted. "Spanx? Those giant underwear things?"

"If you're planning a three-way in the bathroom, allow plenty of time."

"Thanks for the advice." He looked me up and down, this time with more interest. I didn't miss the way his gaze hovered on my cleavage—cleavage that came thanks to the fancy padded bra Romi had sourced. "Hey, Cinderella. You want a three-way in the bathroom?"

My mouth opened, but no sound came out. He was joking, right?

But then a weird thing happened. Batman and Deadpool both backed away in a hurry without waiting for their drinks. Batman gave a little wave of...apology? Regret? What had I done? Did my breath smell? I'd brushed my teeth right before I left home.

"Can I buy you a drink, Cinderella?"

I swivelled to find Prince Charming leaning against the bar. He grinned.

"Are my teeth still okay?" he asked.

Instinct got the better of me, and I pushed him away. Or at least, I tried to. He didn't move an inch, probably because his chest was made of granite.

"Stop it," I told him.

"You wound me. About that drink?"

"This is a free bar. I can get my own drink."

"And there I was trying to be a gentleman."

I recognised his type. I'd come across a hundred Prince Charmings at the events I coordinated—although most of them didn't wear gaudy gold epaulettes—and he was no gentleman. A more appropriate noun would be "player" or "womaniser" or "manwhore." Pheromones oozed from his pores along with expensive cologne, and if Kayleigh and

Lillian hadn't been running around after Hadley Carpenter, they'd have been basking in his aura, fluttering their eyelashes and knocking back his free drinks.

Instead of replying, I turned to the bartender. "Could I get a glass of water, please?"

"Certainly, ma'am."

"Water? We're at the party of the year, and you're drinking water?"

"This is hardly the party of the year."

"Really? But it said so on the invite."

No lie; it had. The word "humble" wasn't in Hadley Carpenter's vocabulary.

"Hadley is prone to exaggeration."

He barked out a laugh. "That much is true. I mean, there isn't even any food."

"The food will be served right after the speeches."

"Speeches?" Prince Charming groaned. "Who makes a speech at a birthday party?"

"The man holding the purse strings."

Or maybe not.

Kayleigh and Lillian stepped onto the stage, beaming now that they were in their favourite place—the limelight. Kayleigh tapped the mic, and everyone winced at the screech of feedback.

"Ladies and gentlemen, thank you all for coming tonight to help us celebrate Hadley's twenty-fifth birthday. Hadley and I—and Lillian—have been friends since we met on Pierre's yacht, which was a night to remember, I'm sure you'll agree, but at least this evening, there's no risk of anyone falling overboard." Hadley's cronies laughed. Her father didn't. "Over the past four years, we've watched Hadley grow from a newbie make-up influencer into a travel blogger with over two million followers, and what a journey that's been. It hasn't been an easy path—who can forget the lost luggage in Tanzania or the thing with the monkey in Marrakesh?—but Hadley has come out the other side stronger and more beautiful than before. Please join me in raising your glasses to wish our lovely friend the best birthday ever!"

Applause erupted as Kayleigh drank her entire cocktail in one go. Did she think her job was over now? Because it was just beginning. Clean-up after an event like this one was no easy task, and I wasn't only talking about the trash. By midnight, at least one woman would have lost her shoes, someone would be on the verge of alcohol poisoning, and there wouldn't be enough cabs available.

"And now I'm thrilled to announce that dinner is served in the Redwood Room."

Wait, what? Tobias Carpenter hadn't made his speech yet, and he was looking, well, mutinous. The guests moved en masse in the direction of food, and Hadley's father made a beeline for the twins. Oh, I had to hear this.

"Excuse me," I said to Prince Charming. "I need to...uh, be somewhere else."

One of the hotel staff was sweeping up a broken glass next to the stage—someone had dropped it in the stampede to the buffet. What was her name? Jeannie? No, Jeannine. She wasn't a local, and I'd only spoken with her once or twice before, so I headed in her direction on the assumption that she wouldn't recognise me.

"Excuse me?"

She looked up, her eyes tired. "Can I help you, ma'am?"

"Do you have a lost property office?"

"Did you lose something?"

"My bracelet. I'm not sure when, but I definitely had it when I arrived."

"What does it look like?"

"It's silver with blue crystals."

"We don't have a lost property office, but if you wait right here, I can go ask the duty manager."

"I'd really appreciate that."

"I'll be back in a moment."

Staff at the Peninsula went above and beyond, and asking the duty manager about lost property was standard operating procedure. Now I had the perfect excuse to hang around by the stage and listen to Tobias Carpenter berating Kayleigh. Lillian had seen trouble coming and made a hasty exit, the same way she always did. Nothing was *ever* Lillian's fault.

"What happened to my time slot?"

Kayleigh looked at Mr. Carpenter blankly.

"For my speech," he prompted.

"The... Oh, yeah, the speech. I, uh..." Forgot it entirely? "I moved it to after dinner."

"Nobody wants to listen to speeches after dinner. I specifically requested the pre-dinner slot to wish my little girl a happy birthday, and you hijacked my time."

"Well, when was *I* supposed to wish her a happy birthday?"

Me, me, me. Kayleigh was the most self-centred person I'd ever met. She'd inherited her mom's ego, while Lillian got the spiteful streak.

"At the end of the night, after you'd run the event to the agreed timetable."

"It was just a speech. Why don't you get a drink and loosen up? They're free."

"They're not free. I'm footing the bar bill. And if you think I'm forking out for your unilateral timetable revisions and bad attitude, you can think again."

Kayleigh stayed silent for a moment as his words sank in. Did she even understand what "unilateral" meant? Finally, it dawned on her that she might not get paid, and she resorted to her default mode: whining.

"Hey, you can't do that. We signed a contract."

Tobias Carpenter turned away. "Sue me," he said over his shoulder.

Did Kayleigh realise he was a lawyer specialising in commercial litigation? I had to assume not. She hurried after him, still complaining and totally unaccustomed to not getting her own way. In the battle of Tobias versus the evil twins, I knew who I'd be cheering for. Hashtag Team Tobias, rah, rah, rah. Okay, so I'd quit the junior cheer squad when I was eight years old to focus on dance, but I'd still be willing to pick up a pair of pom-poms if Tobias followed through on his threat.

I was about to follow and see if I could overhear any other delicious snippets of Kayleigh's comeuppance when I spotted her cell phone on the edge of the DJ's makeshift desk—she'd set up a regular table and stacked books from the hotel library under the legs to achieve the required height. Did Nico know about the sacrifices his leatherbound hardcovers were making? I very much doubted it. On impulse, I swiped the phone and hid it in the folds of my dress to pile a little more pressure on my cousin. When she noticed it was missing, she'd freak. She wouldn't be able to call Lillian, or post to Instagram, or... Hmm, Instagram... All of her #nofilter pictures came courtesy of careful photoshopping—maybe I could add something slightly more realistic? One of her many duck-face selfie outtakes? She always took a hundred shots before she settled on the final version.

"I'm afraid nobody found the bracelet, ma'am, but if you leave your number, someone will call if it shows up."

Jeannine offered me a lost property form and a pen, so I shoved the phone into my tiny purse and conjured up a smile.

"Thank you, I appreciate it."

Instead of my own number, I jotted down the number for the Craft Cabin—I knew it by heart because I bought a lot of supplies there. Or at least, I used to before I was unceremoniously fired for refusing to plan Charmaine Wilson's wedding, which promised to be an *absolute* shitshow. How long before Kayleigh noticed she didn't have her phone? Only a minute or two. She couldn't—

"What's your name?" Jeannine asked. "I should add that."

"S...Lisa."

"Slisa?"

Crap, I was terrible at subterfuge. I'd almost told her my real freaking name. "Just Lisa."

Although Lisa wasn't much better. I mean, it was also my real name; I just didn't use it. Not anymore. Not since I arrived in Baldwin's Shore and Justine Baldwin told me that Saralisa was too much of a mouthful, and so was Baldwin-Forlani. I would henceforth be known as Sara Baldwin, she'd decided. It would help me to "fit in." I'd gone along with the plan because nine-year-old me had figured it would be harder for the monster to find me with a new name. *The monster.* I understood now that he was human, but in the moment he shot my mom, I'd been convinced he was the devil himself. And later, when he showed up in the hospital to kill me as well, I'd been frozen, too terrified to do anything more than tremble and wet the bed when he pressed the pillow over my face. Then I'd heard voices, muffled at first, but one grew louder and more insistent. Demanding. *I don't care about visiting hours. Take me to see my granddaughter right now.* Grandpa had been the most tolerable of the Baldwins —other than my dad, of course—and the only one I cared to spend any time with, but he'd still been fond of throwing his weight around. His sense of superiority had saved me that day. As he got closer, the monster had put the pillow down and slipped out of the room, but not before he made me a promise: if I talked, he'd find me.

He'd find me, and he'd finish what he started.

I hadn't talked.

For sixteen years, I hadn't breathed one word about what happened that night.

And now here I was—very much alive, about to forfeit the inheritance I'd been counting on for a fresh start, and half wishing the monster had kept the pillow in place for just a minute longer. The past decade and a half had been hard. Every time I saw a glimmer of light at the end of the tunnel, it turned out to be a freight train, usually with one of my relatives driving it. So many times, I'd cursed the fact that I was born a Baldwin. My father had had the right idea —he'd gotten as far away from his family as possible.

Maybe it was time to cut my losses and leave? If not for the fledgling friendships I was starting to form in Baldwin's Shore, I'd have done just that.

"You're in the way." Frankie Flux glowered at me, arms folded. "I'm about to start my set."

On any other night, I'd have apologised and scuttled away, but I was sick of being Sara-the-doormat. Tonight, I was Saralisa.

"Didn't your momma teach you that politeness costs nothing?"

"Nah, she didn't."

"Neither did mine. You look like a jackass in those sunglasses."

I turned on my heel and strode out the doors to the terrace, shaking. Speaking my mind was a rush, but I couldn't let myself get too used to it.

5

______

SARA

Kayleigh hadn't changed her PIN in years. I tapped out 1-2-3-4 on her phone screen, and it came to life. Sheesh, she took a lot of photos. Thousands and thousands, and at least fifty percent of them were selfies.

I sat on the low brick wall surrounding the fountain on the terrace and pulled my shawl tighter around my shoulders. There was a definite chill in the air tonight. Beside me, water splashed into a shallow pool, and hundreds of coins glinted beneath strategically placed spotlights, mostly nickels and dimes but a few quarters too. People tossed the coins into the water for luck. I wasn't superstitious, but I fished through my purse until I found a quarter and threw it in with the rest. Grandpa Baldwin had always said that the Lord moved in mysterious ways, and I might as well cover all the bases.

Back to the phone... I needed a picture of Kayleigh with her eyes closed, or one with smudged mascara, or one where she had spinach stuck in her teeth. Hmm, there was one with her underwear showing... No, she'd probably be proud of that.

"Are you going to keep running away all night?" a voice asked from beside me, and I jumped out of my skin, dropped the phone, tried to catch it, and ended up batting it into the water. Crap!

"I thought the fountain was meant to be lucky," Prince Charming said, holding out a glass of champagne.

"Shut up."

Was the phone salvageable? The screen was still glowing, but it also looked cracked. Was it safe to pick the thing up? Or could it electrocute me underwater? I mean, it wasn't plugged in or anything, but how much voltage was in a battery? Or was it the current that was dangerous? Darn it, I should have listened harder in science classes.

I'd just stuck a hand in the water when I heard the worst sound in the world—a cross between a screech and a whine, and it was coming from Kayleigh's mouth as she strode in my direction.

"You! Yes, you—Cinderella. Where's my phone?"

Quickly, I blocked her view of the water with my puffy skirt and borrowed my mom's Texas drawl.

"I don't know what you're talking about."

"My phone is missing, and Malinda saw someone dressed as Cinderella pick it up."

Crap on a cracker, I had roughly three seconds before Kayleigh recognised me. I opened my mouth to stutter a reply, but Charming got there first.

"There are at least three other Cinderellas here tonight, plus two Elsas, who look kind of similar, don't you think? When did your phone go missing?"

Charming sounded so cool, so self-assured that Kayleigh hesitated. "Uh, maybe fifteen minutes ago?"

"Then you have the wrong woman—I've been talking with this Cinderella for the past half hour. Why don't you try the buffet? Most people are hanging out there."

She backed away, delightfully unsure, and I let out the breath I'd been holding. Pheeeeeew. But that left me with a new problem, and I waited until Kayleigh had disappeared into the ballroom before tackling it.

Prince Charming.

Why did he keep appearing wherever I went?

"Is that Kayleigh's phone?" he asked, motioning toward the water.

"Uh, maybe? I swear I was just gonna post an outtake to her Insta and then give it back."

He nodded approvingly. "Good plan."

"Why did you cover for me?"

"Because the Baldwin twins are a pain in everyone's ass. She should put the phone down for a while and go touch grass." He glanced toward the ballroom. "Along with most of the other folks in there."

"If you don't like them, then why did you come?"

"As a favour."

"To who?"

"To my father. I'm supposed to make sure my little brother doesn't do anything dumb. Which is..."—he sighed —"easier said than done."

"Where is he now?"

"Inside with his girlfriend." He rolled his eyes. "The one trying to eat cake in a Power Ranger mask."

The pink Power Ranger who was hanging out with Hadley? Okay, Charming was right: Hadley was notorious for doing dumb things, dumb things that often ended up on the internet, and it was entirely possible that her lack of judgment was contagious.

"So shouldn't you be inside, keeping an eye on him?"

"Absolutely. We can do that from the dance floor."

I'm sorry, what?

"We?"

"My brother doesn't know I'm here. It's your turn to be my cover story, Cinderella."

"Oh, no, no, no. I'm not dancing."

Charming held out a hand, and darn, that smile was intoxicating. My heart thudded against my ribcage as I tried to come up with a way to get out of this new predicament.

"One dance, Cinderella. I can lead."

"So, uh, I can't go back in there. I...I just called the DJ a jackass."

"And I'm sure he deserved it."

"Yes, he did, but now I have to avoid him for the rest of my life."

"No, you don't."

"I—"

"If you modify your behaviour because of him, it won't matter what internal battle you're fighting. He'll win the war."

"Battles and wars and behaviour modification? What do you know about fighting?"

"Quite a lot, actually."

"Are you a psychologist or something?"

"No, but I'll let you into a secret..." He leaned closer, and his voice dropped to a whisper. "I know plenty about winning too."

Charming's ego was bigger than Texas. My head said run, but my heart dragged its heels. It was strangely exhilarating to have the ego on my side for once.

"I can't leave Kayleigh's phone here in the fountain."

An Insta notification popped up on the mangled screen,

reminding me that I was a bad, bad person. Two wrongs didn't make a right, Grandpa used to say, although one wrong didn't feel any better, in my opinion. And Charming, it seemed, was a proponent of the "three wrongs" theory. He reached past me, plucked the phone from the water, and threw it into the shrubbery.

"Problem solved," he announced. "What's your next excuse?"

"You can't do..."

I trailed off because he just had, hadn't he? And Kayleigh could certainly afford a new phone with the inheritance she was about to steal from me. Charming was an arrogant douche, and if his brother was a part of Hadley's crowd, he was probably a trust fund baby too. Everything I usually despised. But just for tonight, with Kayleigh on the warpath, I decided to step into his world. If nothing else, I could use him as a shield.

This time when Charming held out a hand, I took it. And when he offered me the champagne again, I drank it.

"I'm leading," I informed him, perhaps a little haughtily. "And if you tread on my toes, you're on your own."

"I won't tread on your toes."

He led me back across the terrace and into the ballroom. Frankie Flux was playing a dance track, one of his remixes that had topped the charts last year, and although the man had the personality of a porcupine, I had to concede that he made catchy music. The dance floor was already half-full. Hadley livestreamed from the stage as the pink Power Ranger held up a ring light, and the Lone Ranger had passed out on a chair beside them with a bottle of champagne still clutched in his hand. *Just another day in the life of an event planner.* Charming led me to the edge of the dance floor, and I figured he'd start flinging his arms around like all the other drunk morons, but he just looked at me expectantly.

"Have you ever even taken a dance lesson?" I asked, stalling for time as my toes shrivelled inside my shoes.

"One or two."

He lied. I knew within thirty seconds of being on the dance floor that Charming had taken more than a couple of lessons. He was no Marcin, but my toes were safe, and I was regretting my decision to lead. At least everyone else was too drunk to notice the way he moved his hips. But *I* noticed. I couldn't tear my freaking gaze away as we salsa'd our way through the rest of the track.

"Eyes on me." He raised my chin with a finger. "Don't slouch."

I straightened as if I'd been electrocuted. Yes, we'd been holding each other as we danced, but that innocent touch felt somehow more intimate. I swallowed the lump in my throat and forced myself to focus on Charming's face.

"One or two lessons? Really?"

"My Puerto Rican grandma ran a dance school, and she says all young men should know how to impress a lady." He threw in a few samba steps. "Even now, she can out-shimmy a woman half her age."

"I should send her a bouquet. My last dance partner thought salsa was a type of dip."

It was true. Brooke told me. Paulo thought we were going to Coos Bay to binge on nachos until she sent him a link to Casa de Salsa's website.

"My grandma likes peonies. So, Cinderella, what's your story?"

"My...story?"

"You've taken more than one or two lessons as well."

Now I wished I hadn't started along this path. "That was in another lifetime. Can't we just dance?"

"Do I get to lead this time?"

On any other day, I'd have made an excuse and left, but today... Today was different. I had a front-row seat to the twins' screw-ups, plus Charming was taking me on a trip down memory lane, and strangely, I was enjoying the journey. As long as he kept his feet moving, I could ignore the frat-boy aura.

Although his cocky smile did soften as we improvised our way through song after song. Several people gave us weird looks, and Frankie Flux perfected his glower, but I took Charming's advice and tamped down my sensitivities. Nobody knew who I was, and after midnight, I'd never have to see this man again. Which was a good thing.

Right?

Even if he offered me his number, I absolutely wouldn't take it.

I *wouldn't.*

"Hydration break," he announced. "And there might be some of those cake pops left. Let's go and liberate them."

"I can't."

"Why not?"

"People will think I'm greedy."

"Name one person here whose opinion matters to you."

You.

"I...I can't."

Charming steered me toward the remains of the buffet with a palm on my lower back. His hand hadn't strayed toward my butt during the whole time we'd been dancing, which I was kind of surprised about, and definitely *not* disappointed. No siree.

"Strawberry or chocolate?" he asked.

Why was that even a question? "Chocolate."

He handed me a cake on a stick and took one himself, also chocolate. I didn't argue. Nico Belinsky's pastry chef was an angel in human form, and who knew when I'd come back here? My budget didn't run to the Peninsula's prices at the moment.

"The food's better than I expected," he said, passing me another glass of champagne. "I heard on the grapevine that this place was one to avoid."

"That probably came from a bitter local. There are still folks who wish the hotel hadn't been built."

"Why?"

"The previous owner let everyone use the land. People walked their dogs here and picnicked in the summer."

"Maybe I'll come back here for dinner someday."

"I'd recommend it. The head chef trained in Paris."

Jacques had a temper, but Nico once told me that the occasional smashed dish was a small price to pay for soufflés more addictive than crack.

"One time, I had to chaperone my brother at a party on some French guy's boat, and we both got food poisoning." He rubbed his chin. "That might even have been one of Hadley's shitshows. She's fond of fucking around with European assholes. How do you know Hadley, anyway? You don't seem like one of the usual suckers from her entourage."

"Suckers? Isn't your brother in her entourage?"

"Yes, but he has an unfortunate habit of making poor life choices." If that was the main criteria, then technically, I did qualify. "Let me guess—you're sorority sisters?"

"That's actually quite insulting."

"You're one of her skiing buddies?"

"I've never been on a pair of skis in my life."

"You're her dog's au pair?"

"That's not even a thing."

"Swear on my grandma's grave that it is."

"I thought your grandma was alive and shimmying?"

"My other grandma."

I reached over to squeeze his hand. "I'm sorry for your loss. It's never easy when a loved one passes."

"Yeah, well." Charming made a face. He didn't get along with his family? "Are you on Hadley's beach volleyball team?"

"Are you serious? Do I look as if I play beach volleyball? Does *Hadley* even play beach volleyball?"

"It was the only reason she didn't get kicked out of college. She's actually pretty good, and if you don't know that, I'm gonna guess the two of you aren't close."

Damn him. Charming was smart, much smarter than me. Now I had to confess or lie, and I'd already proven I was a terrible liar. Would he tell security if he knew I was there uninvited? I didn't think so. We'd grown closer over the past two hours—quite literally—and he didn't seem to have much affection for Hadley and her crowd.

"I heard there was free food, and nobody was checking invites at the door."

"You crashed Hadley's birthday party?"

"The cake pops were worth it."

Charming looked me up and down. "You sure did make an effort with your costume."

"What, this old thing?"

He threw his head back and laughed. "I like your style, Cinderella." Then he leaned closer and whispered, "This is the fourth party of Hadley's that I've snuck into, but the first I haven't wanted to leave right away."

Charming had been keeping an eye on his sibling all evening, even while we danced. Little bro always had a drink in his hand, and at this moment, he was in the far corner of the ballroom, unsteady on his feet as he tried to play beer pong with top-shelf liquor. Charming hadn't touched a drop of alcohol. Was he the designated driver as well as the responsible big brother? Nico Belinsky appeared in the doorway, and he didn't look happy. I'd go as far as to say he looked a little scary. Brooke had once hinted that he had a dark past, and although she hadn't elaborated on the details, I could believe it when I looked at him now.

"Have you seen Lillian Baldwin?" he asked the inebriated bumblebee beside us.

Her antennae waggled as she shook her head.

"She went out to the terrace five minutes ago," Charming told him. "I haven't seen her come back in."

Add "observant" to his list of qualities.

"Thanks." Nico's smile was tight, his frame rigid as he strode past.

"That should be an interesting battle," I murmured, half to myself.

"My money's on that guy." Charming nodded in Nico's direction. "Want to go listen in?"

A man after my own heart.

"Won't that look weird?"

"Not if we do it properly."

"Have you always been this nosy?"

"I prefer the term 'well-informed.' Knowledge is power, Cinderella. Are you coming?"

"Of course."

Was it weird, being partners in espionage with a man whose face I'd never seen? Heck, I didn't even know his name. But if I asked him for personal details, then he'd reciprocate, and I'd told enough lies for tonight.

I froze when he wrapped an arm around my waist, jolted when he stroked a thumb across my hip, but he just leaned in close to whisper, "Relax."

"What are you doing?"

"Going out to the terrace to eavesdrop is a social faux pas. Going out to the terrace to talk privately with a beautiful woman is perfectly acceptable."

He...he thought I was beautiful? That was just a line, right?

"Are you saying that you're a beautiful woman?" I joked.

Charming chuckled. "Now you know my secret, Cinderella."

"Liar."

The word popped out before I could stop it, but I'd been pressed up against him on the dance floor too many times to count. Either he carried a zucchini in his pants, or he was all man.

"C'mon, we don't want to miss the show."

I leaned into him as he walked us outside again. The temperature had dropped, but Charming gave off more heat than a furnace, which was absolutely the reason I was sweating. What did he look like without the mask? Probably devastatingly handsome if the bits of his face that I could see were any indication. The temptation to find out was almost great enough to make me stay past midnight, but if the twins found out I was here, they'd be furious. And I'd be homeless. They'd already tried to evict me from the pool house once, and only Parker putting his foot down had stopped them.

Lillian was standing by the fountain, hands on her hips as Nico had words. I strained my ears to hear, and Charming sidestepped us closer, one hand cupping my cheek as he looked into my eyes.

"If there's a problem, you follow procedure," Nico said. "You report the issue to the duty manager. You do *not* harangue my staff and make them cry."

"Your staff are clumsy. That woman trod on Kimberley's foot."

"Because another guest pushed into her."

"So? She was in the way. Servers shouldn't be mingling with the rest of us."

"Define 'us.'"

Oh, that threw her.

"You know...*us*."

"You'll have to clarify—are you being racist or classist?"

Her jaw dropped. Of course, Lillian was both of those things, but she didn't like when people pointed it out.

"*Us*." She gestured around the room. "Paying guests."

"I understood you were also hired help tonight?"

Lillian drew herself up an inch and puffed out her chest. "I am an event coordinator, not a waitress or a cleaner."

"Not a very good one, it seems. Why are my library books propping up the DJ's table?"

"How dare you speak to me that way? Don't you know who I am?"

Charming grimaced. "Did she just...?"

"Yup," I whispered back.

"Yikes. This is like watching a car crash."

My guts seized. He couldn't have realised the effect his words would have on me, and I wasn't about to explain. But he knew something was wrong.

"You okay?"

"I'm fine. Shhh."

He kissed my temple. *He kissed my freaking temple.* I

wasn't sure whether to melt into his arms or slap him, but I did neither because Nico wasn't done yet.

"I know exactly who you are, Ms. Baldwin. Which is why it's easy for me to ban you from setting foot on this property again. We won't accept any more event bookings from LKB, your spa membership is revoked, and you're no longer welcome in the restaurant. And just in case you get any ideas about pretending to be your sister, I'm adding her name to the 'persona non grata' list too."

"You...you can't do that."

"Yes, I can."

"My family owns this town. We *are* this town."

"Strange, I thought half of your family was in prison now."

Lillian's expression turned mutinous. "You'll pay for this. You'd better watch your back."

Nico took a step forward, crowding her space, and my poor dumb cousin paled a shade.

"Thanks for the warning. When you take your shot, you'd better not miss." He leaned in closer, and I could barely hear his next words over the background noise. "Because I never do." Nico straightened. "Enjoy the rest of your evening."

If I hadn't been wrapped up in Charming at that moment, I might have run after Nico Belinsky and kissed him. Wow. The twins were low-key obsessed with the aromatherapy hot-stone massages at the Peninsula—the spa had been rated ten out of ten by *Imagine* magazine—and now they'd probably have to drive to Portland to get their pampering fix. All hail King Karma.

"That was fun," Charming said. "Maybe he could do my brother's girlfriend next? She's a pain in the ass."

"Do you have to play chauffeur to her this evening too?"

"Thankfully no. Her father had a meeting in Coquille this evening, so he said he'd swing by afterward. Which means we can go back to the dance floor and celebrate Lillian Baldwin being blacklisted. Did I mention that a year ago, one of my buddies went on a blind date with her?"

"Please convey my deepest sympathy. How bad was it?"

"She talked about herself for two straight hours, then interrogated him about his family and finances. He told her his dad was a hospital administrator and his mom sold handicrafts."

"Smart move." Lillian would never date anyone whose father wasn't either employed at C-suite level or independently wealthy. "What do his parents really do?"

"His dad is CEO of a hospital group, and his mom is a renowned sculptor."

"Oops. Hey, maybe you could introduce me? I might need medical attention if Kayleigh finds out who took her phone."

Again, I'd been joking, but Charming's smile dropped. "Introduce you? No, I don't think so."

What was I thinking? Of course he wouldn't set up his rich friend with a no-name party-crasher who revelled in others' misfortune. And although it hurt to get a reminder of my shortcomings, his words broke the spell that had befallen me this evening. I stepped out of Charming's arms.

"I'm going back inside."

I didn't bother to check whether he was following. And when I reached the ballroom, I forgot about him completely. Because Kayleigh was on the stage, microphone in hand, basking in the limelight as she made another speech. Hadn't she learned from the last one?

"Okay, you lovely folks. It's a little early, but we're all sick of wearing these masks, aren't we? Poor Elina's barely taken a drink this evening. So why don't we fast-forward to the good part?" Whoops and hollers came from the crowd, and my stomach plummeted through the floor, heading for the earth's core. I barely heard the rest of the announcement because I was already hightailing it out of the ballroom. "Three, two, one... Masks off at midnight!"

It was barely eleven freaking thirty. Kayleigh couldn't even respect time, the one constant in this messed-up dumpster fire of a world. I dashed across the terrace and around the corner, vaguely aware of shouts behind me. Was that...Charming? He was chasing me? Or had I attracted the attention of Nico's security team? I turned to look, only to stumble and smack straight into a wall.

"What's the hurry, little lady?"

Oh, crap, it wasn't a wall. It was a person. A man, to be precise, wearing a dress shirt and a sports jacket as he hung out in the smoking area at the side of the main hotel building. His hair was greying at the temples, and his slightly imperious tone said that he belonged at the Peninsula while I didn't.

"Sorry. I'm so sorry."

He blew out a lungful of smoke. "You should slow down if you don't want to trip."

"I will, I—"

I glanced at the man standing next to him and found myself looking into the eyes of a monster.

No, not *a* monster.

The monster.

I'd never forget those eyes. They were burned into my psyche like craters from a nuclear bomb. Hooded ice-blue eyes that narrowed as he studied me, assessing. Was he trying to work out where he'd seen me before? Or did he already know? Had he followed me here tonight? Did he suspect I wasn't holding up my end of the bargain? All those years ago, he'd promised someone would always be watching.

Instinct took over, the inbuilt fight-or-flight response ingrained into my DNA, and I ran. I was no fighter. I ran, praying I didn't fall because death was a very real possibility. I ran, my only goal to get as far from the monster as possible. I ran, and when the heel of my left shoe caught in a drain grate, I abandoned it, pulled off the other, and carried on barefoot.

Where was I going? Away. I had no idea beyond that. I just had to get away.

"Hey!"

The shout barely registered.

"Sara?"

This time, I slowed a fraction.

"Sara, wait!"

I turned to see Brooke jogging toward me, her car abandoned in the driveway with the door open. *Get to the car.* If I could reach the car, I'd be safe.

You weren't the last time.

Then Brooke grabbed my wrist and I nearly shook her off but then she was pulling me toward the car and I was crying and my thoughts were tumbling over and over and over.

"What happened? Where's your other shoe?"

When I didn't answer, she pushed me into the passenger seat and crouched alongside. The remaining shoe dropped out of my hand and into the footwell.

"Sara, what happened? You're scaring me?"

"He shot her."

The words slipped out in a raspy whisper, and fear sent

the contents of my stomach slithering up my throat. Brooke jumped out of the way as I heaved.

"Who shot who? I'm calling Luca."

"No! Don't call anyone."

"But you said someone got shot?"

"Please, just drive."

Brooke looked around, probably for the gunman I'd been foolish enough to mention, and I desperately tried to undo the damage I'd done.

"Hadley's friend decided we should play one of those murder mystery games and...and... I got carried away." Would that work? "The drinks were free, and I wish I hadn't touched the liquor because it went straight to my head, and I feel so, so sick. Can we just go? Please?"

Brooke didn't look as if she believed me, but she did at least skirt around the pool of mushed-up cake pop and head to the driver's side. The whole time, I watched the corner of the building, waiting for the monster to appear with a silenced pistol in his hand the way he had at the car wreck. Mom had saved me that day. At first, I'd thought the monster was there to help, that he was a Good Samaritan, but Mom had shushed me and told me to hide. She'd known what was coming.

And now so did I.

When Brooke started the engine and turned the car around, I was finally able to breathe again. But what if he'd seen us leave? What if he tracked Brooke down, and she told him what I'd said? I'd have to stay away from her. From everyone I cared about.

"Why don't you stay at our place tonight?" Brooke asked. "Aaron makes a great hangover breakfast. Romi swears by it."

"No! I mean, thank you for the offer, but I need to go home."

"Are you sure?"

I made an effort to quell the fear in my voice. "Yes, really. I just want to sleep in my own bed."

And make plans to leave Baldwin's Shore. Now I had nothing to stay for and every reason to go.

6

———

GARRETT

"Did a woman dressed as Cinderella come through here? Blue dress, blonde hair."

Full, kissable pink lips, an ass to die for, and footwork that would give Ginger Rogers a run for her money. I still wasn't quite sure what I'd said or done, but she'd taken off like an Olympic sprinter.

Congressman Mandell sucked in another dose of carcinogens and blew out smoke. Guess his latest attempt to quit his twenty-a-day habit hadn't worked out.

"She playing hard to get?"

"Something like that."

He chuckled and pointed toward the front of the hotel. "The girl went that way. Good luck, son."

When I rounded the corner of the building, there was no sign of her, but something up ahead caught my eye, glinting beneath the floodlights that made night seem like day at the Peninsula. A shoe. More precisely, one of Cinderella's shoes. The crystals on the heel had jammed it tight into a drain grate, and she'd just...left it there? I didn't know a whole hell of a lot about women's footwear, but I'd picked up enough snippets of information from my sister over the years to realise that this was an expensive designer brand.

I stuck a finger into the grate and gently wiggled the heel free, keeping an eye out for its owner.

The optics weren't lost on me—was this some kind of joke? Cinderella had run off at midnight—well, close to it—and left Prince Charming in the dust. Hell, I wasn't even meant to be Prince Charming tonight. I'd reserved a Prince of Darkness costume, but the girl at the costume store made a mistake, one she'd blamed on autocorrect, and here I was. Dressed in fucking ruffles.

With a shoe in my hand.

Did Cinderella expect me to chase her? Because I didn't chase women. They chased me, and I was the one who did the running.

Or had my brother realised who was behind the blue velvet mask? I'd stayed out of his way, but I hadn't exactly kept a low profile this evening, not once I'd set eyes on Cinderella and then realised she could dance. If Trey was playing a prank, it wasn't funny. I half expected one of his idiot friends to pop up with a camera, filming me for their next TikTok video as I made a fool out of myself.

Where was she?

I stilled the way I used to on patrol when I needed to evaluate my surroundings. Waiting. Watching. Barely breathing. *Feeling.* She wasn't there. Cinderella had vanished.

Gone.

Like a ghost in the darkness.

I should go find Trey. That was the reason I'd come here

tonight, the reason I'd dismissed Johannes's idea to fly to Aspen for the weekend and blow off some steam. I should toss the shoe in the trash.

But I didn't.

Instead, I placed it carefully into the trunk of my car and began to plan.

"Why'd you have to be such a dick?" Trey whined, messy brown hair flopping over his forehead. He needed to visit a barber. "It was just a game."

A game that had involved daring each other to strip naked and run into the freezing ocean at one o'clock in the morning while onlookers filmed their antics. It would only have been a matter of time before one of the clips found its way to a journalist. I put down my smoothie and turned to face my half-brother. He'd shown up in the kitchen in his bathrobe, hazel eyes bloodshot, and his breath still stank of stale beer.

"Because Dad doesn't need any more bad press."

"I didn't ask to be born into this family."

"Would you rather be a sheet metal worker in Detroit?"

"I'd rather you and Dad weren't such killjoys."

I took a calming breath and swallowed a couple of Tylenol. "Where's the fun in passing out drunk in the early hours in a pool of your own vomit? Go on, explain it to me like I'm five."

"I didn't pass out."

"You didn't pass out *last night*. Because I was there to stop you from taking things too far."

But he *had* vomited, thankfully before he climbed into

my vehicle. Rain was forecast today, so hopefully the whole mess would get washed away, otherwise we'd probably be joining the Baldwin twins on the Peninsula's banned list. And while I hunted for Cinderella, my brother's girlfriend had escaped the hotel with three of Hadley's equally irresponsible friends and made it all the way to a diner on the outskirts of town because they just *had* to have carbs. Elina had been practically unconscious when her father's head of security carried her to the car. Situation Normal: All Fucked Up. Elina had a tipping point—she'd drink most of the evening and be fine, just a bit giggly, and half a glass of wine later, she'd keel over. I tried to keep an eye on her, but ultimately, she wouldn't listen to a word of my advice, so trying to curb her alcohol consumption was a waste of time.

"You're such a fucking suck-up, always doing what Dad says."

"It's called respect, and you don't have any, not even for yourself."

"Just because I like to have fun instead of being a corporate asshole doesn't mean—"

"Uncle Garrett, can I have banana milk?"

Trey cut off abruptly as our niece meandered into the kitchen. Marlie was eight years old and the apple of everyone's eye—everyone except her mother, anyway. Gracelynn, my older sister, had gotten pregnant after a one-night stand, and she'd insisted she wasn't cut out for motherhood. But because Grandma Margaret had been a staunch Catholic, there'd been no debate over whether Gracie kept the baby.

For a while, we'd had hope. Gracie loved attention as much as the Hadley Carpenters of this world did, and she'd smiled through the first few months of pregnancy when people told her she was "glowing." The baby shower, picking out furniture for the nursery, shopping for tiny shoes... She'd done all that. But just a week after the birth, she'd announced that she couldn't cope anymore, and she was hiring a nanny. And by "hiring a nanny," she meant paying someone to take Marlie off her hands.

Again, Grandma Margaret had stepped in. No grandchild of hers would be raised by a stranger, she insisted, so Marlie had come to live at the family estate near Roseburg. Our lives had been turned upside down. My stepmother—a former flight attendant who was actually a good person and didn't deserve a man-child like Trey for a son—got landed with the bulk of the childcare while Gracie moved to New York to design shoes. What the fuck were you even meant to tell a kid in that situation?

You lied. That's what you did. You lied. And to add insult to injury, Grandma Margaret had shuffled off this mortal coil before Marlie turned two years old.

"Sure you can have banana milk, peanut. Did you eat breakfast already?"

"Letti made me pancakes."

She called my stepmother Letti, the same way I did. No matter how hard Letti tried, she'd never be "Mom" to either of us. Sometimes, I felt guilty about that, but even though my mom had passed away before Dad ever met Colette, she was irreplaceable. Memories faded, but love never did.

I was glad Dad had married Letti when I was still young. If I'd been older, I'd have written her off as a gold-digger, a money-grubber, but she genuinely loved my father. And yoga. And Pixie, a three-year-old miniature pinscher with a bigger wardrobe than mine.

I peeled a banana, broke it into pieces, and dropped it

into the blender, then added ice cream and milk. Banana milkshake was Marlie's favourite, followed by strawberry or blueberry. Chocolate milkshakes were a big no-no. Her refusal to eat anything brown had come after a kid at kindergarten put dirt in her lunch as a prank, and someday, we hoped she'd grow out of it, but she was as stubborn as her mom. Genetics had a lot to answer for.

Speaking of Gracie, I needed to email her…

While Marlie watched cartoons and slurped her milkshake and Trey clattered around making himself fried eggs, I typed out a message to my sister. The rest of the family had more or less turned their backs on her, but I stayed in touch. Why burn a bridge when you might need to cross it later?

Gracie,

I need to find the owner of this shoe, and you're the shoe expert. Please tell me it's some kind of fancy designer limited edition that's only sold in three boutiques where the staff knows every client by name?

The Other G

"Uncle Garrett, will you help me with my Legos?"

"I just need to make a couple of calls first."

"I'll help," Trey offered. "Did you get a new set?"

My half-brother might have been an irresponsible prick most of the time, but there was no doubt that he adored Marlie. He gave her piggybacks around the estate, he sat patiently while she served him cakes from her Easy-Bake Oven, and he'd learned to braid hair.

"Grandma Valeria brought me a rescue helicopter. When I've built it, can I get a real helicopter?"

"Maybe when you're older," I told her.

"Can I fly in your helicopter?"

"Next weekend, okay?"

This weekend, I had a twitching cock, a headache, and a problem with a runaway mystery woman I just couldn't forget, no matter how much I wanted to.

7

SARA

Sara's to-do list:
- Pay phone bill.
- Return jewellery to Brooke.
- Check debit card works in Europe.
- Book flight.
- Pack.

Ten a.m. on Sunday, and an uncomfortable mix of caffeine and stress fuelled me as I paced the living room in the pool house. The monster was here. Here in Baldwin's Shore. My safe space. My sanctuary. I hadn't slept a wink last night, unsurprisingly.

And now, I was getting ready to leave.

To run.

Marcin kept inviting me to stay with him in Gdańsk, so that would be my starting point. I had money saved up, almost fifty thousand dollars from my failed attempt to claim my inheritance. That would sustain me for a year, maybe two if I was careful, and then I could get a job. Start to rebuild my shattered life for the second time, as long as *he* didn't catch up with me again.

If I started another business, I'd make sure I was the sole shareholder, or I could ease myself in gently with some kind of office job. Not customer service, though—I was sick of dealing with difficult people. Perhaps I could be a PA? I was super organised, great at admin, and I knew my way around an accounting program. To-do lists were my favourite thing. Over the years, I'd come up with a system—prioritise five things each morning to give myself a goal for the day.

Five things were always doable.

A list a mile long, that was daunting.

Hey, I could even be a life coach as long as nobody asked for a reference. What was the old saying? Those who can't, teach.

My phone pinged for the tenth time, and I checked in case it was Marcin. I'd messaged him as soon as I got home, teary and still slightly drunk, and I'd been on edge waiting for a reply ever since. The rest of this morning's messages had all come from Brooke, asking how I was, and I had no idea what to say to her. *Oh, hey, last night when I was trying to escape from the hot fake prince I spent half of the evening dancing with, I ran into the guy who murdered my parents, and now I'm moving to Poland. Thanks for everything, and sayonara.* She'd probably call a psychiatrist and have me committed.

MARCIN

> For sure you can come to stay. I got a last-minute coaching gig in England, but I'll be back in three weeks. If you want to come earlier, Andriy is there and he will make you welcome.

Marcin wasn't home? Well, crap. I'd never met Andriy, and although I trusted that Marcin wouldn't be dating a jerk, the thought of spending weeks with a stranger made my stomach sink even further. I felt so...so...fragile. As if I could break at any moment.

What if I travelled to Eastern Europe anyway and just holed up in a hotel? I could order room service, and I wouldn't have to leave the building until Marcin returned. I'd be safe. Wouldn't I? Could the monster track me halfway across the world? I honestly had no idea. The only thing I knew about him was that he was a cold-blooded killer and my parents were two of his victims. I had no idea why they'd been targeted, what they'd done to deserve their fate.

Wait, if I went to see Marcin, would I be putting him in danger? A tear rolled down my cheek as I ran through my options and realised every single one was awful.

Maybe it was time to give up? To accept my fate? I should have died sixteen years ago, and I'd been living on borrowed time ever since.

A knock at the door made me jump out of my skin, and my first instinct was to hide the way I had that night at the side of the road. But my car was in the driveway, and the lights were on, and—

"Sara, are you there?"

My knees went weak with relief when I recognised Brooke's voice. Should I answer? Or crawl behind the couch before she looked through the windows?

"Sara, open the door. We know you're in there," Blue called.

Uh-oh, Brooke had brought reinforcements? I heard Addy's voice next, quieter. "Should we look for a spare key? Or would Parker have one?"

Blue was practically psychic; she'd find the key behind the ugly cherub statue if she looked hard enough. And I absolutely didn't want the Baldwin family involved in this any more than they already were.

"I'm coming," I called weakly.

At least I could return the jewellery, which would check one item off my to-do list. I opened the door and found the three of them standing there. Brooke looked worried, but Blue had her arms folded, which wasn't a good sign.

Brooke wrapped me up in a hug before stepping back to study me. "What happened? Are you okay?"

"I'm fine, honestly. Just"—I yawned for effect—"just tired."

"Liar," Blue said.

Addy glanced through the doorway to my bedroom. "Why are you packing a suitcase?"

"Uh, a friend invited me to go visit. So I'll just get that jewellery I borrowed, and—"

"Where's this friend?" Blue asked, picking up the passport I'd left on the coffee table. "Overseas?"

"I...I..."

Brooke wouldn't let me stay silent. "What happened last night? You said someone shot a woman, but Luca checked, and there were no incidents at the Peninsula."

"And nobody was playing a murder mystery game either," Blue added. "Although Nico was tempted to dig a shallow grave for your cousins by all accounts."

That was it. I couldn't take any more. No more challenges, no more questions, no more kindness. The mask I'd been wearing since I moved to Oregon finally crumbled, and a mess of tears tumbled out.

"I can't... I just can't."

"Can't what?" Blue asked, still thumbing through my passport, and Brooke shushed her as she half carried me to the couch.

"It's okay," Brooke murmured. "Whatever happened, we can fix it."

"You c-c-can't fix it. Nobody can fix it."

"Not if you don't tell us what the problem is," Blue said, and I felt rather than saw her roll her eyes.

The couch dipped as Addy sat on the other side of me. "Should I get you a drink? Water? Coffee? Margarita?"

I shook my head.

Blue tossed the passport back onto the table and folded her arms again. "Well?"

"It's...it's all in the past. What I got upset about, I mean. And...and...you don't need the details."

"Is this something to do with your mom? She was shot, wasn't she?"

My spine went rigid, as if a sadistic surgeon had injected it with titanium. Yes, Mom had been shot, but that wasn't what her death certificate said. The second autopsy concluded that the lump of metal rattling around in her head had been a byproduct of the car crash. That both of my parents had passed away in a tragic accident.

"W-w-why would you think that?"

"I heard a rumour. She was an aide to Senator Colvin, wasn't she?"

"His chief of staff."

The words slipped from my tongue in a whisper. What was the point in lying when Blue clearly knew the answer already? I was beginning to discover that there were definite downsides to having a private investigator in your circle of friends.

One of my earliest memories was sitting on Senator Colvin's lap in his office, the two of us spinning around in his chair while I waited for my mom to finish working. He'd kept a supply of candy in his desk drawer, and he used to slip me pieces when Mom wasn't looking. Back in those days, he'd been a state senator in Texas, and when he got elected to the US Senate, we'd all upped sticks and moved to DC—well, our home had been in northern Virginia—because Mom loved her job and didn't want to lose it. Our new life had been an adventure. Dad was an artist who painted watercolours in between taking me to school and dance lessons. Even while I was practising with Marcin, he'd sit at the edge of the room, sketching ideas in a notepad to transfer to his easel later. As for Mom, she'd worked long hours, but Sundays were always family day, when we went hiking and ice skating and watched movies and baked and planted flowers in our tiny yard.

The end had come suddenly. First, Senator Colvin had passed away, and just a month afterward, the monster had shown up.

"So, last night...?" Blue prompted.

"Why did you research my family?" The thought that she'd been digging into my background, deep enough to find out the truth about my mom's cause of death, made me very uncomfortable. "It's...it's invasive. I don't ask questions about your history."

It was Brooke who answered. "Blue didn't research your family. Some stuff about your mom came up when Brie's team background-checked pretty much everyone in town. I guess they paid extra attention to you because you're a Baldwin."

"I'm not one of them." My words surprised even me, especially the anger they contained. "I'm not a Baldwin. They changed my freaking name."

"Really?" Now Brooke's voice held undisguised curiosity. "What was it before?"

I'd said too much. Far more than I intended. And my

name—my real name—was for nobody but me. It was the last thing I had left of my old life. I'd come from Virginia with nothing, no clothes, no toys, no keepsakes, and I'd never again set foot in my home. It had been in negative equity, my grandfather told me when I was old enough to understand what that was. The whole of my parents' estate had been signed over to the bank to pay the debt.

Marcin was the only person who still called me Saralisa, but someday, that would change. Someday soon. Now that I no longer had a reason to stay in Baldwin's Shore, I could become Lisa Forlani and hide someplace far away where nobody could find me. A fresh start was exactly what I needed.

"It doesn't matter, not anymore."

"Of course it does. Would you prefer if we called you something else?"

"No, really, it's fine."

"Did your grandpa make you change your name?" Addy asked. "Was it some weird kind of power play? Like, he didn't think the town had enough Baldwins already?"

"No, it was Justine's idea."

"Figures. The whole way through school, she thought my name was Abby. Do you remember the time I put dish soap in the fountain? Abigail Berger got the blame, so I know that Justine was the person who reported me to Principal McArdle."

"All the bubbles? That was you?"

"Yes, but Abigail pushed Jennie Martins over in the hallway and told everyone it was me, so she totally deserved the punishment."

Blue had gone quiet. In hindsight, she'd gone *too* quiet, and that meant her mind was working overtime.

"He was there last night, wasn't he? The man who shot your mom?"

Ever felt all the blood drain out of your body? It started as a chill, then I felt dizzy, and I knew that if I looked in the mirror, I'd have been as pale as my mom was after she died in that car.

"Please, just forget everything."

"I'm right, aren't I?"

Blue's expression was smug. It should have been scared.

"You can't get involved in this."

"Are you serious? Someone shot your mom, and you don't want him to go to prison?"

"Of course I want to see him in prison! But it's never going to happen, and I don't want anyone else to die."

"Well, I'm not planning to die."

"You think he'll give you a choice? He forced our car off the road, he shot my mom, and then he tried to kill me too." I was breathing hard, sucking in lungfuls of air as if they might be my last. Thanks to Blue and her refusal to quit asking questions, I'd said far too much, but I couldn't take the words back. Inside, the panic was welling up. "Leave. Please, just leave. If anyone asks you questions, don't tell them a thing. Say I kept my mouth shut."

I tried to push Blue toward the door, but she sidestepped and dropped onto the couch.

"Leave? No way. Not when this is getting interesting."

"Have you lost your mind? There's a literal assassin in town, and you think it's *interesting*?"

"Are you sure it's him? Do you know his identity? If not, we could get Nico to pull the security footage and start from there."

Was I sure? Last night, I'd been certain, but now in the cold light of day, I'd begun to wonder. Could I have been wrong? Or was I just clutching at straws because I wanted to be mistaken?

"I'm ninety percent sure, but it doesn't matter. Sixteen years on, and he's still checking up on me, so I can't afford to say or do anything that might antagonise him, not unless I want a closed casket."

"We'll be careful."

"You think? Because I bet my parents were careful, and they still died."

"If it *is* the same guy, you don't even know that he was there because of you."

"Why else would that monster have been at the Peninsula?"

"He could have been a guest at the party. Or staying at the hotel. Or maybe he just swung by for dinner? When you saw him, was he watching you?"

"I ran into him on the smoking terrace. Well, not him. The person standing next to him."

"So he was there with a friend?"

"I don't know! What sort of person would be friends with an assassin? Are we done yet? I need to finish packing my entire life into a suitcase and one piece of carry-on."

"Don't you think fleeing the country would be a bit drastic if it turns out he was just there for three courses plus wine?"

"How can I take the chance? And now the three of you all know too much, so what if...what if...?"

The words stuck in my throat, and I wiped my face with a sleeve as I sank into an armchair. Life had been so much easier when I didn't have friends. Why couldn't the monster have sunk his teeth into my father's side of the family instead? I wasn't saying that I wished them dead, but if it came down to a choice...

Hey, maybe I should tell Kayleigh my darkest secrets before I left Oregon? She'd never be able to keep her mouth shut, and then the monster would have the distraction of dealing with her plus her three hundred thousand Instagram followers. Meanwhile, I could change my name and start a new life running a turtle sanctuary in the Caribbean.

I'd never do that, of course—I knew nothing about turtles—but sometimes it was nice to daydream.

"You're not the one taking the chance; we are. Give us a couple of days to speak with people from the hotel, and we might be able to get this cleared up." Blue silenced me with a hand when I tried to protest. "You called him a monster, but he's human. He isn't monitoring you twenty-four-seven."

Brooke squeezed my shoulder, offering comfort. "We don't want to lose a friend. If you're worried, why don't you come stay with me and Luca while Blue does her thing? Our apartment has an alarm, and security cameras, and locks on every window."

"I don't want to put you in danger."

"Luca has a gun, and so does Aaron."

"But—"

"Ask yourself 'why now?' If you saw the man you think you did, why would he suddenly start following you now?"

I had to grudgingly admit that their points were valid. Last night, I'd been so sure about what I saw, but I'd only caught a fleeting glance, both yesterday and sixteen years ago. At the car crash, the monster had paused to say a few words to my mom, but the deed itself had been over in seconds. And in the hospital, he'd worn a surgical mask, so I'd only seen his eyes. I thought they were the same, but I'd been drinking champagne. Maybe my subconscious had been playing tricks in the worst possible way?

"I...I don't know why now. Maybe he's been here before and I just didn't spot him?"

"Or maybe he likes spa treatments?" Addy suggested. "The Peninsula hired a new massage therapist, and she's amazing."

"At least let us speak with Nico." Brooke sounded so freaking reasonable. "If there's a psycho staying in his hotel, he'd definitely want to be aware of it."

My head throbbed with the beginnings of a migraine. Hearing other perspectives left me more confused than ever. Nine-year-old me had believed the monster was Satan himself, and the beast who visited me in my dreams every night had taken on an aura of immortality. But Blue's cold logic chipped away at the wall I'd built around my feelings. Fear still dominated, but now anger was nipping at its heels, fuelled by a team of women who refused to take no for an answer.

The realisation that they wanted to help me, even if it meant putting themselves in peril, made my chest swell. Either this was what hope felt like, or I was having some kind of cardiac episode. What were the symptoms of a heart attack?

"So, that's settled." Blue clapped her hands together. "Addy can help you pack, Brooke will make up a bed, and I'll go nose around the hotel. What does this guy look like?"

If I told her, who knew what trouble would be unleashed? Right after the incident, I'd stayed silent because I was scared, but as the years went by, I'd come to understand the bigger picture. Whoever had killed my parents was powerful. Powerful enough to cover up their crime. A doctor had staged a second autopsy, and the results of the first one quietly disappeared. The police had barely investigated. And the man who'd pulled the trigger was free to hang out at the Peninsula while my parents lay in a cemetery overlooking the ocean a mile from here.

Grandpa always said that he'd "brought Peter home." But Baldwin's Shore hadn't been home to my father. He'd left for college when he was eighteen and returned as infrequently as possible, just for holidays, the occasional celebration, and Grandpa's ever more frequent health scares. Even Dad's grave was an insult. The Baldwins had only put half of his surname on the headstone.

Yes, I wanted the man who'd taken so much from us to pay, but at what cost?

"I'm still not sure this is a good idea…"

In fact, I knew for definite that it wasn't. It was a terrible idea. More terrible than the time one of my stupid, dumb cousins had tried to exact revenge on Blue and ended up getting arrested. At least it was all but certain that Easton the Third wouldn't meet his inheritance conditions—he was spending most of his savings on lawyers' fees now.

"Sara, Sara, Sara…" Blue wrapped an arm around my shoulders. "I became a PI because I'm a big fan of justice, and people shouldn't be allowed to get away with murder. If you're right about this man, then he's dangerous, and he was in our town. Maybe he still is? You can help or you can run, but I'm not going to sit back and wait to end up as collateral damage again."

Brooke took my hand. "If you need to leave town, we'll understand, but can you at least tell us what you know first? I don't think Blue's gonna drop this."

No, she wasn't.

I hadn't known Blue for long, but in some ways, she reminded me of my mom. Determined, confident, and a little too impulsive. She'd always stood up for what she thought was right. Of course, my own memories of Mom were hazy, but I'd read more about her online as I grew older. Claire Baldwin-Forlani had spearheaded the movement for equality among staffers on the Hill, even if speaking out had made her unpopular in some circles.

Me? I'd taken after my father. I preferred to avoid confrontation.

Run, don't fight.

But Blue was waiting expectantly, and she'd go wading into the mess whether I talked or not. If I pointed her in the right direction, perhaps I could prevent the ripples she made from turning into a tsunami?

I swallowed hard, and for the first time since the worst night of my life, I spilled.

"He has dark hair. Dark eyebrows, and the left one has a thin scar running through it. Close-set eyes that are such a pale blue they're almost silver. Thin lips. A square face with a sharp jaw, and the bottom of his face is kind of...wider than the top." I took a deep breath. "It's the eyes I'll never forget."

Dead, emotionless eyes with no warmth in them whatsoever. When he scrambled down the bank to kill my mom, he'd angled his car so the headlights bathed the wreck in an eerie glow. And him. I'd watched from the mangled back seat, hidden beneath a blanket and the belongings that had tumbled around the car as it careened to its final resting place. At one point, a flash of lightning had illuminated his face, and that was the frame frozen in my memory. The monster lit by nature's wrath before he fired.

"If I can get hold of a security video, could you identify him?" Blue asked.

I nodded. "Just promise you'll be careful."

"Cross my heart."

8

GARRETT

Garrett,

I could tell you that the shoes are only sold in three boutiques, but I'd be lying. Riya de Leon's pumps are sold in ninety-seven stores in the USA, not including online retailers, plus more stores carry them overseas (I called her to check). Plus they sent out another fifty pairs to models and influencers. I've attached a list of the stores, but Riya can't give out the names of the individuals—she says she's sorry, but she has to respect their privacy.

I can tell you one interesting thing, though—that's not an original Riya pump. The style is called Gigi, and it's been customised. Someone stuck all of those crystals on. I can't find a stylist doing that commercially, and Riya doesn't know of anyone either, but if you find out, she'd like their number because she thinks it's hot.

Why do you need to know, BTW? Have you finally found a girl to buy shoes for? You realise I offer a family discount, right?

The Original G

*I*t wasn't the news I'd wanted to hear, but at least Gracie had given me several leads to follow up. If Cinderella had bought the shoes online, I was shit out of luck, but I could check out retailers in Oregon. If she'd shopped in person, somebody might remember her.

Plus there was the customisation angle. Either a craftsperson had glued all of those crystals onto the shoes, or Cinderella had done it herself. I lifted the shoe up to the light. Since Saturday night, it had been sitting on the desk in my home office, taunting me as I tried to work.

You lost, Garrett.

You lost the first interesting woman to cross your path in years.

I didn't know Cinderella's identity, and I was almost certain she didn't know mine. Women tended to pre-judge when they heard my name. In the circles I ran in, their second question wasn't "Could I get a glass of water, please?" No, it was either "Oh, are you Ellis Dorsey's son?" or "Well, aren't you going to order a bottle of Cristal?"

A thousand crystals glittered under the lights. True, I wasn't a shoe designer like my sister, but to my eye, the workmanship looked exquisite. This was no amateur job. How long had it taken to glue all those gems in place? Hours? Days? A row of larger jewels sparkled down the back of the heel, cut to look like roses. Were those a specialist design? If they weren't mass-produced, then maybe they'd be traceable?

Gracie,

Thanks for the info. The girl's name is Cinderella, and she ditched me at midnight. Any idea where those crystals came from?

The Other G

As soon as I'd sent the email to my sister, a message popped up on my work laptop.

TAWNA

Are you coming to the office this afternoon, or should I reschedule your meeting with David Stoker?

Dammit, I'd forgotten all about the meeting with Stoker, not that I'd been looking forward to it in the first place. Telling a man that at least six of his staff would need to lose their jobs was never easy, but Stoker Apparel had been poorly managed for years, and if Dorsey Holdings hadn't swooped in and bought the company, it would have gone under a month ago when the bank refused to extend the revolving credit facility. At least this way, another thirty jobs would stay in Oregon instead of being shipped overseas.

I'll be there by 1 p.m.

What would I do without Tawna? She'd been keeping me on the straight and narrow since Dad had a midlife crisis and handed over the reins of Dorsey Holdings to me. And by "midlife crisis," I mean that he'd had a heart attack followed by a coronary angioplasty, then decided to run for office. Now he was secretary of state for Oregon, and he spent more time with his personal trainer than he did with his family. He'd quit smoking, he'd quit drinking, he'd lost thirty pounds, and last year, he'd run the Portland Marathon in aid of the American Heart Association.

Garrett,

> *Ha-ha, very funny. Why don't you try a craft store? What's really going on?*
> *The Original G*

Did I want to give Gracie the details? No, not yet. What if I never found Cinderella? I'd look like a fool, hunting down a mystery woman as if I were a fictional character from a children's book.

> *Gracie,*
>
> *Okay, you got me. Johannes talked me into joining a drag workshop the next time we go to Vegas, and I thought the shoes would look sexy.*
> *The Other G*

How much time did I want to spend on this endeavour? A drop in productivity would cost me later in the week, but at the same time, I couldn't stop thinking about Cinderella. There'd been a connection between us. I'd felt it, and I was sure she had too, which made her disappearing act all the more frustrating. Had she worried about getting revealed as a gatecrasher when everyone removed their masks? She shouldn't have—if she was with me, nobody would have kicked her out. But I hadn't explained that, had I? She hadn't given me the chance. Hell, she hadn't even hung around long enough to exchange phone numbers.

I typed "rose crystals" into the search bar and scanned through the results. Rose quartz, desert rose... No, those weren't what I was looking for. I tried "blue rose crystals." Sheesh, there had to be a hundred different types, but none of them matched the ones on Cinderella's shoe. Those were better quality, the detail sharper. The fifth entry on the page was a discussion board, and when I clicked on the thread, I found a long-winded discussion on the merits of various crafting techniques, and wow, these people seemed kind of scary. There was a lot of all-caps shouting going on, as well as a bunch of creative emoji use. But they seemed to like sharing their knowledge, so I moved the shoe to the windowsill for better light, snapped a picture, and uploaded it with a plea: *Can anyone identify these crystals?*

Then I made myself another coffee and waited.

9

SARA

"*I*s this him?"

Blue showed me a picture on her phone, a still from a security camera by the look of it. I recognised the event bar at the Peninsula in the background. My reaction was visceral. It felt as if a semi had run into my chest and squashed the air out of my lungs. My knees buckled, and I fell backward onto the couch in the pool house.

"I take it that's a yes?"

"Just give her a minute." Brooke perched beside me, worried. "Are you okay?"

"How can I be? That monster is here in Baldwin's Shore."

"Was here," Blue said. "Nobody's seen him since Saturday night."

A small mercy. Or was it? Had the monster crawled back under his rock? Or was he lurking in the shadows, waiting to make his move against me? Over the past four days, when the bogeyman didn't show up with a gun or a pillow, the chains wrapped around my chest had loosened just a smidgen. Enough that I could breathe again. A tiny ember of hope sparked inside me, but its future depended on what Blue had found out.

"Why was he there?" Brooke asked. "Was he a hotel guest?"

Blue shrugged. "Nico doesn't know. He was understandably reluctant to divulge details about possible guests, but he had his head of security review every tape from Saturday night, and I can tell you one thing—our mystery man is a pro."

"A pro at what?"

"Being a slippery motherfucker. See that picture?" She gestured toward the still she'd dropped onto the coffee table. "That's the only good image of his face. He kept his head down around all the other cameras, but that one was hidden."

"Why?" Brooke asked, shuddering. "That's a little creepy, having hidden cameras around the place."

I understood why she felt uncomfortable—last year, she'd had her own experience with a stalker, and that stalker had watched her through hidden eyes. I glanced around and shivered myself. When I'd refused to stay with Brooke—despite Blue trying to railroad me into going—Luca had roped Brie's protection team into giving the pool house a thorough security audit, which included checking for hidden electronics and installing motion detectors outside. If anyone was creeping around the property, I'd receive an alert on my phone. And then I'd call Luca, and he'd either come to my rescue or arrange for an autopsy.

He was frustrated with me, I could tell. And if I was being honest, I was frustrated with me too. Luca wanted me to spill every detail I could remember of the night my parents died. But he didn't understand these people. If they could cover up the murder of a senator's chief of staff, then a small-town sheriff's deputy wouldn't worry them, no matter how much military experience he'd had in the past. The monster was untouchable. So all I wanted to find out was whether he'd been in Baldwin's Shore for me or for some other reason. Nothing more. Then I'd know whether to run or to carry on with the same miserable existence I'd survived for the past sixteen years.

But the fear, the terror that had paralysed me for so long before it turned into an all-encompassing numbness, I was struggling to keep it at bay.

"One of the bar staff had his hand in the till," Blue said. "Nico set up the camera to catch him, and he never bothered to remove it."

"Wow. That nice guy with the dimples?" Brooke asked. "I thought he'd just gone on vacation."

"I'm not sure about the dimples, but Nico definitely fired him. Maybe we should send him a thank-you note because otherwise, we wouldn't know that Sara's suspect ordered a sparkling mineral water and a whisky on the rocks. Macallan 18, to be precise."

"The replacement bartender dropped a cocktail shaker when I went to the Peninsula for dinner with Brie last week. Actually, it was more of a toss. I think he was trying to do that fancy trick where you throw it over your shoulder and catch—"

"Can we get back to the investigation?" I asked. Who cared about whisky or cocktails? I didn't, although there was a certain attraction in drinking myself into a stupor right now. Dying from liver damage was probably more fun than being forced off the road and into a tree. "I thought Nico had hundreds of security cameras?"

"That's a slight exaggeration," Blue said. "Cameras cover the exits, the parking lot, the lobby, the hallways and stairwells, the beach area, Nico's private villa, and the inner perimeter around Colt and Brie's suite. Thirty-six devices in total, which is why it took so long for the staff to comb through the footage, but none around the pool or the gardens because nobody wants to—and I quote—make an accidental sex tape. There are guards, though. Four members of Nico's security detail work each shift, plus Brie and Colt have their own team."

All those cameras, all those people, and it hadn't been enough.

"They only caught a single glimpse? There are no other leads?"

"I didn't say that. He wasn't a guest, and he didn't eat dinner there, but we were able to track him around the hotel with a combination of camera footage and eyewitness accounts." Blue rolled her eyes. "That threw up more questions than it answered. He wasn't alone, though. He showed up late in the evening with another gentleman, older. Unfortunately, we didn't get a great look at his face either. Too many shadows. They walked around the corner of the building, heading toward the ballroom, and at some point, your guy"—Blue tapped the photo—"paid a visit to the bar. Then the two of them left together forty minutes later. A security guard saw them standing on the terrace, but they didn't mingle."

"So why would they be..." Brooke started, then trailed off. Probably because she already knew the answer. They'd been there because they were looking for someone.

Watching someone.

"We don't know that they were looking for you," Blue said.

"Oh, sure, it was just a big coincidence."

"Even if they were, all they would have seen was you

dancing with a dude dressed as Prince Charming. Who was he, by the way?"

I put my head in my hands. "I have no idea."

"Really? Because Nico's security guy showed me the video of you two in the bar, and you looked pretty cosy."

"He covered for me when I dropped Kayleigh's phone in the fountain. I owed him a dance."

"You drowned her phone? Hey, good going."

"It was an accident." My whole damn life was an accident. "I should book an airplane ticket."

"No, no, not yet. We still have one lead to follow up."

"What lead?"

"Their vehicle. A black Mercedes S-Class. We might be light on facial IDs, but the camera at the resort's main entrance captured their licence plate."

I jolted as something that might have been hope or sheer terror blossomed in my chest. We were a step closer to the monster, but all I wanted to do was run in the opposite direction.

Brooke didn't share my hesitation. "So we can ask Luca to look up the owner?"

"No need; I already called in a favour."

When I first came to live in Baldwin's Shore, I'd tried telling Justine that the twins were being mean to me. That Easton called me names and Parker told me not to play the piano because it gave him a headache. But she'd just laughed and told ten-year-old me to grow a thicker skin because words couldn't kill me.

But that was a lie.

With one tiny sentence, Blue sent my heart skittering to a halt.

"S-s-so you know who he is?"

"Not exactly. The vehicle's registered to a shell company

out of Delaware, which is a pain in the ass, but it also shows that these people have something to hide. Give me a few days to dig around."

A few days? My nerves wouldn't stretch to a few days. Sitting around in the pool house was like waiting in line for my own death. *Come, take a ticket; it'll be your turn soon.* I'd tried reading to distract myself from impending doom. I'd tried watching movies. I'd even tried dancing a lonely samba, but there weren't enough tissues in the apartment for me to attempt that again, and I couldn't face going to the store. What kind of screwed-up life did I lead when even the good memories hurt?

"I'm not sure—"

Brooke didn't let me finish. "Since you'll be staying for a while, I thought you might be able to help out at the Craft Cabin? Darla's working in Virginia until Saturday, Everly's sick, and Paulo's gone to New York to hook up with his not-so-secret boyfriend, so he won't be back until the weekend either. If I'm on my own, I'm going to struggle to serve customers and teach tomorrow's painting class."

"But—"

"Darla will pay you. I couldn't get ahold of her on the phone today, but she's always fair when it comes to wages, and I know her—she wouldn't want me to try and cope with everything alone."

"What about—"

Blue cut me off. Was this a conspiracy?

"That's a great idea. No way would the guy try anything in public. Think about it—he's been careful to keep to the shadows so far, and he's not going to meander along Main Street, push past Betty Ingram and Elmira Fairbanks while they're picking out yarn, and shoot you at the counter."

Although if he jostled Elmira Fairbanks, he'd be a dead

man, which would solve the problem. Well, one of them. Elmira was a cannonball of a woman who scared the bejesus out of everyone in town, me included, obviously.

"Tomorrow's Thursday," Brooke said. "Which means senior's day at the hair salon, and you know how nosy those ladies are. They all sit there under the dryers, waiting for their curls to set and watching the street outside. If a non-touristy stranger showed up, especially a man on his own, the whole of Baldwin's Shore would find out within five minutes flat. Someone would run out to invite him to a potluck supper."

"And the guy's a cockroach. Roaches hide from the light."

"Okay, okay, I'll come." The watercolour classes I took there had quickly become the only social activity I actually enjoyed. My dad had taught me to paint, but it had taken fifteen years before time dulled the edges of my pain enough for me to pick up a brush again. "Do...do you think you could follow me there and back in your car?"

"Why don't I give you a ride?"

I shook my head. "Two cars, two targets."

"Uh, sure. I'll do that."

She thought I was overreacting, I could tell, but *her* monster hadn't murdered anyone. Mine had gone from zero to one hundred, come straight out of the darkness and killed my parents. I no longer remembered how it felt not to be on edge.

All I could do was fake-smile my appreciation.

"Thank you."

10

SARA

Sara's to-do list:
- Find my size two mop brush.
- Order groceries (Deon to deliver).
- Check on flight availability.
- Avoid nervous breakdown.
- Try not to trip over Darla's cat.

"Ohmigosh, have you ever been to Times Square? I got lost at least twenty times, and the people are weird. Everyone I talked to just looked at me funny, even when I complimented their clothes or wished them a super-duper day. And the lady I sat next to at *The Lion King* kept giving me dirty looks, but apart from that, New York was fantabulous. I spent six hours in Bloomingdale's, and I still barely made it around a quarter of the store." Paulo beamed at Brooke and me. "But I did manage to get gifts for my bestest friends in the whole world. And also for Blue."

Against all the odds, I'd made it through Thursday and Friday at the Craft Cabin and lived to tell the tale. And, even more surprisingly, I hadn't hated being there. After almost a week holed up in the pool house, jumping at my own shadow, spending time among glitter and sequins lifted the veil of darkness. The place was a real Aladdin's cave. And then there was Brooke's unending cheerfulness and a steady stream of customers to take my mind off...well, my mind.

Paulo began unpacking bags, and it seemed he'd bought New York's entire supply of tissue paper and ribbon.

"This one's for you," he said, handing a box to Brooke. "And this is for you."

Shoes. He'd bought me shoes. Size seven Riya de Leon pumps, this time in a dusky pink instead of blue, suede with a maroon velvet ribbon woven around the top.

"You shouldn't have." I mean, where would I ever wear them?

"He didn't. Davis's credit card, right?" Blue spoke from behind me, and I jumped six inches and knocked into a yarn display. Fluffy balls rolled all over the place, and Pickle the cat appeared from nowhere and leapt on the nearest one.

"Hey, hey, let go of that." Brooke made a grab for the cat, but Pickle dodged and ran up a rack of acrylic paints. The whole thing teetered for a second or two, then finally overbalanced, spilling tubes across the floor.

"Shit!" Brooke squeaked, but Blue just laughed.

"That damn cat. She's a pain in the neck."

Paulo turned indignant. "Don't insult Pickle."

Blue was kind of right. Cat-astrophes were a regular occurrence, according to Brooke, but since Pickle belonged to Darla, any breakages just got written off with a sigh.

"No more kitty treats for you," Brooke said as she bent to pick up the mess. "Things went well with Davis, then?"

"Last night, he—" Paulo started.

Blue held up a hand. "Please, we don't need to hear the graphic details."

"I was just going to say that he hired a professional chef to come cook at his apartment, and the truffle risotto was to die for. Sara, do you like the shoes? Brooke said you lost one of the blue ones? I didn't get time to customise them, but if you want crystals, I'm your fairy godmother."

"Paulo, they're too much."

"Nonsense." He winked. "Blue was so right about Davis's credit card. He told me to buy whatever I wanted, and that meant bringing my favourite Cinderella a pretty new pair of pumps."

"Davis French can definitely afford the shoes," Blue put in. "He could afford to buy the whole of Bloomingdale's if he wanted to."

I still wasn't entirely certain how Paulo had hooked up with a wealthy New York businessman, and he was sure keeping quiet about it. I'd only met Davis once, when he was in town visiting with Romi—they were old friends—and he was Paulo's polar opposite. Serious, quiet, distinguished. He rarely smiled, and his favourite colour appeared to be grey.

Brooke stopped stacking paints back onto the rack and opened her gift. Paulo had bought her a purse, a cream leather purse with a colourful scarf tied around the handles. Blue got a selection of fancy coffee and a bottle of perfume. There was no doubt which she preferred.

"Thank you," I said softly. Gifts were a rarity in my world. The last person to remember my birthday had been Grandpa. This year, I'd bought myself a cupcake from the Coffee House, added a single candle, and made a wish that life would be a little brighter this year. Only to get fired two days later by my cousins.

"You're very welcome, sweet pea."

"Who wants coffee?" Blue asked. "I'm woefully under-caffeinated."

Brooke and Paulo raised their hands, and I nodded too. Blue clutched her package of coffee to her chest and headed to the break room at the back of the store.

"So things are going well with Davis?" Brooke asked Paulo.

He turned coy, but nodded. "Is Darla back yet? She called me from the airport to say her flight was delayed."

"Hey, don't change the subject like that."

"If it's hot gossip you're after, you should be asking about Darla, not me."

"What? Why?" Brooke checked the door, and I knew why. Darla had called ten minutes ago to say she was on her way to the store. "Quick, spill the beans."

Paulo lowered his voice conspiratorially. "I think she might have gone on a date."

"Are you serious? Darla doesn't date."

She'd been through a bad breakup before she moved to Baldwin's Shore, and I'd never seen her with a man in the four and a half years she'd lived here. When she was working as Grandpa's nurse, she'd never brought anyone to the house, not a friend and certainly not a boyfriend. At first, she'd spent all her spare time in her rooms—she'd had a small suite in the wing my grandpa had called his own—and after she settled in, she used to go for walks on the beach before Grandpa woke up. In the evenings, she'd knit or crochet or play chess, mostly with Grandpa but occasionally with me. She rarely lost. Grandpa once told me that her mind was wasted at The Lookout. After he died, I'd wondered if she'd sell the house he gifted her and skip town because she'd never really put down roots, but instead, she'd started the Craft Cabin.

Despite the years Darla and I had spent living in close proximity, I didn't feel as if I knew her that well—we were both loners—but if we had one thing in common, it was that the Baldwins, with the possible exception of Parker, disliked both of us intensely.

"A giant asked her out for dinner." Paulo fanned himself. "And holy helianthus, he was a hottie."

"How do you know?" Brooke asked. "I mean, how did they meet?"

"Bradley brought some friends over to help assemble furniture, and it was just a whole parade of deliciousness." He made an exaggerated sad face, lips turned down at the corners. "They were all straight. Anyhow, I might have overheard the hundred-degree hulk asking her if she wanted to go get a burger sometime."

"Aw, that's so sweet. And she went?"

"She said that she'd probably call him, but I don't know if she did because I accidentally ended up in New York earlier than I planned."

"How can you accidentally end up in New York?"

"Alcohol was involved. And Bradley. And a group of rogue drag queens."

Brooke giggled. "Well, I hope Darla did call the hottie."

"So do I, sweet cheeks. So do I."

"Who's Bradley?" I asked.

"He's investing the money to open the new branch of the Craft Cabin in Virginia."

"He's basically Paulo with better hair," Brooke said, and Paulo gasped and clutched at his chest.

"How can you say that? My hair's amazing. I got the ends

frosted in New York." Paulo gave a twirl. "What do you think?"

Brooke giggled. "Are you sure the two of you weren't separated at birth?"

"I wish. If we were brothers, I'd never leave his closet alone. That man could clothe an entire drag queen convention."

"You're out of milk," Blue called from the break room. The aroma of coffee drifted through the open doorway, and the fancy New York beans smelled no different from the regular stuff.

Brooke looked to Paulo, and he rolled his eyes.

"I suppose you want me to go to the store?"

"Either that or you can finish putting these paints back in the right places."

"I'll go to the store."

He disappeared before anyone could say another word, and Brooke laughed.

"I just know he's gonna detour via the Coffee House and come back with cookies, and he'll probably chat for an hour too."

"Good." Blue poked her head through the door and crooked a finger in my direction as the bell above the front door tinkled. "I came here to talk to you."

My good mood vanished in a heartbeat. "Y-y-you did?"

I'd been trying so hard to block the monster and the investigation from my thoughts. The nightmares were bad enough. Brooke glanced toward the group of customers that had just walked in, torn because she wanted to hear what Blue had to say more than I did.

"I'll look after these people," she said, leaving me with no choice but to walk toward the break room with all the enthusiasm of a condemned woman.

Blue handed me a mug of black coffee. I usually took milk, but if Paulo was going to spend an hour on his errand, I might as well drink it before it got cold.

"Did you find something?" I asked.

"Yes and no."

I waited.

"The corporation in Delaware, that's a struggle. Opaque. Whoever set that up doesn't want anyone to find them, and short of hiring a world-class hacker..."

"Do you know any world-class hackers?"

Blue made a face. "Unfortunately not, and if there's one positive thing to come out of this, it's that there's literally no evidence that the man you saw was at the Peninsula because he followed you. Maybe he dropped by to see a friend, or he was travelling to Portland and got thirsty along the way? But I did get curious about the beginning. Before the beginning, actually. Don't you think it's a weird coincidence that your mom's boss died just a month before she did?"

"Mom said he died in his sleep."

Peaceful, that was the word she'd used. It had stuck in my memory for all these years because her death had been anything but.

"He did. The official cause of death was heart failure, and that was what the papers reported. Tragic death, only fifty, blah, blah, blah. But when my old boss died, I inherited his contacts, and one of those contacts is a cop in DC. The part that got swept under the carpet was that Senator Colvin's heart failure was brought on by an overdose of Seconal."

"An overdose? He took an overdose?"

"Yeah. Could have been accidental. The difference between a normal dose of barbiturates and a lethal dose isn't very much at all. And you could see why the family would want to hide it—death by suicide or by a grave error would have led to much more media interest than a heart attack, and who wants grief to be overshadowed by a media circus, especially when there are kids involved? Did you know his granddaughter found the body?"

"Madison?" A fresh wave of sadness rolled over me. "No, nobody ever told me that."

"You knew her?"

"The Colvin family had a compound in Texas, kind of like the Baldwins do here. After Mike Colvin won his US Senate seat, he and his wife spent most of their time in DC, so my family did too, but there were times when we all had to go back to Texas. The Colvins used to let us stay in a cottage on the grounds to save my parents from renting a place. They were like family, I guess. So yes, I knew Madison reasonably well."

Family was important, the senator always said. When he had the time, he used to take us both for ice cream on Saturday mornings, and I used to love playing at the big house. Madison had a dollhouse taller than me, plus her grandpa had bought her a puppy for her eighth birthday, a goofy little thing named Scooter, and I'd been a little jealous because I loved dogs and we couldn't have one since Mom was allergic to fur. Dad would always make me change my clothes right after I got back to the cottage, but Mom would still sneeze.

Madison had been yet another loss in my life.

"Don't you think it was weird that Colvin and your parents died so close together?"

"What are you saying? That their deaths were connected?"

"I'm saying that it's worth keeping an open mind, especially with two hazy causes of death."

The bell over the front door jingled again, this time accompanied by a cheery "Hi, folks." Darla was back.

"We can't talk about this, not here. Not now."

"Later, then."

Possibly. Or possibly not. I'd done my best to block that month from my memory. It wasn't just all the death, it was the fighting. The tension. Mom losing her job had put a strain on everyone, and mixed up in the middle had been Grandpa's eightieth birthday celebration. Our brief return to Baldwin's Shore had put Dad in a foul mood.

I pasted on a smile and went out to greet Darla. "How was Virginia?"

The group of customers were looking at price tags in the sculpture section—the Craft Cabin sold finished work from local artists as well as the materials to make your own masterpiece—and Brooke was already rooting through a bag of candy Darla had brought back.

"The new store's starting to look like a store now. I'll admit that a month ago, I was wondering whether we'd bitten off more than we could chew."

Brooke gave her a sly smile. "I hear you had some help?"

No kidding, Darla went as pink as the muumuu she was wearing, and that thing was *bright*. "Paulo has a big mouth."

"So you *did* go out for burgers with a hot hunk?"

"It was just lunch."

"And? Are you going to see him again?"

Pink darkened to scarlet. "Maybe? He asked me to get pizza with him the next time I'm in town."

Brooke threw her arms around her boss. "That's so awesome! What's he like? Paulo said he's a giant?"

"His name is Alex, and he's a personal trainer. But don't get too excited—it might not go anywhere."

"It's great that you're dating again, though. When are you going back to Virginia?"

"Next month, but we still need to finalise the details." Darla turned to me. "Sara, I really appreciate you helping Brooke out. If you let me have your bank details, I'll make sure you get paid for the hours you worked."

"Thank you so much."

Conversation paused as the customers picked out one of the beautiful wooden boats that were made by Decker Langdon, a local carpenter who did sculpting on the side. They weren't cheap, but they were well worth the money.

"Will you be looking for any more shifts?" Darla asked once the group left. "Because I might need Paulo in Virginia again, and I'm sure Brooke and Everly would be grateful for an extra hand."

My emotions were running so close to the surface these days, and tears stung my eyes. Why did kindness break me more easily than death?

"Can I let you know? I could use the extra money, but right now, I'm not sure how much longer I'll be in Baldwin's Shore."

Darla's expression turned sympathetic. "Is this because of the fight with your cousins?"

Easier to lie than tell the truth. "That's a big part of it."

"Can't say I'd blame you for leaving, hun. You could come back in two years to claim what's yours and then hightail it into the sunset."

"Claim what's mine? You know about Grandpa's will?"

I suppose it shouldn't have surprised me. Darla had been closer to him than anyone in his later years, and they'd obviously discussed his estate because she'd received a part of it. A part of it that everyone except me had contested.

Darla was a mere employee—how dare he leave her with a home?

"We spoke about all sorts of things."

"What does his will have to do with anything?" Brooke asked. "Didn't his estate get divided up years ago?"

I'd always preferred to keep personal business as just that—personal—but what did it matter anymore? Let the whole darn town find out what lying toads my cousins were.

"It didn't get divided up; it got put into a trust. In two years, the trust will be split between beneficiaries who meet Grandpa's conditions."

"What are the conditions?"

"He didn't want any of us to laze around living off the family name, so we have to make at least $250,000 in our own right before we're entitled to a cent of his money—earned, not borrowed or gifted. That's on top of whatever we spend on living expenses. We need to present a bank statement showing the amount to claim a share. I was on track, but when Kayleigh and Lillian fired me, they basically stole my inheritance as well as my job."

"That's...that's..."

"Sneaky? Underhanded? Dishonest? Yup, it is, and there's not a darn thing I can do about it. I have some savings, but there's no way I can make the amount I need in two years."

"Talk about shooting yourself in the foot—Nico's furious with the way they acted at the Peninsula last week, and I bet LKB will end up going bust if you're not running it."

"Probably."

And that hurt too. Everything I built got destroyed. I was twenty-six years old, and I didn't have a single tangible thing to call my own.

"But what about the codicil?" Darla asked. "You don't need \$250,000."

What was she talking about? "What codicil? I don't even know what that is."

"It's a legal document that alters a will," Brooke explained. "I learned that much from Aaron."

"Grandpa's will didn't have one of those."

I'd never known Darla to be anything but cheerful and easygoing, but I caught a flicker of anger in her blue eyes. "Yes, it did. He wrote it two weeks before he died, and I witnessed it."

"But...but..." *A codicil?* "Why didn't Asa say something?"

Asa Phillips was Aaron's mentor, and he'd been Grandpa's lawyer for as long as I could remember. EJ had fired him after the Darla episode, after he'd written the agreement that left her with the house on Valley Drive and the document proved to be watertight.

"East wrote it himself, so Asa most probably didn't know. Your grandfather always was fond of his secrets."

"What did it say?" Brooke asked.

"I can't remember the exact wording, hun, but East was annoyed with Easton the Third in particular, and also with Kayleigh and Lillian. He saw what they were doing to Sara, don't think he didn't. Easton's earnings goal was increased by all the money East had paid to bail him out of his messes over the years—\$176,000 if I remember rightly—and Sara was to get \$200,000 in cash toward her target."

My knees went weak, and I sat down on the nearest semi-solid object, which was a basket of yarn. The yarn compressed, and I ended up stuck with my legs in the air. Crap. Brooke and Darla hauled me up by my arms, and Brooke kept an arm around my waist.

"I-I only ever saw the original will. There was nothing else."

"Darla, do you know what happened to the codicil?" Brooke asked.

"East put it in the safe with the rest of his paperwork. He told me that Asa Phillips had a key, and he'd open the safe and deal with the papers when the time came."

This...this was crazy. "I was right there when Asa opened the safe, and I'm sure he went through all the papers. Why wouldn't he have mentioned a codicil?"

Blue had been listening in, leaning against the wall with a mug of coffee in her hand.

"Well, there are three options, obviously. Either East changed his mind and tore up the codicil, or Asa got paid off by one of the beneficiaries and 'lost' it, or one of your slimy relatives got to the safe before Asa did and made it vanish."

"Strike out option two," Brooke said. "There's no way Asa would have accepted a bribe."

"East was still grumbling about Easton the day before he passed, so he didn't change his mind," Darla chimed in.

"Which leaves option three. Somebody quite literally stole your inheritance. The big question is who?"

11

GARRETT

*D*amn, craft forums were a minefield. I'd assumed there couldn't be much controversy when it came to beads and thread, but it seemed I'd been wrong. Five days had passed since I wrote my plea for help, and suddenly I had answers.

BeadGirl1984: Those roses look like Swarovski to me.

Love2Craft: No, they're GJ florals.

MsSparkle: You're both blind—they're quite clearly from the Naruki Valentine series.

Love2Craft: Are you sure? The Naruki Valentines only come in cotton candy, champagne, and peach.

MsSparkle: They also released two limited-edition colours: Violet Dream and Skybaby Blue. Do your research.

Love2Craft: There's no need to be rude.

MsSparkle: I wasn't. I was being accurate.

Love2Craft: Oh, please. Do your research? You should change your username to MsPassiveAggressive.

MsSparkle: Only one of us is being rude. Why don't you go pintuck yourself?

Click. I closed the browser tab and hoped to fuck I never had to visit the Coffee & Crafts discussion board again. But I had three possible leads, and MsSparkle—who definitely sounded like the kind of pedant I tried to avoid at parties—actually did know what she was talking about. To my admittedly untrained eyes, those roses looked like Naruki beads, and I fired off a message to the manufacturer via the contact form on their website. *Please can you provide a list of your US stockists, in particular, those on the West Coast.*

And then I waited.

And waited.

And waited.

The reply came in the early hours of Monday morning, before I'd had time for my first coffee, written in both polite English and what I assumed was Japanese.

Dear Sir,

Please be advised that we have one official stockist for our products on the West Coast of the United States:

The Craft Cabin,
Main Street,
Baldwin's Shore,
Oregon.

We thank you for your interest in our products.
At your service always,
Aiko Tanaka.

The beads were sold in Baldwin's Shore? Well, holy fuck. A craft store—Gracie had been absolutely right. Looked as if I'd be taking a drive west today.

The bell above the door of the Craft Cabin jingled as I pushed it open, ushering me into a sequinned version of hell. Everywhere I looked, there was glitter, yarn, paint, patterned paper, metal tools that looked more like torture implements, cutting mats, beads, plastic doohickeys, pencils, and a hundred kinds of glue, all wrapped in the smell of turpentine. A black cat sat on the register, washing its paws, and it gave me a dirty look as I approached.

"Can I help you?"

The woman sitting behind the register looked as if she belonged there. Her dress was a long, shapeless thing in mustard yellow, and she didn't stop knitting as she spoke. Her name badge said "Darla" and she'd drawn a ray of sunshine in one corner.

"Do you stock Naruki Valentine beads?"

"Sure do, hun." She waved toward the far side of the store. "They're right over there by the silk flowers, but we're waiting for a fresh shipment to arrive. It should be here next week or the week after."

"I'm actually looking for a lady who purchased some. The blue roses. I appreciate you won't be able to divulge confidential information, but I was hoping you might be able to remember who she was and pass on a message."

"You'll have to explain."

"Maybe it's easier if I show you?" I took the Riya de Leon pump out of my messenger bag and set it on the counter. The cat hissed and ran off. "I'm trying to find the woman who lost this shoe, and the beads seem to be my best hope of identifying her."

"Ohmigosh!" The cry came from behind me, and I spun to find a small, very colourful guy who appeared to be wearing most of the store's products. "Is that Sara's missing shoe? Where did you find it?"

Sara. I had a name.

"You know the woman who owns this?"

"Well, of course I do. I made it for her. Well, not the actual shoe, that came from Romi, but I added the crystals. Isn't it spectacular?"

"Indeed it is. Where can I find Sara?"

"Paulo..." Darla warned. "Don't go giving out people's personal details."

"But this is so romantic." Paulo clutched his hands to his chest. "Don't you think? She dressed up as Cinderella to go to the ball, and now Prince Charming is bringing her shoe back."

"That's a fairy tale. For all you know, this gentleman could be the villain in the story." Darla looked me up and down. "No offence."

"None taken, but I assure you my intentions are noble." I offered a business card. "Garrett Dorsey. I run an investment company over in Roseburg. All I want to do is return Sara's shoe and ask her to have dinner with me."

Paulo gasped. "See? Totes adorbs, just like you and your hot builder."

"Alex isn't a builder. He only came to help out with some

furniture." Darla returned to studying me. "You run a company?"

What could I say? Nepotism had worked out well for me, although I'd still have preferred to keep my old job.

"For my sins."

"Darla, don't be such a party pooper," Paulo chided, then lowered his voice to a conspiratorial whisper. "Come back in two hours. Sara's joining us for the drawing class this afternoon. Hey, we could draw the shoe! The heel's a little mangled, but I'm sure I can patch it up. Yes, that's an excellent idea, and maybe you could pop over to the Coffee House and grab some cookies? Sara likes the double chocolate chip ones."

Darla was right; Paulo shouldn't be giving out Sara's information like that, but I wasn't going to complain when I could turn it to my advantage. Today's trip had been worth the trouble, even if my PA hated me and my freshly shuffled schedule meant I had back-to-back meetings for the whole of Thursday. Two hours, and I'd finally see my runaway princess without the mask.

Two hours.

"I'll get the cookies."

12

SARA

The first thing I saw when I walked into the Craft Cabin with my portfolio case was a plateful of double chocolate chip cookies with a side of cake pops, but my spark of happiness was quickly extinguished because the second thing I saw was my shoe. My left shoe. The one I'd lost. The one I'd abandoned in the shadow of the monster. Good thing I hadn't eaten any of those cookies because they'd have come right up again. I backed away, panic gripping my throat, then let out a little shriek as I stepped on somebody's foot. Arms wrapped around my waist, and I began to struggle as they tightened, my breath coming in fast pants.

Get away, get away, get away.

Blue said the monster would shy away from the light, but she'd been wrong, hadn't she? Because here he—

"Easy, Cinderella. Don't break my nose."

Now I stiffened, but this time not from fear. I recognised that voice. I'd replayed it in my head more times than was healthy over the past week, sometimes in frustration and sometimes with regret.

"Charming? What are you doing here?"

"Returning your shoe. Isn't that how the story goes?"

"That's fiction. If you do it in real life, it counts as stalking."

"Even if I come bearing cake pops? Chocolate, not strawberry?"

"That's playing dirty."

A hand came up to my throat, and his breath tickled my ear. "What if I like playing dirty?"

I swallowed hard. "H-h-how did you recognise me?"

His thumb skated over my bottom lip. "I'd know this mouth anywhere."

Someone coughed, and too late, the spell was broken and I remembered we had an audience. Three of Baldwin's Shore's older residents were staring at us from the art table, their mouths hanging open, and Paulo had his hands pressed to his face like an Edvard Munch painting. Darla cleared her throat.

"Why don't you talk in the break room, hun? It's a bit more private."

"Not a bad idea," Charming murmured, and that asshole was still holding me. I elbowed him in the stomach, taking a small measure of satisfaction in the *oof* that sounded behind me as I strode in the direction of the break room. But I wasn't thinking straight today. I should have run out the front door. By the time my thoughts caught up with my feet, Charming was right behind me, and goosebumps popped out on my arms as I prepared to face him for the first time without the safety blanket of a mask. I hesitated before I turned. Dreams of him had given me a tiny respite from the nightmares, but what if the reality didn't match up?

"So, this is where you've been hiding." Charming's hand skimmed my hip. "Sara."

"We're not on the dance floor anymore." His hand fell away as I whirled to face him. "Keep your distance."

Holy smokes, he was even more handsome than I imagined. Today, his hair was tousled rather than slicked back, and he'd ditched the epaulettes in favour of black jeans, a grey T-shirt, and biker boots. From Prince Charming to the Prince of Darkness, definitely not my type at all. Not that I had much of a type. If there was one characteristic that my handful of past relationships had shared, it was poor judgment.

Meanwhile, Charming was sizing me up, and I couldn't read his expression. Disappointment? Annoyance? Incredulity? He'd gone to the effort of tracking me down, only to find that without my team of fairy godmothers, I was just a dull, mousy-haired nobody who hadn't even ironed her shirt this morning.

He perched on the arm of the couch, arms folded. "You're a hard woman to find, Sara."

"Then why bother?"

"That's a question I've asked myself a hundred times over the past week."

"And what's the answer?"

"I'm not sure," he admitted. "But I don't like unfinished business."

"You've never had a woman walk away from you before?"

"You didn't walk. You ran."

"Aw, did that put a dent in your ego?"

What was wrong with me? I never spoke to people this way.

"A small one, but don't worry; it'll recover." A pause. "I've been to a hundred of those events, and I didn't expect to enjoy anything about that evening." His gaze met mine. "I was wrong."

What was that supposed to mean? "You're...a big fan of cake pops?"

"Yeah, Cinderella, the cake pops were a hit. And so was the woman eating them."

"But...but I'm not her."

"I might be many things, but I'm not stupid. I recognise your voice, indignant then uncertain. I recognise the way your lips flatten in a thin line when I do something you don't like." Charming stood and took a step closer. "I recognise that little flutter of fear in the pulse at your neck."

I also took a step, a big one, backward, and my ass hit the counter on the other side of the break room.

"Well, I mean obviously I dressed up as Cinderella last week, but that wasn't the real me. I don't usually do that kind of thing."

"You're the good girl, huh? You don't crash parties and steal phones and dance sexy salsas with strangers?"

"I only meant to borrow the phone."

"Any comment on the sexy salsa?"

"I don't know what came over me."

"I do. Dopamine, endorphins, and lust." He ran one finger over my cheek, and I shivered. "For one night, you let down your guard and lived for the moment. You might have been wearing a mask, but what I saw *was* the real you." Another step. "And I want to see that woman again."

"She's gone."

"Liar."

Charming left me seriously off balance. I was leaning sideways on a tightrope, about to fall, and there was no safety net. I said I wasn't the woman from the party, but he wasn't the same man either. This version was darker. More commanding.

"I get the impression that sexy salsa is your default operating state."

"I'm more of a dirty tango man."

See? I'd gotten in way, way over my head last Saturday.

"So, uh, thanks for bringing my shoe back, uh... I don't even know your name."

"Garrett."

"Thanks for bringing my shoe back, Garrett. I appreciate you taking the trouble."

Another step. "Have dinner with me tonight."

"I don't think that's a good idea."

"Who's talking now? Sara or Cinderella?"

"Both of us?"

"So many filthy lies coming out of your mouth today. I'll pick you up at seven."

"You don't know where I live."

"You think I can't find out?"

Shit.

"I don't have anything to wear."

"I'm not going to complain if you come naked." My mouth formed an O of shock, which seemed to amuse him, judging by his grin. "In fact, I hope you do."

For a moment, I thought he was going to kiss me, and he sort of did. On the forehead. Which wasn't so much a smooch, more his way of sucking out all rationality.

"Seven o'clock," he said.

"You are *not* picking me up."

"Then meet me at the Peninsula."

The heat in my veins turned to ice in a heartbeat. The Peninsula? Was this some kind of sinister plot? Would the monster be waiting for me again? Just as quickly, the fire in Charming's eyes faded, replaced with...concern?

"Sara, are you okay?"

I managed to shake my head.

"You don't want to go to the Peninsula?"

"I want to go far, far away from here."

"Then I'll take you." He finally stepped back, which should have eased my fears, but it didn't. No, the tension ratcheted up a notch when he held out a hand. "Let's go."

"But I...I barely know you."

"We can change that." His gaze settled over me like a weighted blanket. Oddly comforting. "You always play things safe, don't you?"

"It's the only way I can live."

"Are you really living? Or just existing?"

How did this man, this virtual stranger, distil me down into my essence in a few short minutes? He saw me. Saw *through* me. And maybe he was the first person ever to do so.

He couldn't be part of the monster's world, could he? I mean, if he'd wanted to harm me, he could have carried me off along the beach last Saturday, the two of us embraced by darkness, and delivered me into the ocean's foamy grasp. I would have been powerless to stop him, just as I was powerless now.

"Most days, I can barely breathe," I whispered.

"Then we'll get you some air."

I stared at his hand, and instinct told me that if I took it, my life would be turned on its head. But would that really be such a bad thing? What would another sixteen years of *existing* do to me? Sometimes, death felt like the better option, but what if there was another way? Perhaps Charming would ruin me, but the thought of running terrified me too.

I put my hand in his.

As he led me out of the break room, I felt the crushing weight of the status quo lift, replaced by a new burden: fear of the unknown. But there was also a jolt of something else.

Excitement.

"Where are you going?" Paulo asked.

"I have no idea."

"Ooh, fun. Hey, Prince Charming, if you hurt her, I'll turn you into a human pincushion."

Garrett snorted softly. "Understood."

"Don't forget your purse, hun." Darla thrust it into my hand as I stumbled past. "Text if you need anything."

Text? I couldn't even think. A steady drizzle fell as Garrett towed me across the parking lot and half lifted me into an SUV. Hurrah, my breakdown was complete. My life was officially out of control, and all I could do was hang on for the ride.

13

GARRETT

*W*hat the fuck was wrong with me?

First, I'd found my mystery woman, and then I'd practically abducted her from her art class. I didn't do impulsive. Last year, the *New York Times* had described me as a control freak, a label I didn't particularly appreciate, mainly because it was accurate. I stayed healthy, I worked, I did my damn best to protect my family, and when I dated, the women were carefully selected to be as uncomplicated and as obedient as possible. They got background-checked. They signed NDAs. They moaned in all the right places as I fucked them into submission.

So why was I driving toward North Bend at five miles over the speed limit with a silent Sara in the passenger seat of my Porsche?

Because not one of those women had ever made my blood run hot the way she did.

I *burned* for this brunette.

Why was she so quiet? She hadn't uttered a word since we left Baldwin's Shore. Although, quite frankly, I was afraid of what she might have to say. The flash of fear in her eyes at the mention of the Peninsula, that had been my undoing. I'd put the worry there—I wasn't quite sure how—and now I had to fix it.

She didn't snatch her hand away from mine, at least. That was a plus point. I ran a thumb over her knuckles, and she gave a delicate shiver and carried on looking out the window.

Sara, Sara, Sara. I didn't know anything about her, not even her surname, but I knew she'd spent an entire evening with me, just me, without being aware of who I was, without being in it for the money or the kudos of saying she was dancing with Oregon's most eligible bachelor. No, I wasn't kidding when I said that. Two years ago, much to my irritation, thousands of readers of *Imagine* magazine had awarded me the dubious honour, probably because some journalist—and I use that term loosely—had included details of my family's net worth and a picture of me in my dress uniform alongside the poll.

I was nothing special.

But maybe the woman beside me was?

I'd driven away from the craft store with no decorum and no idea where I was going, and I needed to come up with a plan fast. Should I take Sara to a quiet bar, invite her to share her troubles? My English grandma had always said a problem shared was a problem halved, but she'd caused a good number of the problems, and she hadn't appreciated me telling her that. And Sara didn't strike me as the kind of woman who liked to talk anyway. She hid a thousand secrets behind those hazel eyes of hers.

One by one, I wanted her to confide them all.

But first, I had to win her trust.

"Where are we going?" she questioned softly.

"I'm still figuring that out."

At the party, Sara had made her views on the Hadleys of this world quite clear. She wouldn't be impressed if I simply threw money at the problem, which had unfortunately become my modus operandi over the past several years.

"Are you hungry?" I asked.

"Not really."

I glanced across at her, took in her defensive posture—arms folded, legs pressed together—and the way her body inclined away from me. She was nervous as hell, yet she was still here. At the Peninsula and again at the craft store, I'd felt a connection between us, a pull toward her as if we'd gotten trapped in each other's orbits, and despite a whole mountain of misgivings—misgivings she was right to have—she felt it too.

Today, she was a very different woman from the one I'd first met, and not just in looks. The princess persona was no more, replaced by a girl-next-door vibe. Gone was the carefully coiffed blonde hair, transformed into silky brown strands fastened into a messy bun, and the only make-up she wore was a smear of pink gloss on her lips. The things I longed to do to that mouth... I wanted to strip her out of those leggings and Converse and that fluffy purple sweater and—

Don't run before you can walk, asshole.

Sara was two different people, as was I. Today, I'd abandoned the corporate persona, stepped out of my meticulously crafted world into one that had the potential to liberate me. But instead of feeling nervous the way she did, I felt energised. For once, I was living in the moment and doing something I wanted to do instead of what was best for my family and the business. The last time I'd experienced that freedom had been three years ago in Djibouti, Camp Lemonnier to be precise. I'd belonged in that world. Then I'd been forced to return home and take the helm of Dorsey Holdings so my father could sidestep into politics.

I understood why he'd done it. Supported him because the last secretary of state had been a corrupt sleaze and someone needed to clean house. But that didn't make the sacrifice any lighter to bear.

Didn't make living a lie any easier.

Deep down, I wasn't the clean-cut CEO I pretended to be.

And Cinderella, with her effortless grace and her tempting mouth, with that hint of feistiness under the compliant exterior, made me hard as fuck.

She wanted air, and she wanted distance. A flock of birds swooped across in front of the car, heralding inspiration as well as an incoming storm. Would Eugene be far enough? When we hit Reedsport, I turned right.

"Did you figure it out?" Sara asked.

"Yup."

"And?"

"And, it's a surprise. Do you like surprises?"

"I hate surprises."

Then she must have had a lot of assholes in her life.

"Maybe I can change your mind on that." I brought her hand to my lips and kissed her palm. "Trust me?"

"I don't trust anyone."

"Maybe someday, I'll change your mind on that too."

14

SARA

I don't know what I expected, but it sure wasn't this.
Okay, that was a lie.

I *did* know what I'd been expecting. No matter what most of my family thought, I wasn't dumb, and I knew Charming had money. Firstly, he'd been at Hadley's party, and secondly, he was driving a Porsche. I figured he'd take me to a reasonably nice restaurant and show off by ordering the most expensive bottle of wine on the menu. Or, if this man I barely knew turned out to be a real sleazeball, he'd "surprise" me by skipping the restaurant and heading straight for room service. At a fancy hotel, of course.

But instead... Wait, were we lost? What if we'd simply gotten lost? Hmm, Charming didn't seem to be checking a map. No, he was just staring at me.

"We're going *skydiving*?"

"Indoor skydiving. This place opened a few months ago."

"Are you crazy?"

"I'll take that as a compliment."

"Isn't it dangerous?"

"Not as long as you do what you're told."

I was so, so sick of doing what I was told, but I could see how it might be necessary when my life was on the line. Garrett exited the vehicle, and when he walked around to the passenger side, I still hadn't made up my mind whether to get out or not. Not to be deterred, he reached in and unclipped my seat belt.

"Take a chance." His lips brushed my ear, and I jolted. "Interesting," he murmured.

"Have you done this before?"

"Impulsively driven a woman to a town two hours away? Never."

"I meant skydiving."

"Indoor skydiving? No. Outdoor skydiving? Yes."

"Like, from an airplane?"

He struggled to keep a straight face. "That's generally what's involved, yes."

"Why? I mean, why would you do that?"

"Because I'm a US Marine, and it was a requirement."

My eyes bugged out because that was the last thing I'd expected. The crowd he hung with, the expensive car... "You're a soldier?"

"Absolutely not. Those pussies in the army aren't a patch on Marines."

"Oh." I digested that for a moment. "So, how come you're here? You're on leave?"

"I haven't been on active duty in three years. But once a Marine, always a Marine." He held out a hand, and I took it hesitantly. "C'mon. Step out of your comfort zone."

"You'll go first?"

"Because if someone's gonna die, it should be me?"

Was I that transparent? "Something like that."

"Good to know where I stand. Yeah, Cinderella. I'll go first."

***

The instructor gently leaned me forward into the airstream, and I struggled to keep the smile off my face. Before my first try, I thought I'd hate this. Detest it. But here I was, on my third flight of the day, weightless and spinning, and I could grudgingly admit that Charming had done good. He, of course, had only required a quick rundown of the hand signals before he ventured into the wind tunnel, and now he was standing outside the plexiglass wall, watching me with the faintest smile on his face. I tried to wave and ended up flipping over instead. A shriek escaped my lips, and that smile turned into a full-on grin. Asshole.

But I survived. I survived, and what was more, I had a good time. Perhaps I could suggest indoor skydiving as an idea to Addy? Anything would be better than burlesque. Paulo was already making feathered fans, but thankfully, the instructor was booked up for the next two months, so I had time to think up an excuse not to go. At least if we all went skydiving, I'd be able to wear clothes rather than pasties.

When the instructor signalled that my time was up, I gripped the edges of the doorway and dropped my feet back to solid ground. This whole day had been surreal, thanks to the man who offered me a hand as I walked down the steps. Contact with Charming was becoming...not easier; that was the wrong word. More familiar? Every touch still sent sparks through me, but I was learning to accept the tension rather than constantly fighting it. And those darn kisses... His lips hadn't touched mine, but they got everywhere else. My forehead, my palm, my knuckles, and now my hair as he pulled me tight against his side and pressed another kiss to the top of my head. A head that screamed at me to put a stop to all the liberties he took because this could only end in tears—my tears. Boy, I was a hot little mess of emotions today.

"Thanks for coming today, folks," the instructor said. "Hope we'll see you again."

Garrett gave my waist a gentle squeeze. "That's up to Sara."

Oh, I was no good at this kind of decision. Business decisions, yes, but whenever I tried to take control of my personal life, it just spiralled again.

"I'm not sure how much longer I'll be staying in Oregon," I blurted, and I felt Garrett's fingers tense against my hip.

But outwardly, he kept the easy smile. "We'll let you know."

He was a mass of contradictions. Part of the country-club set, but relatively down to earth. Uptight but adventurous. Pushy but gentle when he held open the door of the flight centre and then the door of his car. But he didn't close it. Not yet.

"You're planning to leave Oregon?" he asked, one eyebrow raised.

"Maybe? I'm not sure yet." He didn't let up with that intense gaze of his. "It's complicated."

A pause, and then he leaned in and grazed his lips over mine. Just that whisper of a touch turned the sparks into a smoulder, and I was acutely aware of the ache between my thighs. That must have come from the skydiving, right? Some weird side effect?

Garrett cupped my cheek in his hand. "Then I guess I'll have to make it more complicated."

What?

What was I meant to say to that?

Now he closed the door.

"Where are we going?"

I thought after we left the skydiving centre, we'd head back to Baldwin's Shore, but Garrett was driving east, farther into Eugene, and he seemed to be looking for a parking space.

"You need to eat."

"I don't understand why you're doing this."

"That makes two of us."

"What does that mean?"

"It means that ever since Hadley's party, I haven't been able to get you out of my head. So here I am, stalking you, abducting you, taking you for dinner, and breaking every one of my damn rules. I know more about women's shoes and glass beads than I ever wanted to, my staff are cursing my name because I keep changing my plans at the last minute, and I'm trying to work out whether to take you for pizza or something fancy and French, because I want to impress you but also not come across as a pretentious prick." He paused at a stoplight and brought my hand to his lips. "*Sara.*"

Oh. My. Gosh.

If tumbling around in the air had sent my pulse racing, Charming's words pushed it into overdrive.

"But...but why? I'm nothing special."

Worse, my whole freaking life was cursed.

Garrett turned to look at me, but I kept my eyes on the windshield as I chewed on my bottom lip. I'd dated three men in the past, and the most passion I'd ever experienced was a heartfelt declaration that my "ass looks great in those pants." Oh, and who could forget the impromptu bunch of flowers from the gas station? But now I was sitting beside a man who shed pheromones like a dog shaking off river water, whose words sent flames licking through my belly and probably incinerated his group of female admirers waiting in the background too.

"Nothing special?" He slowly shook his head. "The worst part is that I think you truly believe it."

"I don't know what to say."

"It's simple. You tell me whether you prefer pizza or French food, and then I take you to an appropriate restaurant."

Simple? No, nothing about this was simple, but I had to stall for time, time I desperately needed to get my thoughts in order.

"Uh, pizza?"

"See, that wasn't so difficult, was it?"

15

SARA

"So, why'd you run out on me last week?"

It was the question I'd been both expecting and dreading, and Garrett waited until the main course had been served—a mouth-wateringly delicious stone-baked pizza topped with pepperoni and artichokes—to ask it. Coincidence? I didn't believe that for a moment. Apart from his little speech in the car, he'd remained steadfastly in control at all times.

"I didn't run out on you. I ran out on the situation."

"You didn't want to take off your mask?"

"I crashed the party, remember?"

Luckily, that answer seemed to satisfy him.

"Shame—you missed the catfight between Lillian and Hadley."

A piece of pepperoni went down the wrong way, and I had a coughing fit. *Way to impress the hot out-of-your-league guy, Saralisa.* A waiter materialised with a glass of water, and I drank nearly all of it before I could speak again.

"Are you serious?"

"That's what happens when you mix alcohol and the glitterati."

"Why? What were they fighting about?"

"A guy. Lillian was flirting—futilely—and Hadley took offence because she's made a number of ill-conceived passes at the same man over the years and thought that gave her some sort of claim on him."

"Wow. I thought Lillian looked slightly bruised on Sunday."

"You saw her?"

Ah, crap. Lillian wasn't the only person who needed to think before she spoke.

"Uh, only in passing. Who was the guy?"

Charming gave a little smirk. "Me. And while I was busy untangling Hadley's hair extensions from Lillian's jewellery, my brother decided to go skinny-dipping, and his girlfriend snuck out the side door because apparently one DUI isn't enough for that brat."

"Did she get pulled over?"

"No, thank fuck, but she lost the side mirror off her friend's car."

I noticed that Garrett was drinking water tonight, even though he'd ordered me a glass of rosé. It seemed he took his chauffeuring duties seriously, and for that I was grateful.

"I'm sorry they gave you trouble. Do you have any other siblings?"

"An older sister. She lives in New York. How about you?"

"I'm an only child." An only child who didn't want to discuss her family or her past. "Have you been to this restaurant before? The food's really good."

This was no cheap chain place. The pasta was home-made, the music was soft and classical, and the furnishings bordered on opulent, although the number of naked flames did concern me. There were three candles on our table alone, and were the padded velvet chairs fire retardant?

He shook his head. "I found it online while you were fixing your hair."

"Mental note: next time, bring more hair ties. Not that I'm assuming there'll be a next time. I mean, a next time with you. I might just go skydiving on my own."

"Unless you flee the state."

"Exactly."

"Why do you want to leave?"

A sigh escaped. "Family trouble. Plus..." I swallowed hard. *Guess we're talking about this whether I want to or not.* "Plus someone from my past showed up in town unexpectedly, and he's not a man I want to be around."

"An ex?"

I nearly choked again. "No! I mean, not an ex, just someone who hurt me as a child."

For once, Garrett's cool facade cracked, and he actually looked a tiny bit scary as he put two and two together and made entirely the wrong number.

"He hurt you? Touched you?"

"No, he didn't touch me, not like that. Please, can we drop this?" My appetite deserted me, and the fork dropped from my hand and clattered to the plate. "I can't... I just can't."

The tension dropped out of Garrett's shoulders, but I could tell the sudden relaxation was forced. Mind over matter. The lines on his forehead were the last thing to disappear as he reached carefully past the candles and twined his fingers through mine.

"Then don't. Why don't we focus on the positive? What's keeping you in Oregon?"

An easier question.

"Friends. I don't have many of those, and I've always found it difficult to, you know, form any kind of relationship. The thought of starting again overseas... I'm in a rock-hard-place situation."

"Overseas?"

"I have one friend in Poland. He moved there a while ago, and he's offered me a place to stay until I find my feet."

"He?"

Garrett had called Hadley out on her jealousy, but I thought I saw a tiny flash of fire in his sapphire eyes. Or maybe it was just the reflection from the candles?

"My old dance partner. Relax, he's gay."

"Do you even speak Polish?"

"I downloaded an app this week."

"It gets damn cold there in the winter."

"You've been?"

A brief hesitation, then a nod. "For work."

Did he mean his old military job or his current one? I didn't get a chance to ask before a girl my age approached the table with a tray full of roses, individually wrapped in cellophane and tied with ribbon. She addressed Garrett.

"Hi, can I interest you in buying a rose for your wife? We're raising money for Live without Limits."

"Oh, we're not married," I said.

"Yet," Garrett added, and my gaze snapped to his so fast I gave myself whiplash. He was joking. He had to be joking, but his expression was unreadable.

The rose seller didn't seem to pick up on any tension. "Well, you make a lovely couple." She not-so-subtly inched the tray forward. "All the proceeds go to a great cause."

"Sure, give me a rose. A red one."

"They're five bucks each."

He pulled a hundred bucks out of his wallet. "Keep the change."

"Wow, really?"

"Really."

She selected another rose, a pink one, and put it beside the red one she'd already placed beside my plate.

"Here, you totally get an extra rose. Hope you have an awesome date."

I didn't miss the long glance she gave Garrett as she moved to the next table, and I couldn't even blame her for it. While my look could best be described as "rumpled" after our skydiving session, the wind had taken his hair from "tousled" to "artfully dishevelled." He'd topped the grey T-shirt with a leather jacket, and every single woman in the restaurant had stared at him when we walked in. I felt like an imposter.

"Is this a date?" I asked.

"What else would you call it?"

"Stockholm syndrome?"

"Have you ever been to Stockholm?"

"I haven't travelled much." Only as far as the Bahamas if we were talking overseas. "How about you?"

"I went to Stockholm once."

"For work?"

He shook his head. "I spent a long weekend there with the family on our way to Sälen. Skiing," he explained when he caught my blank look.

Of course. Skiing. I hadn't grown up poor, but Garrett was in a whole other league. Plus Grandpa had been too much of a penny pincher to ever go on a family trip to Europe. EJ and Marianna used to take fancy vacations, but thanks to Grandpa's inheritance challenge, we'd all been budgeting carefully for the past six years.

Just thinking about the will made me seethe. If Darla was right—and I couldn't see any reason for her to lie—then a member of my family had gotten ahold of the codicil and made it disappear. The truly tragic part? I had no idea who. Every single member of the Baldwin household had a character riddled with flaws.

Easton the Third—Paulo called him Easton the Turd, which was far more appropriate—was the obvious culprit. He'd been mentioned in the codicil too, and by destroying it, he'd have gotten away with all of those bail-outs from Grandpa scot-free.

Who was next on the list? It was a toss-up between Marianna and one of the twins. The twins had more of a motive—they'd needed me to do the work building up LKB for them. But they were also *really* dumb. Would they have managed to find out about the codicil, locate Grandpa's hidden safe key, and sneak in to steal the right document? Even I didn't know where he'd kept the key. Asa Phillips had brought his own when he opened the safe for the will reading.

Anyhow, Marianna had never liked me, plus she was a devious snake. She wouldn't have wanted to lose a cent of EJ's inheritance to someone she didn't even consider family. Justine, EJ's first wife, had felt the same way, and she could have gotten Parker to do her dirty work. Parker had both the opportunity and the brains to get into the safe. As for Uncle EJ, he could have acted on Marianna's orders—it was clear who wore the pants in that relationship—or simply cancelled out my share of the family trust to increase his own.

Whichever way I looked at it, I couldn't trust any of them, and living at The Lookout had become more uncomfortable than ever.

"Sara? You okay?"

"What? Huh?"

"You zoned out there."

Darn it. "Sorry. I just have a lot on my mind."

"Want to talk about it?"

And send the hot guy running for the hills in the middle of a date? Nuh-uh. Although a pack of mountain lions was more fun to hang out with than my family. Wait, did mountain lions hang out in packs? Or was that just regular lions? Not that this *was* a date.

"It's better that I don't."

Garrett gave a one-shouldered shrug. "Take your time. This *is* a date, by the way. Are you having dessert?"

I checked my watch. Seven thirty. "Oh, I shouldn't. We have a long drive back, and this *isn't* a date."

"You keep telling yourself that, Cinderella. Do you have a pumpkin coach to catch today?"

"You know I don't."

"So why rush back? There's a club right around the corner, and I owe you a dirty tango."

If he kept stoking those darn flames, I was going to self-combust.

"How do you figure that?"

"I dragged you away from your drawing class. The least I can do is take you for a quick spin around the dance floor."

"I'm not a car."

"I'm well aware of that. I assume a joke about excellent bodywork would be inappropriate here?"

My eyes rolled all of their own accord. "Who says romance is dead?"

"Romance? So you admit this is a date?"

"I admit nothing." But memories of the night at the Peninsula, of moving to the music with our hips so perfectly in sync, overruled common sense. "Fine. One dance, not a tango, dirty or otherwise, and then you can take me back to Baldwin's Shore."

Not to The Lookout, though. He could drop me at Applejack's on Main Street, and I could get a ride home from the bar. I did *not* want Garrett anywhere near my family.

"One dance," he agreed. "And if you insist, we can save the tango for our third date."

16

——————

SARA

*O*ne dance? Yeah, right.

The Rockfish Club themed its evenings by decades, and tonight, we were in the '80s, dancing to Cyndi Lauper and INXS and Tina Turner and Michael Jackson. Charming did a pretty good moonwalk. The cocktails were two for one, and since Garrett was driving, that meant more for me. I hadn't had a night like this in, well, ever.

The music brought back memories, of dancing around the house in Virginia with my parents on the weekends, of Dad spinning me in the air and Mom singing. Happy memories. And those happy memories were being overlaid with new ones that were every bit as good but a whole lot dirtier. Away from the scrutiny of Hadley's friends, Charming lost the last of his stiffness, and— Actually, no, that was a lie. There was still stiffness, but it was in a different place. The first time his hand slid down to my butt and tipped me against him, I felt it and went rigid myself.

But because the alcohol and the darkness made me both brave and incredibly stupid, I just grabbed handfuls of his T-shirt and pulled him closer. It felt as if I were having an out-of-body experience, except instead of my old soul floating above, a new soul had replaced boring old Sara, and now she was getting a taste of the life she would have lived if *circumstances* hadn't taken over at the age of nine. I'd always pretended to be someone I wasn't, but tonight, I finally came to terms with a truth I'd been denying for sixteen years. I *hated* pretending. Sara was an imposter.

Saralisa was the real me.

I was finally snatching a rare moment of happiness.

In a second-rate nightclub where the floor was sticky and the bathroom walls were covered in phone numbers and the lecherous bartender called everyone "darlin'" and spent way too long reading the slogan on my T-shirt. It was too hot for a sweater, so I was stuck with "Please don't make me do stuff" written across my boobs, words that Charming was studiously ignoring. But none of that mattered, not when he looked at me as if I were the only other person in the world.

Our bodies moved as one, and his hands roamed everywhere, from my ass to my shoulders to my neck. I ran my fingertips down the muscles of his back, relishing the way they rippled under my touch, but then he spun me to face away from him, pressing into me and letting me feel that hardness again. Light fingers skimmed the underside of my breasts, and this wasn't dancing; it was foreplay. Long, loud foreplay.

He plucked my necklace free from my shirt and held it up to the light. "What's this for?"

"A relic from another life." I twisted in his grip, and the little key on its silver chain dropped back to my chest. "Why haven't you kissed me yet?"

It was the alcohol talking, not me.

"Do you want me to?"

"I think so?"

He fisted my hair in one hand but made no move toward my lips. Instead, he just watched me. Waited.

Well, I wasn't waiting. I stood on tiptoes and touched my lips to his, then realised I'd made a mistake because I had no idea what I was doing.

"You need to lead," I murmured against his mouth.

Four small words, but they unleashed a wild animal. Charming's fingers dug into my scalp, holding me in place as he pushed down on my bottom lip with the thumb of his other hand. The last vestiges of my common sense retreated as his tongue advanced, and I melted against his chest. The air between us was electric. Charged. Everyone dancing around us disappeared. His hips rolled against mine, still in time with the music, and my thighs clenched with need. Who was this woman, dancing so wantonly, so...so, uh, sweatily? And who was this man? I still knew barely anything about him, but maybe it was better this way? Relationships—if you could call this craziness between us a relationship—were all about give and take, and I wasn't in a position to give, not with my mind anyway. Therefore I couldn't take little pieces of him either. No questions, no answers.

But he could have my body. I felt the vibrations as he groaned into my mouth, the impossible hardness of him as he pressed against me, the heat that rolled off him in waves. He kissed like a tsunami, full of raw power and energy. Plus he made my panties wet.

Finally, we broke apart, and once again he watched me, but this time, his gaze was filled with promises. Dark, dangerous promises.

"I think I just had a life-changing experience."

"Think?" he asked.

Crap. Did I say that out loud?

"I..." It came out as a croak. "I... My mouth's gone dry."

"Then I'll get you a drink."

He tried to steer me toward the crowd at the bar, but I shook my head. "The bar guy stares at my boobs."

"Want me to punch him?"

"That's a joke, right?"

He nuzzled my neck, and then I felt the bite of teeth on my earlobe. "That depends on your answer."

"No, I don't want you to punch him."

Another nibble, and the pinch of pain zapped downward. By the time it reached its destination, it had turned into pleasure. Huh. How did that work?

"Stay here."

The first bars of "Need You Tonight" played, and I spun away lip-syncing because the words were pretty darn accurate. Garrett took a step after me, but I flicked my fingers toward the bar.

"Down, boy. Drink."

Without his arms around me, I realised just how unsteady on my feet I'd become. Those two-for-one cocktails were a killer, but at least it would be a pleasant death. Might as well throw my hands up and dance before my pumpkin coach showed up. Was it midnight yet? I tried to check my watch, but the numbers blurred together. It wasn't a fancy watch. My mom hadn't been a fan of ostentatiousness, just love. Dad had given her the timepiece for their fifth anniversary, and whenever I got down in the dumps—more down in the dumps than usual—I flipped it over and read the inscription on the back.

LOVE ALWAYS WINS.

Since they died, I'd never experienced love, so maybe that's why I was such a loser?

Someone jostled me, and I stumbled to the side, head spinning. Room spinning. Whole darn world spinning. But then hands steadied me, strong hands, and hips ground against my ass. Wow, had Charming's dick finally deflated? I mean, I wasn't an expert on male genitalia, but surely it was unnatural to be hard for hours on end?

"You're hot," a stranger's voice rasped in my ear, and the horror slowly became clear as my new dance partner breathed stale beer over me.

These are the wrong hands.

Yeuch.

Instinct took over, and I whirled and slapped the guy before reason caught up. His cocky smile slid away, replaced with a scowl.

"What was that for, bitch?"

"Get your hands off me."

He reached for my hips again. "A prick-tease like you needs to learn a lesson. Don't offer what you're not willin' to deliver."

"I'm just dancing, you jerk."

"Got a better use for that smart tongue of yours, little lady."

"Let go!" I ordered, but his grip tightened as I struggled. "Get away—"

A fist flew past my face and smashed into the jerk's jaw. His head snapped sideways, his eyes rolled back, and he crumpled to the floor. An arm snaked around my waist, and I twisted to check it was the right one this time. Phew. Well, kind of. In that moment, Charming looked anything but charming. In fact, he looked positively pissed.

"Drink this." He tilted a high-ball glass toward my lips.

"What is it?"

"Water."

A small crowd had gathered around us, and a brunette with coloured ribbons woven through her braids crouched beside the jerk, wailing.

"What did you do to him? What did you do?"

Charming gave her a sharp look. "Taught him that dry-humping my girl wasn't a smart idea."

"He would never—"

"He did. Take my advice: you can do better." Charming turned his attention back to me. "Drink, Cinderella."

He practically poured the water down my throat, and I coughed on the last mouthful, but then I was in his arms and we were walking out into the chill night air. So much drama. So much alcohol. This was why I didn't drink very often. Because things went all fuzzy and people sounded weird and my stomach felt bleurgh.

"You didn't have to hit him."

Charming avoided answering, just carried on walking until we reached his SUV. *Bleep-bleep.* He bundled me into the passenger seat and clipped the seat belt into place. Why did he keep doing that? He thought I was incapable? Okay, so maybe he was right at the moment because I was seeing two of most things, but the other times, I could poke the thingy into the hole. I was an expert on car safety. The best. There was no better way to learn than through personal experience.

"Did you know...that airbags don't always work?" I asked Charming as he started the engine. "Sometimes, they just don't go off. You know the sensor thingies? Not rebib... relab...repliable."

"Any component can fail."

"Yup. Fail. And then your head goes splat on the windshield like my dad's did."

"Your dad had a car accident?"

"I was in the back seat, even though I wasn't supposed to be. Always buckle up, folks."

"Fuck, Sara. I'm sorry."

"Me too. Sorry for so, so many things." I hiccuped. "Oops. Are we going to have sex now?"

"Why? Do you want to?"

"Yes? I mean, I think so? I only had sex two and a half times before, and it was pretty terrible. The first guy lasted *nineteen seconds.*"

"Nineteen seconds?"

"Yup!" I leaned across the centre console as we took a bend. We'd left the lights of Eugene behind now, and the darkness wrapped around us like a shroud. "I counted. Nineteen seconds is bad, right?"

"Appalling. How can you have sex half a time?"

"Well, the second time, we were on the guy's couch—a different guy, not the nineteen-second one—and he was sort of thrusting away in that gap between my thighs and my...my..."

"Your pussy?"

"Yes, that." My cheeks heated because Grandpa always said I should act like a lady, and ladies didn't swear or use words like "pussy." Or perhaps it was the alcohol causing me to flush? I'd consumed quite a large amount of it, hadn't I? "And after a while—maybe a minute?—he grunted and asked how it was for me, and I had to, uh...break the news to him...but he didn't take it well."

No, he'd stormed into his bedroom and slammed the door, and since I'd never found myself in that position before, I'd been at a loss. In the end, I'd located some cleaning products under the sink and sponged the mess off the couch, and when he still hadn't reappeared after an hour, I'd slipped quietly out of his apartment. We'd never spoken of the incident again, which made buying kosher party food a little awkward because he worked at the deli in Coos Bay and never seemed to take a day off. The last time I needed salami, I'd feigned a migraine and made Parker go.

Charming glanced across at me, and he almost did a smile.

"Do you think that counts as half a sex or a whole sex?" I asked him.

"I don't think it counts at all."

"Really? In that case, I've only had sex two times. Also, I'm never doing it on a velvet couch again. Leather's the way to go."

"Duly noted. Dare I ask about the third time?"

"I thought it would be better, you know? We took things slowly. The whole second base, third base, whatever. He used to do this thing with his tongue that felt like...like he was stroking my lady parts with a dead fish, and then he asked if I was enjoying it. Are you meant to lie in that situation?"

"Not if you want it to get any better."

"Oh, crap."

"You lied?"

"Just a tiny bit? I panicked and told him it made me see stars, and he asked which ones, and that was how I learned he was into astom...astrom..."

"Astronomy?"

"Exactly. He had a telescope on his roof."

"So, which stars did you see?"

"With the tongue thing? I didn't know a whole lot about stars, so I told him the Big Dipper, which I thought was okay, but I guess it wasn't because after we had the actual sex, like, a week later—also bad, by the way—I saw him kissing a blonde woman at a party that *I organised*. They snuck into the bathroom between the main course and dessert."

"Did you spit in his dessert?"

"Ladies don't spit. I scraped the chocolate crumb off the top and replaced it with dirt from the parking lot." A truck came toward us, and its headlights highlighted the planes of Charming's face. I reached out to stroke his cheek. "You're so pretty. I bet you've had sex a lot more than two and a half times. I mean two times. Are you sure the thigh thing doesn't count?"

"I'm certain."

"Should I be disappointed?"

"No."

"Okay. Good. Hey, is this thing still hard?" I reached for his crotch, and wow, it was. "Is that normal?"

He spoke through gritted teeth. "No, it's not normal."

"Maybe you should see a doctor?"

"Fuck my life," he muttered, then lifted my hand back onto my thigh. "Not tonight, Cinderella."

"Well, obviously. What doctor is going to be working at this time? Uh, what time is it?"

"Twelve thirty."

"At least I didn't lose any shoes today, huh?" I leaned over to double-check, and that made my head spin again. "Nope, both still there."

"What a relief."

"Are you annoyed? Did you know that when you're annoyed, you sound a tiny bit British?"

"Probably because I went to college in England."

"Wow, really? I didn't go to college at all. One of my

cousins tried going to college, but he dropped out, and now he's in jail, so I think that maybe it's overrated? Do you think it's overrated?"

"It depends on what you want out of life. What do you want out of life, Sara?"

"I...I used to think I knew, but every time I make a plan, it ends up in the toilet, so now I'm just going to live for the moment. Isn't that what you told me to do? Live for the moment?"

"Indeed I did."

"And speaking of toilets, I need to pee. Where can I pee?"

"At this time of night? There might be a bar open in Cottage Grove. I'll stop when I see somewhere."

"How far is that?"

"Ten minutes."

"What if there's nowhere open?"

"Then you'll have two options—hold it or find a bush. Please don't piss on my car seat."

"I won't. I swear I won't, but I really need to go."

And maybe I wanted to puke too? My stomach felt all churny, and everything was a blur. The trees, the car lights that zipped past, Charming's handsome and slightly grouchy face. Why was he grouchy? Didn't he have a good time tonight? I had a good time apart from the last bit where he punched the guy, and had he bruised his knuckles? I tried to check, but my vision was super weird. Kinda hazy and black around the edges. My eyes began to close. Perhaps sleep was the better option?

Yes, sleep.

Sleep was good.

17

SARA

My temples throbbed as I turned over in bed, and I just knew that today's headache was going to be a monster. Over the past several weeks, I'd suffered from more headaches than usual, but that was perfectly understandable. It wasn't every month that a girl's life fell apart completely. That was why I'd started leaving a bottle of Tylenol and a glass of water on my nightstand, ready for action in the morning. I'd swallow a couple of pills, then burrow back under the covers and wait for them to work their magic.

I reached out for the bottle, but instead of the comforting presence of over-the-counter medication, my hand landed on...flesh? Warm flesh? My eyes flew open, and I gasped so hard I almost choked on my own tongue.

There's a man in bed with me.

Horror clawed its way up my throat as I asked myself a thousand questions. Who was he? How had he gotten into the pool house? What did he—

Wait.

This wasn't the pool house.

Light filtered in through gauzy drapes, and among the soft shadows, I picked out the silhouette of a pair of couches and a coffee table on the far side of the room. A studio apartment? Through an open door to the right, reflections bounced off a bathtub, but the most notable thing was space. This apartment took minimalism to a whole new level.

The guy beside me turned onto his back, and I recognised Charming. Even in semi-darkness, there was no mistaking the line of his jaw. He'd brought me home with him? Had we...? I lifted the sheet and found myself wearing an oversized T-shirt and a pair of sweatpants, neither of which belonged to me. He'd changed my clothes? I mean, abducting me from work was one thing, but what gave him the right to strip me and touch me? I pressed my thighs together, testing, but everything felt normal down there. Sex in the past had never been comfortable, so if we'd—

Are you sure the thigh thing doesn't count?

Oh. My. Gosh.

What had I told him last night?

Hazy memories flitted back, of me running my mouth in the car, of me groping him, of him hauling me out of the passenger seat, pulling down my leggings, and holding me up by the armpits as I squatted to pee in the grass at the side of the road. Of him twisting my hair back as I puked up my poor judgment. Of him carefully clipping my seat belt back into place and sighing as he shook his head. Of him carrying me into an elevator sometime in the early hours.

Oh boy, had I messed up.

And by "messed up," I meant that I'd taken my fairy tale and run it through the garbage disposal, then shoved the sorry remains through a wood chipper, doused them in gas, and set them on fire. And after that, I'd swept up the ashes, encased them in concrete, and tossed them into the ocean. Charming had taken me skydiving, bought me dinner, and danced with me for hours, whereupon I'd thanked him by vomiting on his shoes.

I need to get out of here.

The walk of shame would be, well, shameful, but at least I'd been too inebriated to blurt out my home address last night. Being delivered into Parker's and EJ's loving arms would have been the icing on the cake, and the twins would have undoubtedly found some way to make my stupidity go viral on social media. I crept out of bed and found my phone charging on the nightstand. I also realised I was still wearing my bra and panties, thank goodness, and—bizarrely—my socks. The rest of my clothes had disappeared, but my purse was on the coffee table, wallet intact. I had a credit card. A cab home from...wherever this was would probably be expensive, but my inheritance ambitions were dead. What did it matter if I spent my savings? Heck, I should swing by the Coffee House for donuts on the way to The Lookout because Addy said that carbs were a girl's best friend in the event of a breakup. Not that this was a breakup, exactly. More the loss of a-dream-that-might-have-been.

I found a door and tiptoed out of it, but instead of finding myself in a hallway, I was in a room even larger than the one I'd just left. Holy crap, Charming's bedroom was bigger than the entire pool house. And the great room, that was a vast space dominated by floor-to-ceiling windows and a significant number of oversized canvases. Paintings. Mostly women—naked women—and a few couples. Kind of abstract, but there was no mistaking what they were meant to be, and some of the poses made me blush. What was this, the Kama Sutra? I tilted my head to one side, trying to work out how one pretzel-like position was even possible. Those people must have a good chiropractor.

Before I left, I fished through my purse for a pen and paper. Yes, I needed to get home and cry, but Charming deserved an apology first. I scribbled out a note and left it on the dining table.

A handful of lamps guided me to a lit foyer, and I paused to study a statue on the central table before I hotfooted it out the door. A couple, the woman bent over on all fours and the man... Okay, time to go. The door opened from the inside without a key, and I practically ran to the elevator in the hallway outside. Oh, it was the penthouse. Why was I even surprised? I jabbed at the button for the first floor and let out the breath I'd been holding only when the doors opened in the foyer. Then groaned when I saw a man watching me.

"Can I help you, ma'am?"

Was he a concierge? His badge said "Jorge," and his expression said he didn't often get scruffy women stumbling out of the elevator at this time in the morning.

"Uh, I was staying upstairs, in the, uh, in the penthouse, and I was wondering if you could help me to find a cab?"

"You're a guest of Mr. Van de Kamp?"

That was Garrett's surname? What was it, German? Dutch? "Yes, that's right."

"If you'd like to take a seat, I'll arrange for a car to pick you up. Where will you be travelling to?"

"To Baldwin's Shore."

I figured I'd sound like a fool if I asked where I'd be travelling from, so I took a seat on the pale grey couch at the front of the foyer and prayed that Garrett wouldn't show up in the elevator. That was a conversation I didn't want to have, and I especially didn't want to have it with a hangover.

Far better to leave quietly and never speak of this monumental disaster again.

Out of curiosity, I searched for Garrett Van de Kamp while I waited, but nothing came up. He was probably one of those quietly wealthy people who liked to keep a low profile, so it was fitting that he'd worn a mask when we first met. It had been a metaphor for his life. Mine too. But if nothing else, last night had taught me a little about the type of person I wanted to be going forward. I was sick of trying to please other people at the expense of my own happiness. Friends were different, and I'd go above and beyond to help Brooke, Addy, Paulo, Darla, Brie, and Romi, Luca, Colt, and Aaron, but my family could go to hell.

And as for the monster... I hoped Blue was right and he wasn't in town for me, but if I was still on his radar, then I'd have to take my chances.

My old life had been no life at all.

18

GARRETT

"So she just ran out on you again?" Johannes snorted around a mouthful of cheese. Behind him on the screen, Anouska—his latest girlfriend-slash-muse—lounged on a couch, topless. Neither of the pair had any inhibitions whatsoever. The two of them, blessed as they were with trust funds and a complete lack of responsibilities, had taken an impromptu trip to Courchevel to catch the end of the ski season. "Did you ever stop to ask yourself whether it might be you?"

"She left a note apologising for throwing up on me."

"Okay, maybe it *is* her."

"I shouldn't have let her drink so much. Where's your laundry soap? She also puked on herself, and I need to wash her clothes."

"Do you even know how a washing machine works?"

"I'm sure I can figure it out."

"If you're washing her clothes, does that mean you're going after her?"

"Of course."

"The thrill of the chase?"

"Something like that."

Johannes wouldn't understand what I was feeling. Hell, I barely understood it myself. He was happy with superficial relationships that were never intended to go the distance, and for years, I had been too. I'd actively sought them out. Better to date an unashamed party girl who understood her place and signed the paperwork to prove it than a gold-digger intent on getting her claws into a fortune. But even the party girls had grown tiresome. When I returned to the US full-time, I'd joined Nyx, a club created for men like me. The hostesses were beautiful, bound by NDAs, and willing to do anything a dick could desire. But although I'd learned a lot about my own sexual proclivities, lately I'd found myself wanting more. I needed the whole package, not just one part of the fantasy.

And I thought Sara might possibly be that package.

"I'll probably need to borrow your apartment again," I told Johannes.

"Whatever, bro. Don't want to introduce the new girl to the fam yet?"

"If you were a Dorsey, would you?"

My father would interrogate her, my stepmother would smother her, and my half-brother would either hit on her or insult her, depending on which side of the bed he'd gotten out of that morning. If I was going to stand any chance with Sara, I needed to build a solid footing for our relationship before I walked her into a nightmare.

Johannes snorted. "Hell, no."

"How long are you staying in France?"

He turned to Anouska. "How long do you want to stay here, babe?"

A shrug, and she arranged her fine blonde hair over one breast. "I'm bored with snow. I want to visit Vittoria in Milan."

Translation: Anouska wanted to shop, and Johannes would go along with the plan because Vittoria was always up for a three-way. Or a four-way—I knew that from experience. They wouldn't be back for at least a week.

"Don't do anything I wouldn't do."

Johannes grinned and picked up his wine. "That doesn't leave much out."

"It leaves out breaking your leg off-piste again."

Always the optimist, he just laughed off the comment. "If I'm confined to the chalet, I'll have plenty of time to paint and fuck."

Anouska smiled in the background, and I struggled to keep a straight face. "Don't get any ideas, Nous."

"I always have ideas. Garrett, if you like this woman, you should take her a gift. A purse, a scarf, a necklace. Women love gifts."

True, but Sara wasn't a woman I could buy with diamonds and pearls. The line between impressing her and insulting her was wafer thin and as dangerous as a high wire. One wrong step, and I'd lose my balance. I blew Anouska a kiss and ended the call.

Challenge accepted.

Mary's Coffee House was just along the street from the Craft Cabin, and if I sat at a table in the window, I could watch the craft store's parking lot and the people coming and going. With luck, Paulo would be working today—he'd been the most willing to talk. But the only staff I'd seen so far were Darla and a younger woman with dark brown hair and a ready smile. The brunette had helped a couple of customers carry bags out to their cars.

Tawna's sharp inhale had told me she was far from amused when I'd asked her to reschedule yet another day of meetings, but I paid her to do the impossible, and finding Sara—again—was more important than speaking with reps from the hundred companies who wanted my family's money. Dorsey Holdings had plenty of investments. I only had one Cinderella.

My phone vibrated with a message.

TAWNA

I told them you were sick, and I've cleared what I can from tomorrow in case you need more time.

Appreciated.

Tawna was one of the few people I trusted to have my back, and I made a mental note to send her flowers. Or maybe I could take her a box of pastries from the Coffee House? If I had to spend much time here, I'd need to fit in extra gym sessions.

One car in the parking lot interested me: a dark green Toyota Corolla. It had been there yesterday when I picked Sara up—that sounded much better than abducting her— and it didn't look as if it had moved overnight. Was it hers? I couldn't make out the licence plate, but if she didn't show up in the next half hour, I'd take a walk over there. Dorsey Holdings kept an investigator on retainer, and he'd be able to find out who owned it.

"Can I warm up your coffee?" Mary asked, approaching

with a jug. A plump, grey-haired woman, she wore a row of bangles on one wrist that jingled every time she moved.

"Thanks."

Mary topped off my mug, but she didn't move away. Curious? I hadn't missed the glances she'd been casting in my direction all morning.

"Waiting for someone?" she asked.

"Just killing time before a meeting." This was a small town. Plenty of tourists passed through thanks to the Peninsula, but there couldn't be too many permanent residents. How many Saras were there? Surely not more than one or two? I had questions of my own, but I also didn't want people gossiping, not about either of us. I glanced at my watch. "Sara emailed to say she was running a little late."

"You mean Sara Baldwin?"

Jackpot.

Wait a second... Sara *Baldwin*? As in Kayleigh and Lillian Baldwin? Was there a connection? I fought to keep my expression neutral, something I'd luckily had plenty of experience with.

"That's right. I got the impression she's feeling slightly fragile today, so I told her to take as much time as she needed."

"Fragile? Well, I'm not surprised after what those cousins of hers did. Firing her from her own company—it just wasn't right. A meeting, you say? Is it about an event you want planned?"

Little pieces of the puzzle began to click into place. Last night, Sara had said asswipe number three cheated on her at a party she'd organised. Had that been her job? Event planning? If so, it would also explain her presence at Hadley's party. She'd been there to spy and to sabotage. No wonder she'd wanted to keep a low profile.

"A corporate team-building day. Sara's services come highly recommended."

"She'll do a wonderful job, but take my advice and stay away from LKB Events. With the Baldwin twins running the show, nothing will ever get done, and I can't imagine they'd be easy to work with either."

"I'll take that on board. Could I get a box of your cookies to go? Say, two dozen? The folks at the office would go crazy for those."

Mary beamed at me. "Of course, of course. I'll pack them up right away."

Sara, Sara, my pretty Cinderella. As soon as Mary was back behind the counter, I began searching on my phone. Sara didn't go in for social media, but it seemed the twins were as efficient at updating their company website as they were with everything else. The "About Us" page listed the two of them as directors with professional pictures and highly inaccurate biographies, and underneath, there was a candid snap of "Sara - Assistant." I'd found her.

I'd found her, but fuck, this had the potential to complicate things. I didn't want to get tangled up with the Baldwins. The whole family was toxic. Another piece clicked—Sara had said her cousin was in prison, and Trey once mentioned that Easton Baldwin had been jailed for shooting at a carful of women last year. One of them had required surgery.

Even so, I could hardly hold Sara's family against her, not when I was related to Trey and Gracie. But damn, I'd have to be sure about Sara before we went public with any relationship. People would talk. They'd judge. Thankfully, Sara seemed happy to keep our dalliances under the radar, and Johannes didn't need his apartment back any time soon.

Sara Baldwin. Assuming she lived somewhere on the

family estate, finding her would be easy. Hell, I'd even been there before to pick up Trey. Getting her to talk with me, that would be the hard part.

I finished my coffee, paid the check, and thanked Mary for the cookies. Then I went to find my girl.

19

———

SARA

Someday, I'd have to go and pick up my Toyota from the Craft Cabin, but today was not that day. No, today was the day to weep into my pillow, eat all the chocolate left in the pool house, and rehash every painful detail I could remember from last night. Not that I *wanted* to do that last part. It just happened, and short of drinking myself into oblivion again, I didn't know how to stop it.

I crossed out *Retrieve car* on my to-do list and replaced it with *Buy Tylenol*.

Brooke had obviously heard from Darla or Paulo what

happened at the store yesterday, and she'd called once and texted twice, but beyond reassuring her that I was still alive and back home, I'd kept quiet about the details. How could I possibly explain what I'd done? The mistakes I'd made? Parker brought over the bag of groceries Deon delivered while I was out, but at least he didn't ask questions. That was one good thing about Parker—he simply didn't care. Usually, I hated his cold demeanour, but today, it had worked in my favour. It was too chilly for Kayleigh and Lillian to swim, and Uncle EJ hated exercise, so I had this little corner of the estate to myself. I was free to wallow in misery, safely tucked away between high hedges and trees just coming into leaf.

By mid-afternoon, I couldn't stand the lingering smell of vomit any longer. I hadn't managed to identify the source, and it might even have been my imagination, but I stood in the shower and scrubbed myself until the water ran cold and mixed with still-warm tears. Tomorrow, I'd pick myself up, but this evening, Netflix was calling. Why keep crying over a man when I could sob my heart out over a chick flick? My weakness was Hallmark movies, the more Christmassy the better, even though I knew the ending before I started watching. Surprises sucked. Apart from skydiving. That hadn't sucked.

I walked out of the bathroom in a robe because getting dressed seemed like too much effort today. Where was the remote? I spotted it on the dining table and turned on the TV. What was the point in even having a dining table? It seated four, but three of the chairs had never been used because it wasn't as if I ever had visitors, and I mostly ate on the couch with a plate balanced on—

Wait.

Wait, wait, wait.

I froze as movement outside caught my eye, and all the air left my lungs in one suffocating *whoosh*. Someone was sitting at the table under the portico, watching me through the living room window.

And that someone was Garrett freaking Van de Kamp.

Anger trumped fear, and I yanked the front door open.

"What are you doing here? How did you find me?"

He held out the roses I'd left in his car last night. "You forgot these. You also have a gap between two of your motion sensors, and you need a better lock on your door. I'll fix it in the morning."

How could he act so calm? So infuriatingly calm?

"You can't just trespass on private property. It's…it's *rude*."

"If you'd stayed for breakfast instead of disappearing without a word this morning, I wouldn't have had to."

"When I woke up, you were in the same bed as me. Don't you understand the meaning of boundaries?"

"I figured that after you fondled my cock, certain boundaries had been crossed. And besides, I didn't want to take the risk of you choking on vomit if you decided to throw up again."

His words were a pin, and I was the balloon. All the fight went out of me.

"I'm so sorry. I'm sorry for everything. For puking, for groping you, for the whole urinating-on-the-nature-strip thing."

"For running out on me for the second time?"

"I thought it was for the best."

"And yet you didn't think to consult me, despite the fact that I was lying a mere six inches away?"

"Sorry."

"Are you going to invite me in? You're getting cold."

"I'm fine, honestly."

The robe was plenty warm enough, plus that fire inside me was flaring into life again. And was having Charming in my space really a smart idea?

No.

No, it wasn't.

"Okay, then you're getting turned on," he said.

"You can't make assumptions like that."

His gaze dropped to my traitorous nipples and stayed there, focused on two stiff peaks jutting against the fabric.

"Oh."

"How long are you going to keep fighting this?"

"Could you give me a moment? I'm still trying to work out if I'm hallucinating because I just don't understand why you'd be here after I made a complete fool out of myself."

"I'm here because you're real."

"But are you?"

"Come over here and find out."

He crooked a finger, and so help me, I went. Then I was back in Charming's arms, and his lips crushed mine in a kiss that bordered on punishment. He picked me up, hands under my thighs as he pressed me against one of the stone columns and took his fill. Our tongues didn't dance today, they duelled, him fighting for the upper hand and me just fighting to breathe. His cock was freaking granite. *Has it been like that since yesterday?*

"No, Cinderella, it hasn't. I've jacked off twice today, and both times, I was thinking of you as I came."

Oh. My. Gosh.

"I need to gag that stupid voice inside my head."

"No gagging, not this evening. I have plans for your dirty mouth. Are you ready to take this inside yet? Or shall we go for third time lucky right here against this column?"

"Are you talking about sex?"

"I'm not talking about playing the lotto." He trailed kisses down my jaw. "If 'pretty terrible' is your baseline, I can raise it with one finger."

"That's just a figure of speech, right?"

He shook his head. "That's all I need to find your G-spot."

"Isn't that a myth? I'm almost certain I don't have one of those."

"Do you want me to show you?"

I chewed on my bottom lip—a bad habit—and he let out a low groan.

"How long would it take?" I asked.

"Longer than nineteen seconds."

I glanced in the direction of the main house, but all was still. If the Baldwins saw Charming here, they'd lose their collective minds.

"Then I guess you should come inside."

As soon as the door closed behind us, I pulled the drapes in every room to hide the evidence of my illicit activities. The last thing I wanted to do was answer awkward questions.

"Where's your car?" I asked him.

"In the parking lot by the beach. I was heading up to the main house when I saw footprints leading this way and got curious."

"Why didn't you drive in through the front gate?"

"If I'd buzzed the intercom, would you have answered? Or would you have hidden behind the couch and waited for me to leave?"

How did this man I'd only just met know me so well? When I didn't answer right away, he raised an eyebrow.

"Okay, fine, the second one. Did anyone see you come here?"

"No."

"Are you sure? Because if you found me, then you must have worked out who I'm related to."

"Uncle Sam spent a great deal of taxpayer money teaching me how to sneak behind enemy lines. Trust me, nobody knows I'm here. Are you done stalling now?"

"I..." What could I tell him but the truth? "I'm scared."

Charming's gaze softened, and he took both of my hands in his. "Tell me what worries you, Cinderella."

"You," I whispered, unable to look at him. "What if I do something wrong? The more time we spend together, the more terrified I get that I'll lose you. Not that I really have you, but—"

"You have me."

"I do?"

"Yes, you do. And there's no right or wrong in sex, just what feels good and what doesn't. Every person has different tastes, and the only way to find out what you like is to experiment. And communicate. No lies."

"No lies," I agreed. But I reserved the right to omit certain details. Telling Charming the truth about my messed-up life would only push him away, no matter what he said.

"Now kiss me."

I obeyed.

20

GARRETT

I circled Sara in the living room of her cute little home, and I could tell she wanted to turn with me. Her feet fidgeted, and her shoulders tensed. But one word—*no*—and she stayed still.

I can't tell you how much that pleased me.

Her lustrous brown hair was damp, and she smelled faintly of citrus. Lemon and lime, but the scent of her arousal enveloped her like a cloud, and I knew that when I made a move to stroke her oh-so-elusive G-spot, I'd find her wet already. My Sara. So responsive.

But I took my time, watching her closely as I unknotted the belt of her robe. She didn't try to stop me, but her breathing grew rougher when the flimsy fabric fell open and I drank her in. Last night, when I'd dressed her in a pair of Johannes's sweats, I'd forbidden myself from taking a good look because somnophilia wasn't my thing, but today, we had all the time in the world. When she was barefoot, I had to look down at her, but put her in a pair of Gracie's heels, and she'd be almost as tall as me. She had a dancer's legs, toned and slender, and small, high breasts that were each a perfect mouthful. Those rosy pink nipples were hard already and so incredibly tempting. I leaned in and circled one with my tongue, then blew cool air over the pebbled tip, pleased when she shivered.

"Beautiful," I murmured, and from the way her eyes lit up, in surprise and then in hope, I suspected she didn't receive many compliments. The men in Baldwin's Shore must be blind. Or stupid. Probably both.

I nudged the robe off her shoulders, and it pooled at her feet, leaving her naked before me. Still she hadn't moved a muscle. My cock was so hard it ached now, straining against my jeans in a plea for freedom. But I had patience, and hell, I'd need it with Sara. She was like an onion. So many layers, and from the glimpses of pain I'd caught last night when she was off guard, there would be tears as I peeled them away.

"Where have you been my whole life?" I whispered.

"Right here." She looked up at me from under those long lashes of hers. "Waiting."

Her words undid me, and I had to kiss her. Had to get another taste. The urge to pick her up and throw her onto the nearest flat surface was almost primal, not helped by the way she mercilessly ground against me as she cupped my face in her hands and gasped as our tongues tangled.

This woman was going to be the death of me.

I picked her up, cupping her ass, and found her thighs were slick already as I carried her to the bedroom. Fuck, if she kept this up, maybe I wouldn't make it past that nineteen-second benchmark after all.

"Stay there," I murmured against her neck, then left her kneeling on the bed while I fetched a towel from the bathroom to go under her damp hair. I wanted to see it spread out over her pillow as I fucked her, gently at first because that was what she needed, but then as hard as she could take.

I laid her back on the bed and arranged her as I wanted her, but her arms quickly snaked around my neck when I kissed her again. This time, I let her do it. She had an old-fashioned iron bed frame, and someday, I was going to cuff her to that and force her to focus, helpless, as I extracted every drop of pleasure her body contained.

My fingers roamed over her, learning every curve of her as she writhed underneath me. Whenever the rough denim of my jeans came into contact with her sensitive clit, she gasped, as if she knew where she wanted to go but was uncertain how to get there. I would take her. She tunnelled fingers through my hair as I kissed my way down her body, getting distracted by her breasts on the way because what red-blooded male wouldn't?

The first time I ran my tongue between her folds, she arched off the bed with a cross between a yelp and a scream, and then her nails dug into my scalp and pushed my head downward. Sara might not be so good at telling me what she wanted, but her actions didn't lie. My own pulse was hammering, my cock throbbing, and out of all the women I'd been with, all the wild things I'd tried, I knew this was the encounter that would stick with me forever. My tongue circled her clit, and I savoured her sweet taste and breathy moans as I fought not to shoot my load in my pants.

"Just to check, are you getting any fishy vibes here?"

Her eyes flew open. "Huh? No! No fish."

"And how about stars?"

"Stop talking and…and…"

"Eat?"

She blushed a deep red. "Yes."

Eating was an understatement. This was no afternoon

snack. I feasted on Sara, wishing my mouth could be in two places at the same time so I could swallow every one of those gasps and groans. I added a finger into the mix, and she bit that bottom lip so hard I feared she'd draw blood. A few strokes in the right place, and she detonated with a scream, going first rigid and then boneless as the orgasm surged through her. Yes, this sight would be burned permanently onto the insides of my eyelids.

"Told you that you had a G-spot."

And there were the tears. "I had no idea...no idea it could be like that."

"We've barely gotten started, Cinderella."

I dragged my shirt over my head and crawled back up the bed. I needed to feel her skin on mine, needed to soak in her sweat-slicked heat. She rested her head on my chest and wrapped an arm around me, and in that brief moment, everything was right with the world. I wiped her tears away with a thumb.

"Don't cry."

"I can't help it. Everything's just so...so...overwhelming."

"Yeah, I know the feeling."

"Do you? Nothing ever seems to faze you."

"Maybe my mask is just fixed on tighter." I'd promised her no lies. "This is out of character for me. I've never done this before."

"Which part? The stalking? The abduction? Trespassing on private property?"

"Any of it. You're the first woman who's ever gotten under my skin enough for me to care."

A long pause. "Why? I'm a nobody."

Honestly, I struggled to put it into words. "As I said, you're real. A regular—but beautiful—person with flaws and hang-ups and opinions. Sometimes you fight me, and other times…" I trailed a fingertip down her cheek. "Other times, you submit."

"You could probably have any woman you wanted."

"I know, which is why I'm in your bed right now." I palmed myself through my jeans. "Fuck, I need to do something about this."

Sara swallowed hard, and it looked as if she was steeling herself.

"I'm ready."

She didn't sound ready.

"Are you sure?" I freed her lip from her teeth with a thumb. "You're the one with the power here."

"I am?"

"Give me a safe word."

"A…safe word?"

"If you say it, I'll stop whatever I'm doing in a heartbeat." I laid a hand on her chest. "Because that's what I need to protect: your heart."

She thought for a moment, then smiled. "Shark."

"Shark?"

"Fish and sex don't mix. You'll really stop?"

"I promise." Shark? I loved that even amid her uncertainty, she hadn't lost her sense of humour. I captured her mouth for a searing kiss. "I promise."

I didn't bother to take my jeans off completely, just unzipped and shoved them low enough to free my painful cock. I couldn't wait. Not any longer. There was a condom in the wallet in my back pocket, and I ripped the foil open, then rolled it on. Sara watched me carefully, and that lip was between her teeth again. She'd make a terrible poker player.

We locked gazes as I slid my cock into her, inch by desperate inch. She was so fucking tight, and the way her walls gripped me, I almost joined nineteen-second-guy in the losers' corner. But I wanted more than a participation trophy. I gritted my teeth and held still until the urge to explode subsided.

Instead of chasing my own pleasure, I focused on her. On her silky skin, on those pink buds, on the full lips I'd never get enough of. I brushed fine hair away from her eyes with one hand and pressed a kiss to her forehead.

"Okay?"

"Yes."

This time, she was telling the truth, and I began to move with smooth strokes, never breaking eye contact. Her eyes gave so much away. When she finally relaxed, they unfocused slightly, and despite the fading light outside, they seemed to brighten. Sara burned from the inside out. As her hips started to buck against me, I slipped a hand between us and found her clit again. She gripped my arms, her fingers digging in.

"Don't fight it, Cinderella. Just give in and let it happen."

"I...I can't."

"Why not?"

"Because—"

I shifted the angle of my hips, and her eyes widened as she gave a soft, involuntary cry. A curse slid from her lips, and not "heck" or "darn." The loss of control made me smile. If I could get Sara to shed her inhibitions, to unleash the sense of adventure that she'd locked down deep inside, there was nothing we wouldn't be able to achieve together.

Another thrust, and her walls pulsed around me, shuddering as she came for the second time. I couldn't hold out any longer, didn't want to, and I followed her over the edge with several curses of my own. The periphery of my vision went black, and I peppered kisses across her flushed cheeks as I waited for my pulse to steady.

"You were saying?" I murmured when I could speak again.

"I…I have nothing."

"A lie. I'm going to give you everything. I'm going to give you the world, and don't you dare ask any dumb questions like 'why?' You know why." Reluctantly, I withdrew from her snug warmth. "I have to get rid of this condom."

I lost the jeans too. We weren't done yet. I'd give Sara a few minutes to recover before I made her come again, but tonight, she was mine, and I intended to remind her of that fact in every possible way.

21

———————

SARA

Whenever Brooke and Addy and Romi—not Brie because she'd never kiss and tell— would sit around and giggle about how one of them couldn't walk properly or laugh that they'd been thoroughly ruined in a pleasurable way, I'd smile and nod along, but I didn't truly believe it. Until now. Who knew? Who knew that sex could be so utterly and splendidly mind-blowing? I was thirsty as heck, but I wasn't sure I'd be able to make it to the kitchen, so when Charming reappeared from the bathroom, this time completely naked—oh my—I just curled into his side and rested my head on his shoulder.

Which gave me a terrific view of his abs. I thought they only looked that way in movies, all that chiselled perfection. And was his dick hard again already?

I nodded toward it. "I thought we just fixed that?"

"Deflation lasted about three seconds. Around you, this is situation normal."

Twenty-six years old, and this was the first time I'd cuddled properly after sex with a man, and the fact that the man was Garrett Van de Kamp shocked the crap out of me. I hadn't expected him to have a tender side. A soft snort escaped as a memory came back, and I buried my head against his chest.

"What? You think it's funny that you make me hard?"

"No, no, no. I was just thinking, uh, you probably don't want to know."

"Tell me."

Well, he asked for it… "So, I was just thinking that the last time I was in this position, the guy said he had to run home and feed his cat, but the week before, he'd told me he was allergic to cat dander. That was when I began to realise I'd made a really big mistake."

"Was that the nineteen-second asshole or the jackass with the telescope?"

"The jackass with the telescope."

"And how big was the mistake?" Garrett held his thumb and finger half an inch apart, smiling. "This big?" He widened the gap infinitesimally. "This big?"

"Definitely kiddie-sized." I realised what I'd said and clapped a hand over my mouth. "Shit! I mean, shoot! There was no paedophilia involved, none. He was five years older than me. I'm so bad at this whole snuggling-pillow-talk thing. Truly terrible. I'm so sorry."

Garrett was openly laughing now. "See what I mean? You're real. For the record, I don't have any pets of my own, and if we're talking about our pasts, then every single one of my exes would have been in the bathroom at this moment, fixing her make-up."

"I don't wear much make-up. Only when I'm working, which is never these days."

"Because of your cousins? Kayleigh and Lillian?"

I let out a decidedly unsexy groan. "Please don't remind me that I'm related to them. I do my absolute best to forget."

"You have the twins; I have Trey."

"Do you work with him?"

"Not really."

"That's not a proper answer."

"Dad gave him an office and a fancy title, but he rarely shows up more than once a week."

"That sucks."

"It's better for both of us that way."

"That also sucks."

"It does. And do you know what else sucks?"

"What?"

Before I could blink, I was on my back underneath him again.

"Allow me to show you."

My head fell back as Garrett went to work with his tongue. He took over my senses, my body, my mind. I got lost in him, and what was more, I loved it. For so many years, I'd fought in vain to retain some semblance of control over my life, and only now did I discover that giving in to his mastery and obeying his soft commands to drop my knees to the side, to hold on to the cool iron of my bed frame, to turn over and raise my ass in the air could bring relief. Relief that I was finally able to surrender responsibility to somebody who wanted to give rather than take.

I barely knew him, and nothing about what we were doing could be described as normal, but in a strange way, I trusted him. Trusted him not to screw me over. Well, of course he was screwing me, but we'd waited until the third date, so that was good, right? Respectable? Third sort of date, anyway. Was this even a date? He'd just shown up and—

The sting of his hand on my ass sent that train of thought skittering into oblivion.

"If you're thinking of anything but my cock right now, stop."

"Sorry." It came out as a whisper.

He ran a hand up my back slowly, ass to neck, then fisted it in my hair, tilting my head and turning it so he had access to my mouth. Instead of kissing me, he pulled my bottom lip between his teeth and nipped hard enough to sting, watching me closely for a second before he let it go.

"I've needed to do that for a long time."

I wasn't prepared for the rush of heat that burned through me at his words and the tiny bite of pain. That wasn't normal either, was it? To enjoy that sort of thing? The ache between my legs didn't lie, and with that feeling came shame because I was learning so much about myself tonight and I wasn't sure—

"When we're fucking like this, you think of me and only me, Cinderella."

This time, there was no gentle easing. He slammed into me, and I gasped at the sudden intrusion. He was bigger, I was fuller, and there was room for nothing else.

"Fuck!"

"Better."

I heard the smile in his voice as he pulled on my hair, arching me up against him. He cupped my breasts in both hands, first caressing gently, then surprising me with a hard pinch as he caught my nipples between thumb and forefinger.

"Oh!"

One hand moved downward, and the release was like nothing I'd ever experienced. In a good way. The best way.

"What's your safe word?" His lips brushed against my ear, and the vibrations went straight to my core.

"I—"

"Tell me."

"Sh-shark."

"Do you want to use it?"

And have him stop? Have this dark journey of discovery end? "No."

A hand came to my throat, but he didn't apply any pressure, just held me against him, my back to his front, while he circled my clit maddeningly slowly with those magic fingers of his. I clenched around him, and this time, the groan was his.

"You're everything I hoped," he whispered.

Before I could process that, he lowered me back to the bed so I was on all fours, and he began to move in short, measured thrusts, all the time working me with his fingers. Who said men couldn't multitask? My legs began to tremble, and my breath came in short gulps as those first little tendrils of an orgasm wrapped around me. I gave myself over to him. Let him do whatever he wanted because I knew I'd want it too. When that heady bliss finally rocketed through me, Garrett held me up with an arm around my waist, and that was the only thing that kept me from collapsing into a sweaty heap when he pulsed into me a moment later.

"Holy freaking hell," I murmured, mostly to myself.

"My sentiments exactly."

Garrett withdrew smoothly, and with one soft kiss to my cheek, he morphed into his usual sweet self. Gone was the Prince of Darkness. Charming was back.

"Am I allowed to think about other things now? Because what the heck was that?"

Rather than answering, he fluffed the pillows and settled me against them, then retrieved the quilt from the floor and tucked that around me as well. I got an excellent view of his ass as he walked to the bathroom, and the toilet flushed a moment later.

"Are you hungry?" he asked when he reappeared. "Thirsty?"

"Thirsty."

"What do you want to drink?"

"Anything but alcohol."

He returned with a glass of orange juice and another of those dangerous forehead kisses, totally unashamed of his nakedness as he studied me. Not that he had a thing to be ashamed of. He was so beautiful I had to pinch myself. No, really.

"What was that for?" he asked.

"Just checking you're real."

"In that case, shouldn't you be pinching me?"

"I wasn't sure you'd appreciate that."

The bed dipped as he settled onto the edge and took my hand. "I'm very real."

I took a sip of juice and tried to gather my scattered thoughts. "You didn't answer my question. What was that?"

"That... That was a little more of myself than I'd intended to show you tonight."

"Oh."

"I need to know how you're feeling."

How could I tell him when I didn't even know myself? "Mixed up?" Dirty, slightly guilty that I liked it, sated in a melting-into-the-mattress way, scared that I'd never get to experience Charming's magic again. Scared that I would. "Is it always like that?"

"Do you want it to be?"

Did I? What happened, it had been so intense. So incredibly, deliciously wrong that for one blessed evening, everything was right in my world. When I'd walked away from the men of my past, all I'd felt was relief. If I had to walk away from Charming, my soul would be wrenched from my body.

Slowly, I nodded. "Yes, I do."

He let out a breath I hadn't realised he'd been holding. "You have no idea how happy that makes me." His grip on my hand tightened. "I've never wanted any woman the way I want you."

Was he serious? Or did he say that to every woman he bedded? "Is that just a line?"

"It's anything but a line, Cinderella."

"But what if...what if I'm not enough? If in a month or two months, you discover I'm really not that interesting and—"

"Are you talking about breaking up before I've even had a chance to take you white-water rafting?"

"White-water rafting? I'm not the best swimmer, and what if—" I realised he was joking and shoved him in the chest. "It isn't funny."

"No, it isn't."

"We barely know each other."

"So, let's change that."

"I'm a perpetual screw-up. My life has basically been one big mess since I was nine years old. I don't have a job, or—"

"Good. No job means you have no excuse not to come back to Roseburg with me tomorrow. Now, what do you want for dinner? I have two dozen cookies from the Coffee House in the car, or I can pick up takeout, or I can cook."

Charming liked to call the shots, that much was clear,

and not just in the bedroom. I could have fought, but what was the point? My mouth watered at the thought of Mary's cookies, and I was in no state to make dinner myself, not when I couldn't even walk to the kitchen. I didn't hate the idea of escaping Baldwin's Shore for a day either.

"Okay, you win. Let's see how good you are with a stove."

Losing an argument had never felt so good.

22

SARA

There was something thrilling about all the subterfuge. About throwing clothes into a duffel bag and sneaking away from The Lookout without a word to my family. About texting Brooke to let her know I was being whisked away for a dirty break and not to worry. About spending time with a man I suspected had as many skeletons in his closet as I did.

This morning, Charming was sitting opposite me in a diner halfway between Baldwin's Shore and Roseburg, eating scrambled eggs and checking emails on his phone as I covered my pancakes in maple syrup. It all seemed so normal when last night had been anything but. I smiled inwardly. We each had our own secrets, but now we shared some too.

"What do you actually do?" I nodded at the phone. "For work, I mean."

"I took over running the family business three years ago when Dad decided on a change of direction."

"And what's the family business?"

"Investing. Dad made a bunch of money in software

when he was younger, and after he cashed out, he began financing other entities he believed showed promise. I basically oversee a family office, albeit a fairly complex one."

"Like a bigger version of Baldwin Estates? That's our family company. Well, not mine—I don't have anything to do with it. My cousin Parker is in charge now."

"Not your uncle?"

So, Garrett had done at least basic research on me.

"Uncle EJ isn't business-minded. His wife used to run things with Parker, but she won't be getting out of prison any time soon."

"She's in for murder?"

"Google is your friend, huh?"

"Just doing my due diligence. I'm surprised you haven't googled me."

"I tried. There was nothing."

His eyebrows dipped in puzzlement. "Did you spell my name right?"

"Maybe not? I tried Kamp with a K and a C, but neither of them got any hits."

"Kamp?"

"Garrett Van de Kamp?"

He burst out laughing.

"What? The concierge at your apartment said you were Mr. Van de Kamp."

"Try Garrett Dorsey. D-O-R-S-E-Y."

Oh. I typed the new name into my phone, and holy crap. Words jumped out from the screen: *billionaire, playboy, eligible bachelor, elite, party lifestyle, mysterious.* There was Garrett in a tuxedo, Garrett in a suit, Garrett in a military uniform. I dropped the phone, and it landed in a pool of maple syrup.

"Why didn't you tell me? Why didn't you tell me who you were?" I scrolled farther. "Wait, your father is the secretary of state for Oregon?"

"Would it have made a difference?" he asked as he rescued my phone and wiped it with a napkin.

"Duh, yes? I couldn't... I mean, I wouldn't... You're a *billionaire*?"

"No, that's Dad. And maybe that's why I didn't tell you. I wanted you to see the real me, not my reputation or my family or the bullshit the media writes. I'm just a man, Sara. A man who's very much into you."

"Well, you were last night." A slightly hysterical giggle escaped. Thankfully, we were sitting in a quiet booth at the back, an old-fashioned circular one with high walls. "And this morning."

Garrett checked his watch. "And roughly an hour from now. Are you going to finish those pancakes?"

"Yes." I took another mouthful. "Who's Mr. Van de Kamp? Is that an alias?"

"He's a friend. A friend who's currently screwing his way through Europe's beau monde, so the apartment's ours for a week. I have a few meetings, plus a commitment on Saturday I can't change, but I'm yours for the rest of the time."

I nearly choked on the pancake. "A week? What are you planning to do, keep me there as your sex slave?"

"Why? Are you offering?"

Instinctively, I opened my mouth to say *no way*, but the words stuck in my throat. Would it really be so terrible to spend days in the huge bedroom with the couches and the en-suite and be fucked into submission by a living god every night? Garrett would feed me, right? He'd done a reasonable job with the spaghetti bolognese last night.

"More coffee, sir?"

The server's arrival brought me back to reality. I needed to find a new job, map out my future, and probably seek therapy. Of course I couldn't spend a week naked in Roseburg.

"My girlfriend would like more coffee too," he said, and I caught the edge in his tone.

"Uh, yes, yes, sure."

The flustered waitress topped off my mug, and I wanted to sympathise, to say I knew just how she felt in Garrett's presence. But...wait a second.

"Girlfriend?" I asked the moment she was out of earshot.

"What else would you call this?"

"Illicit sex?"

"Right here, right now? I'm game, but we might get kicked out of the diner."

That morning, I learned an important lesson. Never sit next to Garrett Dorsey in a restaurant. I'd just forked another piece of pancake into my mouth when his hand slipped into the front of my leggings, and maybe that "playboy" tag wasn't bullshit because he knew exactly what he was doing. I nearly sucked the pancake into a lung.

"Hey, warn me next time!" I hissed, coughing.

"Where's the fun in that?"

He barely gave me enough time to take a mouthful of coffee before his finger resumed its dirty dance. I pressed a hand over his, trying to stop him, but that only made the sensation more acute.

"You're always so wet for me, Cinderella," he whispered, then gave my earlobe a gentle nip.

"This is a diner."

"I'd noticed."

"We're in public."

"Are you using your safe word?"

Was I? A ripple of pleasure ran through me, and rationality flew out the window. I wanted this. Needed this. Needed him.

"No," I whispered, letting my legs part a little more. "Hurry up."

Charming had unlocked a side of me I never knew existed, and now lust was running so close to my surface that it didn't take much to make it spill over. I fell apart. In a freaking diner. He muffled my moan with a kiss, then withdrew his hand a moment before a group of people walked past us to sit at the next table.

Sheesh.

"Just think how many times I could make you come in a week," he murmured.

"Fine. *Fine*, I'll stay." At least if I was hiding in someone else's apartment, I'd be safe from the ghosts of my past. "But can we try to take things slowly? I'm not feeling myself at the moment."

"Sure, you can feel me instead."

"Be serious, Charming. I mean it. The sex is good, better than good, but I need to know who you are."

His expression grew sober. "We can take things slow, I promise. We'll talk. I haven't had a relationship like this one before, and you haven't had one at all, so we'll have a lot to figure out as we go along. Okay?"

"Okay."

"I want this to work."

So did I, perhaps more than I'd ever wanted anything in my life.

"Kayleigh drank so much at one event that I had to hide her in a closet until the host went to bed, and then I nearly gave myself a hernia lifting her into my car."

"Trey pissed in a Greek shipping tycoon's pool once."

"Isn't that quite a common thing to do?"

"Not from the diving board."

I dissolved into laughter and nearly spilled my champagne. We'd christened Johannes's grand piano, which was an interesting and not particularly comfortable experience, Garrett had made calls for work while I took a much-needed nap, and now we were curled up on the couch —the *leather* couch—playing a game of "my family's more messed up than yours" over pizza and champagne. I never usually spoke about the Baldwins, but in this little bubble of a borrowed apartment, I felt safe. Safe to speak my mind.

Charming seemed content to keep what was happening between us quiet, and for that, I was grateful. Firstly, I wasn't convinced this relationship would last, and the last thing I needed was for my impending heartbreak to be broadcast all over town. And secondly, if by some miracle we did survive as a couple, the gossip mill would run on overdrive, not just in Baldwin's Shore but beyond. I could see the headlines now. *Member of disgraced Baldwin family has fling with billionaire's playboy son.* The twins would go into meltdown and surely try to find a way to turn the situation to their advantage. Dollar signs would flash in their eyes like a malfunctioning slot machine.

"You want to see?" he asked. "As always, there's a video."

"No, I absolutely do not want to see. Uh, how high was the diving board?"

"Three metres. The tycoon's daughter was a competitive diver, and she used the pool for practice."

I snorted. "Easton the Third puked in a bowl of

potpourri once, but Marianna liked to keep the house at a tropical temperature, so the mess dried out overnight, and if you just gave a quick glance, it was hard to tell. The living room smelled funky for a week before anyone worked out where the stink was coming from."

"Trey puked in the glove compartment of my car."

"Yeuch."

"Not the one I have now. I had it detailed four times, and it still smelled weird, so I sold it."

At least I'd only managed to puke on Charming's shoes. Go me.

"What about your sister? You said you had a sister, right? Is she a party girl?"

His smile faded. "Gracie. She's a year older than me. And no, she's not a party girl. Not anymore."

"I didn't mean to pry."

"You're not prying. It's just...difficult."

"Do you want to talk about it?"

"Not really." He put down his glass. "But I also don't want there to be any secrets between us. I meant it when I said I want this to work. The issues with Gracie are family business. Private."

"Nothing goes further than this room, I promise. I know I'm talking about the Baldwins here with you now, but I swear I'm not a gossip. This is a first for me." I squeezed his hand. "You've taken so many of my firsts."

"Why do you always call them the Baldwins? Why not your family?"

Trust him to pick up on the little things. I'd found a true unicorn: a man who listened. And he was also right—if this was going to work, we had to share our secrets.

"I guess I don't...I don't feel like one of them. Until I was nearly ten, I'd only met them a handful of times, and although my dad was a Baldwin, we used to drop that part and just use Mom's surname. Then my parents died, and I was sent to Oregon, and the Baldwins tried to turn me into someone I wasn't."

"Words aren't adequate, but I'm sorry."

"So am I." My eyes began to prickle. "I miss my mom and dad so much, and for years, I couldn't even talk about them."

"Too painful?"

"Nobody to listen."

Charming gathered me into his arms and attacked my defences with another forehead kiss.

"A little late, but I'm here now, Sara not-a-Baldwin."

"Saralisa. My name is Saralisa Forlani."

"That's what you'd prefer me to call you?"

I nodded. "Someday, I want to reclaim my identity. Does that sound dumb?"

"You need to do what feels right, but why someday? Why not now? And why have you stuck around in Baldwin's Shore for so long? Not that I'm complaining because if you'd skipped town, we'd never have met, but I'm curious."

"Well, it all happened because my grandpa was a bit of an asshole." I took a deep breath and told Garrett about the will, about the way Grandpa just had to keep meddling from beyond the grave in a strange quest for immortality. "Basically, he couldn't stand the idea of us benefitting from the fruits of his labour without making any effort ourselves. Originally, I planned to get some experience—because even a minimum-wage job demands experience these days—with LKB and use it as a springboard into the events industry, and the twins were bearable at first. Then LKB did well, really well, and the conditions of the will meant I had to make a deal with the devils, which of course backfired." I gave a soft laugh. "Two years ago, I almost quit, right after they left me to fish a turd out of a swimming pool at some brat's sweet sixteen party, but Parker talked me out of it."

He'd shown a rare glimmer of humanity that day. Said that if I stood back and let the twins win, let them steal my share of the inheritance, then I'd look back in a decade and wish I'd done things differently. His pep talk had sent me back into battle, and now I wished I hadn't listened.

"In the Marines, I got shot at on a number of occasions, but it still sounds more fun than working with your cousins."

"I stayed for the money. I realise how materialistic that makes me seem, but I looked upon it as compensation. Payback for putting up with the Baldwins for so long. If everyone met their targets, then I'd have gotten about two million dollars—a quarter million for each year of Grandpa's challenge that I endured—and I'd have been lucky to find an entry-level position that paid a fifth of that. Plus I could live rent-free at The Lookout. On paper, it was a straightforward decision, but now I have regrets. So many regrets."

"In your position, I'd have done the same thing."

"Isn't two million bucks back-of-the-couch money for you? Anyhow, it's over now. Time to move on and find a new job."

"Is it?"

"There's no way I'd work with the twins again. Even if they realised they'd made a huge mistake and offered me my old job back tomorrow, I wouldn't take it. They'd screw me over again, except they'd learn from the past and do it better this time. They're not entirely stupid, just lazy and arrogant. Oh, and back-stabby, don't forget that."

"But would you stay in the event-planning industry?"

"I'd like to, but I also want to leave The Lookout and make a clean break, so I'll take whatever pays me enough money to do that. I have plenty of transferrable skills. Organising is my superpower. Although I haven't made a single to-do list today, which is unusual."

"Getting withdrawal symptoms?" he joked. "You want me to find you a pen and paper?"

"Maybe? I also have an app on my phone."

"You want me to find you a job too?"

I stiffened. "Is that...is that a joke?"

"Not at all. If you need to earn enough to claim your inheritance, I can make it happen. As you so sweetly pointed out"—he paused to kiss the tip of my nose—"that much is a rounding error for my family."

"I..." What was I meant to say to that? He was offering a solution to a problem I never thought I'd be able to solve, but at the same time, it felt...wrong. I'd sold out once for money and lived to regret it, and the idea of being beholden to a man I was sleeping with, dependent on him for everything, left me uneasy. "Can I consider it? We've known each other for such a short period of time, and if you were my boss, then the whole dynamic between us would change, and...and I want to keep *this*."

"Take as much time as you need, but the offer's there." Another kiss. "Enough of the serious stuff... Wait here for a moment."

He rose from the couch and opened a hidden cupboard on the other side of the room. Everything in this apartment was tucked away, leaving the surfaces clean and clutter-free. This was the expensive kind of minimalism, the type that came not from being unable to afford things but from having enough money to hide all the junk.

A minute later, Charming returned with an artfully wrapped box. "For you."

A gift? He'd brought me a gift? "Thank you, but I haven't gotten you anything, and—"

"Shh. We're not running a scorecard, and besides, this present benefits both of us. Open it."

Shoes. He'd bought me shoes. Dance shoes, to be precise, black Latin dance shoes with laces that criss-crossed over my feet and tied at the ankles. They were beautiful, undoubtedly expensive, higher than I was used to but unbelievably sexy.

"I'll cue up the playlist while you put them on. I *will* get my dirty tango, Saralisa."

At that moment, I'd have given my prince anything he asked for.

23

SARA

"What do you want for dinner this evening? I can pick something up on the way back."

I hadn't left Johannes's apartment in two days. Nor had I spoken to our absent host, but Garrett informed me that several of the paintings on the wall in the great room were self-portraits, so I already felt I knew the man far better than I needed to. He was an artist, Garrett said, an artist and a trust fund baby who had an uncanny ability to convince women to remove their clothes. One of the paintings slid to the side to reveal a hidden studio flooded with natural light from skylights above, and I suspected that the paint-covered bed in one corner was used for more than just staging. Garrett claimed there wasn't a surface in this apartment that wasn't intimately acquainted with bare flesh, so I felt that was a fair assumption to make.

I also sanitised all the kitchen counters and the dining table while he chuckled from behind his laptop screen.

Garrett was surprisingly easy to spend time with. The darkness, the intensity that both unnerved me and turned me on, he seemed to be able to switch it on and off at will. It rarely made an appearance during daylight hours, and I secretly wondered whether he might be part vampire, but so far, he'd been drinking coffee and wine rather than blood. He had a sweet side too. All those chaste kisses, the grazes of his fingers that made me shiver, the little gifts he brought me. Okay, so this morning's surprise had been a pair of leather handcuffs, but it was the thought that counted, right? I took a bite of croissant and studied the man opposite me as he sipped his morning latte and checked his emails.

A week ago, the idea of being tied up in bed would have horrified me, but now I could divide my life into two parts: before Charming and after. If he wanted me to wear the cuffs, I'd wear them, and I trusted him to make sure I enjoyed the experience. Sheesh, I was getting *that* ache just from thinking about it.

"I'll eat pretty much anything except seafood. I'm not a big fan of slime."

He smiled, and my heart skipped. "Noted."

"Are you sure you can't stay here and try out those cuffs?"

"If I could, I would, but this is one commitment I can't cancel."

He hadn't told me where he was going, and I hesitated to ask. We were sharing parts of ourselves, but we were still at the stage of picking and choosing which snippets to divulge. I had to respect his privacy. There were still pieces of my past I couldn't bring myself to speak about, so the reticence went both ways. Meanwhile, I was planning a Netflix marathon in front of Johannes's giant TV with popcorn, ice cream, and the box of chocolates Garrett had bought for me yesterday.

I hopped down from my stool and went for payback with a kiss to his cheek.

"I understand, but I'll be waiting."

His phone buzzed, and I glanced at the screen. I didn't mean to be nosy, but it was right there, and now...now that roller coaster of emotions I was on took a nosedive. Because I'd read the message before Garrett got to it.

MARLIE

When are you picking me up? x

Right, well, at least now I understood his hesitation with the details. That little lick of pain from the *x* at the end hurt worse than anything he'd done in the bedroom, and my stupid eyes began to prickle. *Dumb, dumb, dumb.* We hadn't said we were exclusive. I'd just assumed, and of course it stood to reason that he had other women waiting in the wings. *Playboy, womaniser, confirmed bachelor.* Thank goodness we were using condoms.

I backed away, and when he reached for my hand, I moved sideways like a rook on Johannes's checkerboard floor.

"It's not what you think."

"Honestly, it's none of my business."

"Don't walk away from me, Saralisa."

That was one command I didn't obey. "I'll see you later."

"She's my niece. Marlie is my niece."

I stopped dead in my tracks. A niece? Garrett hadn't mentioned a niece. From what I'd heard about Trey, I couldn't imagine him parenting a child, which meant the girl was Gracie's. But didn't she live in New York?

"Sit down. Please."

This time, I did as Garrett asked, and he sighed as he leaned against the counter.

"Marlie is my niece. She's eight years old, and she lives with us here in Roseburg because Gracie decided she didn't want to be a mom."

This time, it was me who reached for him. "I'm so sorry."

Sorry that I'd backed away, sorry for what Gracie had done, sorry for a young girl who had to grow up without her mom. I knew how hard that could be.

"I can't pretend it's been easy, but things have gotten better over time. Letti—my stepmom—stepped in, and most people assume Marlie is hers."

"Wow."

"Yeah. Once a week, I take Marlie out to do something fun to give Letti a break and also to show Marlie that not everyone in the family has abandoned her. Letti's mom minds her when Letti is busy, and my dad and Trey help out too."

"Trey?"

"He's actually pretty good with her, probably because he's a big kid himself."

I swallowed hard. "Thank you for trusting me enough to tell me."

Garrett didn't answer, just wrapped his arms around me and kissed my hair. That was the moment I realised I was in big trouble, or at least, my heart was. For all his darkness and his bossiness, I could quite easily fall for Garrett Dorsey.

"I hope the two of you have a great time today. Don't worry; I'll be absolutely fine here with Netflix."

"I won't be back late."

"Doesn't matter if you are. You should reply to Marlie's text, though. Tell her you'll be there soon."

He typed out a message, then raised his coffee mug in a mock toast. "To fucked-up families."

I held up my own mug. "To making a little girl feel wanted."

Because I hadn't been. Marlie and me, we were opposites—she had a mom who didn't want her and a family who did, while I'd lost the love of both parents and been made to feel like an intruder for the rest of my life. That Garrett was willing to give up half of his weekend to spend time with his niece made me so freaking happy.

I was loading breakfast plates into the dishwasher when he reappeared ten minutes later in cargo pants, sturdy boots, and a lightweight down jacket.

"You're going hiking?"

"Marlie wants to visit Fall Creek Falls and explore the trails there."

"You look so rugged." A halfway house between Charming and Darkness. "I like it. If you're looking for your keys, you left them on the table in the foyer."

"Thanks." He kissed me—with too much tongue for a goodbye—then headed for the door as I fanned myself. But he only made it two steps before he turned back. "Come with us."

"What?"

"Come hiking with us."

"But...but... I can't. We haven't known each other for long enough, and what if—"

"There you go with the 'what ifs' again. In case I haven't made myself clear, this isn't a short-term fling, and Marlie's gonna like you as much as I do."

Now I wanted to cry again, but this time because my heart was so full that it threatened to overflow. If Garrett wanted me to start meeting his family, that said a lot about his intentions. Of course, the move wouldn't be reciprocated in the near future—I wanted him to meet the Baldwins at around the same time that hell froze over—but I knew he'd understand why.

"Is the path okay for sneakers?"

"The path's good, and I have a jacket you can use. Marlie's going to have a whole bunch of questions because I've never brought a girl to meet her before, and I'll warn you now, she couldn't keep a secret if her life depended on it." He led me toward the guest room closet. "So no tongues in front of my niece."

***

"Say cheese."

Marlie mugged for the camera and Garrett stuck his tongue out, then I held my breath as they climbed down from the fallen tree they'd both clambered onto. Once they were back on solid ground, Marlie grabbed her phone and checked the pictures, then ran off to perform her next death-defying stunt.

"She's a real daredevil, huh?"

Garrett took my hand and watched her go.

"Just like her mom was at that age," he said, and I didn't miss the sadness in his voice.

He'd introduced me to Grandma Valeria—who was his stepmom's mom—as "my friend Saralisa," and she'd stared with undisguised curiosity. I'd struggled not to do the same. Valeria was about five feet tall, and even at home in the daytime, her make-up was flawless and she wore flowers in her hair. Her dress was the colour of poppies, and her shoes matched perfectly.

"Why didn't you tell me you were bringing someone?" she asked. "I would have made tea."

"You never make me tea."

"You can make your own." She'd taken both of my hands in hers. "Tell me, how did you meet Garrett?"

"Uh, we were at a party, and we ended up dancing together."

"You dance?"

Garrett rested his chin on my shoulder. "Saralisa's the salsa queen."

I found myself dragged away from him as Valeria twirled me around her living room, past a cabinet full of trophies and photos of her dancing when she was younger. Now I saw where Garrett got his fast feet from. On the second circuit, he grabbed ahold of my hand and claimed me back.

"Don't scare her off, Valeria."

"I won't; I like her." She turned toward the doorway. "Marlie, *llegas tarde otra vez!*"

Apparently, Marlie was always late. Easily distracted, Garrett said, and I could see why. She had to balance on every log, turn over every rock, and examine every leaf. When we reached the waterfall, she wanted to paddle in the pool, but the water was too cold, so Garrett promised her a piggyback instead. This was yet another side to him, the carefree kid who larked around without a care in the world.

As for me, I wasn't quite so adventurous, but I did find my worries slipping away, albeit temporarily. Who could be downbeat when there was nature, pizza, the man of my dreams, and a super-cute little girl to hang out with? Even though they weren't related by blood, Valeria's influence on Marlie was clear—the little girl loved bright colours, and her smile was infectious. I suspected she was a whiz at salsa dancing too, the same as I'd been at her age. In some ways, the afternoon was bittersweet, because in her, I saw the child I'd once been before disaster struck. But Marlie wouldn't suffer the way I did. Nearly all of her family adored her.

And I thought she was warming up to me, although I knew nothing about kids. At the pizza place, she squished my cheeks between her palms and giggled, then knelt on the seat next to me and begged Garrett to take a picture. My squashed smile was genuine.

"You looked as if you had a good time," he said in the car on the way back to Johannes's apartment.

"I did. I really did."

"Marlie's a great kid."

How could Gracie abandon her? The words were on the tip of my tongue, but of course I didn't say them.

"The sweetest, but you need to have eyes in the back of your head."

"Tell me about it. When she was six, she loved to play hide-and-seek, and the day she snuck into a delivery driver's truck, we thought she'd been kidnapped. Dad called the police, and apparently the guy nearly had a heart attack when he got back to the depot and found her."

"I bet he did. You need to handcuff her to—" I clapped both hands over my mouth. "Shit! Sorry! I didn't mean to say that. Your kinks are a bad influence."

"If it helps, all I've been able to think about for the past three hours is you naked and tied up in my bed."

"Tied up? Like, with rope?"

"Would you object to that?"

"With you, I'll try anything once."

24

SARA

And so the roller coaster continued with the highest of highs and the lowest of lows. After Garrett had stroked me and teased me and sucked me and kissed me and fingered me and spanked me and finally fucked me as I lay bound beneath him, I fell asleep in his arms, sated, shattered, and just a tiny bit in love.

Then *he* came.

The monster.

He'd stayed out of my dreams for a week, which was a record, but as I settled into life with Garrett, that beast pushed his way back into my subconscious. It was the same as always. The crash, the blood, the fear, the gun. The panic as he pushed the pillow over my face. The whispered threats.

But it was also different.

Because instead of sobbing to myself in the dark, I was shaken awake in a room bathed in the soft glow of a bedside lamp with Garrett's worried face watching over me.

"Are you okay?"

I tried to offer a reassuring smile, but it didn't work out. "Just a nightmare."

"Do you get them often?"

No lies. "Yes."

"Anything I can do to make it better? Do you want a glass of wine? Milk? Should I leave the light on?"

Last night, he'd turned my ass delightfully pink, but now he was back to being sweet again. "There's nothing you can do. They'll just keep coming. If..." I squeezed my eyes closed to clear the tears. "If it disturbs you, I can sleep in another room."

"I'm not worried about me; I'm worried about you. Have you tried seeing a doctor? Taking sleeping pills?"

"No, no, no. No doctor." Several years ago, I'd pilfered a handful of prescription pills from Marianna's medical cabinet and discovered that the only thing worse than a nightmare was a nightmare I couldn't wake up from. "I just... I'm used to it."

"Is it always the same dream?"

"Always," I whispered.

"Do you want to talk about it?"

No, I didn't, but if I didn't tell Garrett now, then when would I tell him? How many more times would he have to hold me in the middle of the night without understanding why?

"I... It's the night my parents died. The car crash. I keep reliving it, over and over and over."

"You said you were in the accident with them?"

I nodded, my throat swollen and my eyes fuzzy.

"Hell, princess, I'm so sorry. Were you hurt?"

"Just bruised. But...but it wasn't an accident."

"What?"

"S-s-someone ran the car off the road."

Now anger mixed with the shock. "Someone killed your parents?"

"I'm...I'm so scared. I'm not meant to talk about it, and I don't want to put you in any danger."

"You won't, I promise. In the Marines, I was special forces, and I'm not meant to talk about that either, but understand that I can look after myself."

"I've never told anyone the whole story, just...just pieces."

"Whatever pieces you want to share, I'll listen, and I won't tell a soul. I want to make this better, princess." He wiped my tears away with a thumb. "I don't like seeing you cry."

"I-I-I don't even know where to start."

"How about at the beginning?"

Charming gathered me against him, arms wrapped around me, and small miracles did happen because for once, his dick wasn't hard. This was serious Garrett.

"In the beginning, I was a little like Marlie. I loved to play hide-and-seek. My parents were going out for dinner, and I was meant to stay with the babysitter. Vicky." I made a face. "She mostly ignored me, and after Mom and Dad left, she always used to sneak her boyfriend over. I didn't know what they were doing on the couch at the time—I was only nine years old—but of course I do now."

Garrett shook his head in disgust. "Marlie stays with me sometimes, so I'd better get a lock installed on the bedroom door."

I added "responsible" to his list of qualities.

"Well, Vicky didn't care what I overheard, and I didn't want to stay at home and listen to grunting. So when Mom forgot her scarf and went back to the bedroom for it, and Dad stepped into the kitchen to take a phone call, I snuck into the garage and hid under a blanket in the back of the car. I figured that if I stayed quiet until they got to the restaurant, they'd let me have dinner with them instead of taking me back home. But we never got to the restaurant. And now...now I'm not even sure that's where they were going. There was... We ended up heading out of town, on deserted roads, and Mom and Dad were fighting. Until that month, they'd never fought. *Never*. Not in front of me, anyway. I think maybe they were meeting someone? But they never got there because a vehicle hit us from behind. Mom screamed, and I screamed, and I'll never forget the horror on her face when she realised I was in the car. She just kept yelling at me to put my seat belt on. It all happened so fast. The headlights behind us, the jolts as the other vehicle hit us, my parents shouting at me and each other. Then Dad lost control, and we swerved off the road and hit a tree."

"I'm so fucking sorry, Saralisa."

"It got worse. So much worse."

Garrett's soft kisses soothed me, but nothing would ever take the hurt away completely. Talking, though, talking helped. It was strangely cathartic, putting my nightmares into words, knowing that nothing would go beyond this room. He was like a sponge, soaking up all my pain.

"I think Dad was already dead at that point, but Mom, she was still alive. She asked if I was okay, if I was hurt, and I could hear her moving around, trying to get free, but she was stuck. And she kept talking, telling me things I didn't understand, random words and numbers mostly. I didn't realise what was happening. I saw lights shining over us and thought help was coming, but Mom knew it wasn't. She told me to hide again, hide and shush, and then *he* was there. I call him the monster, but he was human. I'll never forget her last words. *Burn them.*" She'd said them desperately, angrily, and I'd never been sure whether they were aimed at me or the monster, or what exactly she meant. "And then he shot her."

Garrett was holding me so tightly I could hardly breathe, or perhaps that was just the band of tension that had been suffocating me for years? The pillow was damp with tears. I gulped in air, trying to get some much-needed oxygen to my lungs.

"Tell me they found the person who did that. Tell me he got the death penalty."

Garrett didn't just sound angry, he sounded furious, and that fuelled me to keep talking. Because I was furious too. Furious that my family had been stolen from me, furious that I'd lost everything I loved, furious that I hadn't even been able to speak about this for sixteen damn years.

"They didn't. They didn't because the police thought it was an *accident.*"

"How the hell could they think that? Couldn't they find evidence of an impact? A gunshot? What about you? You were a witness."

"When I say I've never told anyone, I mean *anyone.*"

He cursed under his breath. "The cops should have brought in a trained interviewer. Someone used to speaking with kids."

"I still wouldn't have talked. He told me I'd die if I did."

"He?"

"The monster."

"He spoke to you?"

"Not that night, not in the car. I was stuck there for hours. The doors wouldn't open, and even if they had, where would I have gone? We were in a freaking forest. A man found us in daylight." A kind man. He'd told me everything would be okay—a lie—and stayed with me until the fire service cut me out of the wreckage. The creaking, the groaning, the ear-splitting *screech* of tearing metal…it all stayed with me. "They took me to the hospital, and I guess the monster realised his mistake. If he'd seen me in the car, he'd have killed me too; I'm absolutely certain of that." The sea was blue, the sun rose in the mornings, and assassins tidied up loose ends. "He came to the hospital the next day and tried to suffocate me with a pillow before he got interrupted."

My tone had turned matter-of-fact now. The more I talked, the easier it got. Now I was narrating my own life, a tale I'd had the misfortune to live, a memoir. *Orphan: The Saralisa Story*. But as I became calmer, Garrett became more agitated. He rolled out of bed and began pacing.

"It's not too late. There's no statute of limitations for murder. Where did this happen? My father has influence in Oregon, and if the cops aren't doing their job, he'll sure as hell find a way to make them."

"Don't. Please don't. I'll be risking my own life if I go after them, and part of me thinks I'm selfish for that, for not going after justice, but I want to live. I have dark moments, but I want to live. And Mom and Dad would want me to live too."

"But this is an old case. How long ago did it happen?"

"Sixteen years."

"Sixteen years." Garrett raked a hand through already messy hair. "There's a new generation of cops, new investigative techniques. The perp might not even be alive anymore, but don't you want to try? Don't you want closure?"

"He's alive."

Garrett's head whipped around. "How do you know that?"

His tone was clipped, almost staccato, and I began to fear he was angry with me. Angry that I wasn't as brave as him.

"Because that night at the Peninsula, I wasn't only running from you. I was running from him too."

"This motherfucker's *following* you?"

"I don't...I don't know. He was just there. And don't suggest interrogating the hotel staff because I have a friend who's a PI, and she already did that. The only thing we know is that he arrived with another guy in a car registered to a shell company in Delaware. They weren't guests, and they weren't there for dinner. It's a dead end."

"They were at Hadley's party? At that dumb fucking unmasking ceremony? I can get a guest list."

"No, not at the party. At first, I ran because I didn't want the twins to recognise me, and the monster was outside on the smoking terrace with another man. I figured they were there for me and I freaked out, okay? That's when I lost my shoe. But Blue —that's my friend—she says there's no evidence either way, so maybe it was all some big coincidence? Whatever, as long as he thinks I'm keeping my mouth shut, he leaves me alone, and I just need to bury this. Bury it deep, where somebody with enough power and influence to tamper with autopsy results and shut down a police investigation wants it to stay."

Garrett was stock still now, his gaze absolutely piercing, and I wanted to hide under the quilt the way I'd hidden in the back of Mom and Dad's car all those years ago.

"How certain are you that the man you saw at the Peninsula was the same man who killed your parents?"

"I don't know! At the time, I was sure, but it was a gut

reaction, so maybe I got it wrong? The eyes...the pale, pale eyes were the same. But isn't everyone meant to have a doppelgänger? Please, can't you come back to bed? I wanted to explain my nightmares, not start a chain reaction that neither of us would be able to control."

He began pacing again. Great.

"Please?" I begged. "Please? A week ago, my life didn't matter so much, but then you came back into it and promised me a future that I never thought I'd have, and I just want to live. I want to live with you."

Finally, he stilled by the bed. "You want to live with me? Guess I'd better clear out half of my closet, then."

The anger dissipated, and I could tell he was trying to lighten up for my benefit.

"Can we change the subject now? Just fuck me. Tie me up and hold me down and take my mind off this. Take my demons away."

The energy rolling off Garrett in waves changed. There was still anger, but now he channelled it, and I felt the raw strength of him when he picked me up and threw me onto my stomach.

"You'd better be ready for this."

I told one more tiny but oh-so-necessary lie.

"I'm ready."

25

GARRETT

I'd promised Saralisa no lies, but today, I'd lied. I'd fucked her into exhaustion and then told her something urgent had come up at home, but now I was in my office, alternately pacing and googling everything I could find about the Baldwin-Forlani family because what she'd told me last night was insane.

Crazy.

I'd dated a fantasist before, a woman who'd claimed to be the daughter of an English earl before the background check revealed her to be an out-of-work actress from London. The dalliance had lasted less than two weeks before I sent her packing, and I hadn't cared one way or the other. She'd been nothing, a nobody, a warm pussy to sink my cock into while I waited for the right woman to come along. If she'd asked, I'd have given her a reference because her acting skills had actually been pretty good.

Saralisa wasn't a fantasist. She hadn't misrepresented herself, and all the revelations she'd made last night had been intended for my ears only. Fishing for sympathy? No, that didn't strike me as her game either. But I wasn't convinced her recollections were correct.

The part about the car crash was true; I'd found out that much. Claire Forlani and Peter Baldwin had died in a car wreck sixteen years ago in northern Virginia. Their nine-year-old daughter (name withheld) had been found the following morning and taken to the hospital suffering from shock and hypothermia but otherwise unharmed. There was no mention of a shooting, no mention of a murder attempt on the kid. A short obituary talked of a loving mother who'd worked on Capitol Hill and a doting father who'd followed his dream to become a painter. I checked out a number of his works, and they sold for a tidy amount these days.

As for Saralisa herself, she seriously underplayed her dancing achievements. I'd found old videos of her in competition, and although the quality of the footage wasn't great, there was no mistaking the girl who'd turned into the woman currently unconscious in Johannes's spare bed.

The basic facts were all there, but her tale of murder and cover-ups, of silence and surveillance, that was the part I couldn't swallow. I believed that she believed it—there was no way she'd faked her fear last night as the story came spilling out—but was there any truth in it, or had her mind created the scenario because it was easier to accept than her father's mistake? Cars were easy to crash. I'd wrapped one around a tree myself when a deer ran out in front of me. Whiplash, a mild concussion, and I'd walked away, but not everyone was so lucky.

My phone buzzed, and I answered the call.

"I'm here."

"Come on up."

Two minutes later, Carson Broad walked into my office

on the third floor. His name didn't suit him. He was a tall, wiry man with eyes that missed nothing and a mean left hook.

"Thanks for coming."

"What's so important on a Sunday?"

"I need a background check on a woman."

"Another one?"

"This one's different."

"Aren't they all?"

"I also need a second check on a man."

"Planning to get adventurous?" Carson chuckled at his own joke as he headed for the coffee machine in the corner. *If only he knew.*

"It's complicated. I've learned a considerable amount about the woman already, but there's one particular aspect of her life I'm interested in."

"Which is? Do you have any more of those Colombian java pods?"

"In the cupboard underneath. Her name is Saralisa Baldwin-Forlani, and she was orphaned approximately sixteen years ago. I need to understand the circumstances of her parents' death. It happened in a car crash. The police say it was an accident, and she says it was murder."

Carson found the blend he wanted and pushed the pod into the machine. "Murder? Isn't that the kind of thing the police would look into?"

"At best, she believes they dropped the ball, and at worst, there was a cover-up."

The coffee machine beeped, but both of us ignored it as I laid out the story Saralisa had told—not all the personal details, just the bare facts. Nobody needed to know about the babysitter issues or her parents fighting or the absolute shitshow that was the Baldwin family. Carson made notes as he listened, and only when I was done did he retrieve his mug.

"That's a big allegation," he said.

"Precisely. And I don't want it to come back to bite either of us later on. Discretion is vital."

"As always. Who's the guy?"

This was where it got tricky. "Seth Harless. He's Graham Mandell's head of security."

"Congressman Mandell?"

"Yes."

"And is this a separate project?"

"No, the same project."

"So how do the pieces fit together?"

I took a deep breath and opened Pandora's box. "Because Saralisa thinks Harless is the man who murdered her parents."

Carson gave a low whistle. "That's..."

"Fucked up? Yes." When she described the encounter at the hotel, I'd known right away who she was talking about because I'd been hot on her heels. "But the allegation is out there, and if Saralisa and I stay together—which I hope we do—she's going to run into Harless at some point. I need to get any misunderstandings cleared up before that happens."

That they would meet was inevitable. My dad and Graham Mandell were old friends. Trey was dating his stepdaughter. Our families got together for cookouts and galas and Sunday lunches, and I wanted Saralisa to be a part of that, but first, I had to prove that what we were dealing with was a case of mistaken identity. Seth Harless was a family man. He had two daughters himself.

During my university years, I'd hooked up with a psychology student a couple of times, and I had a vague recollection of her working on some sort of project about trauma response. She'd mentioned false memories. Now I wished I'd actually listened to her, but I'd been young and horny and far more interested in her body than her brain. What was her name? Lizzy? Libby? Johannes might remember—he'd probably painted her.

Anyhow, the upshot was that trauma could lead to false recollections, and I suspected that was what had happened in Saralisa's case. Would she be open to therapy? I'd gladly pay for all the treatment she needed if it would help her to lay those demons to rest.

But what I wouldn't do was ruin Seth Harless's life with unfounded allegations. Maybe there was a resemblance to a figure in Saralisa's past? His eyes were unusual, I'd give her that. Pale blue, almost silver, and they had a way of boring into anyone he wanted to intimidate. More than once, he'd turned them on Trey. But that was his job.

My half-brother's relationship with Elina Mandell could best be described as rocky. Sure, there was chemistry there, but Elina was a spoiled brat and Trey refused to admit that he made mistakes, let alone learn from them. They fought loudly and often. Twice, they'd split up, and secretly I'd hoped each time that the parting would be permanent. But three weeks before the infamous party at the Peninsula, I'd gone to use the swimming pool and found them banging in the cabana. Perhaps it would be third time lucky?

"I'll take a look into Harless's background. The accident was in Virginia, you say? Hopefully, we can show he was working here in Oregon at the time."

"Fingers crossed."

"I'll have to link up with a colleague over there to do some of the legwork—licensing requirements, you know the deal—and since this is an old case, the costs might be a touch higher than usual. Depends how much is computerised."

"The cost doesn't matter. Getting Saralisa the help she needs, that's what matters. I'll need regular updates."

"You'll get them. Is that everything?"

"For now. Please see yourself out."

After Broad closed the door, I rocked back in my chair and hoped to fuck I was doing the right thing. I was falling for Saralisa, but I had to protect my family and, by extension, Elina's family.

If Broad could dig into Harless's past and prove he had nothing to do with the events in Virginia, I'd also be able to reassure Saralisa that whatever she thought happened sixteen years ago was in the past and nobody was following her now. And if nobody was following her and she accepted my offer to find her a job, there would be no reason for her to leave Oregon. My comment last night about closet space had been a joke, but I found I didn't hate the idea.

Domestic fucking bliss, emphasis on the fucking.

I'd never lived with a woman before. Until her, I'd never wanted to, but everything was different now.

Well, not quite everything.

My phone rang, and it was Dad.

"You need to get over to the house. We're in damage limitation mode."

Ah, fuck. "What did he do this time?"

"Got into a bar fight, and allegedly a bag of coke fell out of his pocket. Burford will make any charges disappear, but you just know some asshole's gonna leak the details to the press."

"I'm on my way."

I could hear Trey in the background, whining as usual. *It was only one line, I don't see the big deal.* But for once, I wasn't mad that Trey had travelled down the path of irresponsibility yet again. A little drug bust was nothing compared to some of his past escapades. And thanks to his screw-up, I had a genuine emergency at home, a real excuse for leaving Saralisa in bed alone this morning.

Damn, this was a mess.

26

SARA

"Tell us everything."

Brooke rested her chin on her hands across the table and regarded me with gleaming eyes. It was girls' night at Applejack's—well, girls' night plus Paulo—and I had an audience of six. Even Brie had shown up for the gossip tonight. Her security team hovered in the background like hot Scandinavian ninjas.

"Maybe she needs another cocktail first?" Addy suggested.

"No, really—"

Too late. Addy was already topping off my glass from a jug of the house special—applejack, blue curaçao, and lemonade garnished with apple slices. On any other night, I would have ignored the alcohol and switched to water, but Garrett had promised to rescue me at the end of the evening and make sure I got home. Which would be the pool house tonight. Darla was working in Virginia again this week, and Brooke had offered me some shifts at the Craft Cabin. I still hadn't decided whether to accept Garrett's offer. Five weeks after I puked on his shoes, things were going good between us, better than good, but this was all so new. So strange. Plus he had to take a trip to Los Angeles for work next week, and I'd feel a bit weird staying at his place by myself, especially with his family so close by. And I missed my friends. I even missed Baldwin's Shore a tiny bit, something I'd never thought would be possible.

"Did you change your hair?" Brie asked. "It looks nice."

I nodded. "I've changed so much—my hair, my clothes, my outlook on life. It was time. I'm sick of being a doormat."

"Good for you."

"Now spill the tea," Brooke instructed. "We googled your new guy, and ohmigosh..." She fanned herself with a menu. "You met him at the masked ball?"

"We both crashed the party and ended up dancing together, then one thing led to another and he ended up charging into the craft store and taking me skydiving."

"Uh, what? *Skydiving*?"

"Indoor skydiving."

I gave them a brief rundown of events, leaving out any mention of handcuffs, riding crops, and nipple clamps. To be honest, I still wasn't sure about the nipple clamps. We'd only tried them once, and although the after-effects were exquisite, actually wearing them hurt a little more than I was comfortable with. Garrett was going to pick up a different pair to see if they were any better. Anyhow, I focused on the sweet stuff, the parts that wouldn't ruin reputations if they got picked up by the papers. Not that I didn't trust my friends. None of them would knowingly sell a story, but Paulo in particular had a big mouth, although Brooke said he'd learned to zip it after he began seeing Davis French. Did Davis have a nervous PR lady the same way the Dorsey family did? Her name was Angela, and I'd met her in the aftermath of Trey's latest scandal. Luckily, his bag of "coke" had turned out to be a mixture of baby laxatives and powdered vitamins, and he'd been more upset about getting ripped off by his now ex-dealer than the potential drugs charge.

Angela had also given me a lecture on the importance of protecting "the family," and when I'd made a joke about the Mafia, she hadn't cracked a smile. But she did have a minor breakdown when she realised I hadn't signed a nondisclosure agreement, then Garrett walked in and said I didn't have to because he trusted me, which had sent a whole other kind of warmth through my veins. But I also didn't want to get off on the wrong foot with Angela, so I'd insisted on signing the NDA anyway.

Brooke gave me a sappy grin. "Aw, he takes you dancing? That's so romantic."

"That salsa class we went to sure paid off," Paulo said, nearly taking his eye out with a swizzle stick. "Was it my excellent footwork that helped you to hook your man?"

"I hate to break it to you, but I was actually a junior dance champion before I moved to Baldwin's Shore. Only national, not world."

Six jaws dropped.

"Oh, sure, only national." Ah, there was Blue's snark.

"So, do you know any hot dancers?" Addy queried. "Asking for a friend."

"Not anymore. My old dance partner was the son of the Polish ambassador, and he moved back home years ago."

"Aren't you the dark horse," Blue muttered.

"My mom worked on Capitol Hill and my godfather was a senator. Practically all of our family friends were connected to politics, but my dad and Marcin's dad met at an art exhibition." I took a sip of my cocktail. "I miss my old world, and I'm going to start taking steps to reclaim whatever I can from it. Dancing, art, my old name. I'm sick of hiding away."

Romi looked puzzled. "Wait, your name isn't Sara?"

"It's Saralisa, and my surname is Baldwin-Forlani. *They* made me drop the Forlani, but I think it's time I dropped the Baldwin instead."

Brooke held up her hand for a high five. "Go you."

"So, if you're taking up dancing again, does that mean you'll join the burlesque workshop?" Addy wanted to know. "Brie will be out of town, Darla's a no, and we need to have at least six people."

"Why not?" Time to live dangerously.

"Darla did offer to help with the outfits," Paulo said. "I'm going to have sequins everywhere."

"Everywhere?" Blue snorted. "Sounds painful. I'll stick with sportswear."

"Party pooper."

"Have you thought any more about work?" Brie asked. "There's definitely going to be a gap in the market for an event coordinator around here soon. Your cousins are messing up every job they work on."

"Where did you hear that?"

I'd barely spoken with the Baldwins in a month. Parker checked in every couple of days, but the twins were avoiding me and EJ had just made a sarcastic comment about me treating The Lookout like a hotel.

"From Nico. He hears things. They organised a party in Coquille last week, and the host's wife went into anaphylactic shock because they didn't take her peanut allergy seriously."

The smugness I'd been feeling vanished, replaced by horror. "Was she okay?"

"Luckily, she had an EpiPen. Nico says LKB will

probably get sued, so it's a good thing you're out of there, but if you're thinking of getting back into events, then I'd like to hire you."

"*You'd* like to hire me?"

"Just for a small thing—Kiki's birthday party. It's four months away, but I want to make it special."

"Uh, sure. Sure, I'd love to help. Do you have any ideas for a theme?"

"This month, she loves cats and ice skating. We're hoping the new house will be finished by then, so maybe we could do something in the grounds? That would be easier from a security perspective."

"Depending on your budget, a synthetic skating rink might be possible? With, uh, cat costumes?"

Brie laughed. "Why don't we catch up over coffee during the week?"

"I'd love to."

Paulo clapped his hands together. "Isn't this fabulous? We should drink to Sara's new events company. What are you going to call it?"

"I'm not—"

"What about Aardvark Events? That way, you'll always be at the top of the listing."

Blue shook her head. "That's dumb."

"Okay, fine, let's go hipster. Avocado Events."

"Honestly, I'm still not sure I'll be starting a full-fledged events company myself. Garrett...Garrett offered to find me a job. Not necessarily one that I'll love, but one that would pay enough for me to claim my inheritance by the deadline."

Brooke held up her glass in a toast. "That's awesome! To Sara's new job and sticking it to the Baldwins."

"I haven't decided if I'll take it yet."

"Why wouldn't you?"

"Because I'd be tying my entire life to his, and...and if our relationship doesn't work out, I'd lose everything again."

"Don't be such a Negative Nelly," Paulo said, but Romi was nodding.

"No, I get it. I love Aaron, I really do, but if we had to work together, we'd end up killing each other."

Support for that point of view came from Blue too. "I used to work for my ex, and when we broke up, he trashed my reputation and I ended up handing out flyers in a wiener costume. I'm with Romi: don't do it."

"At least think it through for a little longer," Brie suggested. "There's a honeymoon phase in any new relationship."

Brooke nodded. "You know that's over when your boyfriend says he has a dirty surprise for you and it turns out to be a compost tumbler."

Romi rolled her eyes. "Tell me Luca didn't..."

"He did."

"I'm gonna kick his ass."

Brooke got a compost tumbler, and I got a glass-handled flogger that looked more like a piece of art than a sex toy. But I definitely wasn't going to announce that in a crowded bar.

Brie's suggestion was the best so far, and the time spent in Roseburg had given me room to think. Physically, I could be in a worse position, much worse. I had a roof over my head, no debt, a small cushion of savings, friends who cared, and a supportive boyfriend. Mentally, I still felt fragile, but every day, my foundations grew stronger. The monster was back in his cave, sharing my secrets with Garrett had lightened the load I carried, and I spent most days floating on a cloud of dopamine.

"I think I'll take some more time to consider my options."

"Marrying a billionaire is a perfectly acceptable career move," Addy told me. "Just saying."

"Garrett isn't actually a billionaire. It's family money."

"So, have you met his family yet?"

I nodded.

"And?"

"They're nice."

His father had been intense but surprisingly amenable. I'd expected to feel intimidated and way, way out of my depth, but he'd been polite and asked about my hobbies and life in Baldwin's Shore and the work I'd done in events. There were a lot of questions, a *lot*, but nothing about the Baldwins themselves, and I suspected Garrett had briefed him not to mention them. And Letti was lovely. The kind of stepmom I wished I'd had. She'd invited me out to lunch when I felt ready, or to the spa, or shopping. Garrett's biological mom had died when he was young—from cancer, I'd found out on the internet—and he said memories of her were like a faded photograph. He felt her love, but her face was faint, dulled by time.

Accepting, that was the best way to describe the Dorsey family. They didn't judge me for not having blue blood or money and seemed happy that I was a part of Garrett's life. When I'd blurted that out to Garrett in a moment of honesty, he'd laughed and said everyone was just relieved that I wasn't a reckless fool like Trey's girlfriend.

I'd only crossed paths with her once, other than at Hadley's party, and she was the one person who'd been snooty with me. Elina Mandell was definitely the type of person to judge a book by its cover.

"Has Garrett met the Baldwins?"

"Not exactly."

"What does that mean?"

"He's familiar with the twins and Easton from the party circuit, but that was before we met. I'm hoping to put the formal introductions off for as long as possible."

"But the Baldwins know you're dating him?"

"Nope. Parker knows I'm seeing someone, but not who. The others don't care." Or at least they didn't right now, but that would surely change when they realised the Dorseys' net worth. "Let's talk about something else. The Baldwins have occupied way too much of my headspace."

"We should eat," Paulo announced. "Who wants to share a plate of nachos?"

A burger, a plate of nachos, an ice cream sundae, and far too many cocktails later, Prince Charming came to rescue me. We'd made it to the tiny dance floor by then, and I was desperately trying to avoid Paulo's feet when I felt hands on my hips.

"Fancy meeting you here," he whispered in my ear in a faux English accent.

"I'd meet you anywhere."

"Are you ready to leave?"

"I—"

Addy wasn't so lucky with Paulo's feet, and she staggered past us on her way to a spectacular face plant. Garrett made a grab for her and missed, but luckily, Deck Langdon was closer. He caught her a moment before she hit the floor and set her back on her feet.

"Careful, Addy."

"Oops." She stroked his face. "Delicious Decker, you're so purdy."

"You might want to ease up on the cocktails."

Addy clung to Deck with one hand and reached for me

with the other. "I'm good. We're good, right? Sara? We're good?"

That was debatable. My feet hurt, but at least I was still able to stand upright. "Good-ish."

"Is that your shexy hot man? He's purdy too. Gary?"

Thankfully, Garrett seemed more amused than annoyed by her antics. "Garrett." Then he addressed Deck. "Want me to take her off your hands?"

"She needs a glass of water."

"I see that." He gave Deck a closer look. "Have we met before?"

"Not that I'm aware of."

"Gary, I need to pee," Addy announced, giggling.

Garrett looked to me for help as Deck beat a hasty retreat. "Can you handle it?"

"I'm almost certain I can do that."

My purdy hot shexy man was an angel in human form. Two glasses of water and a bathroom break later, he carried Addy out of the bar and then drove her back home to Coos Bay. Between us, we got her into bed and made sure she had a bottle of Tylenol close by for the morning.

"Think she'll be okay?" he asked.

Addy just snuffle-snorted and tucked the quilt around herself.

"Yup. I'm really sorry about this."

"It's a good thing I love you."

"You...you love me?"

He gave me the sweetest, most heart-melting smile. "I do."

His heartfelt declaration was met with a loud fart from Addy, and I couldn't help it—I just started giggling.

"Fuck," he muttered.

"I'm... I... Oh my gosh. I don't know what to say."

"How about telling me you love me?"

"I love you."

"There, that wasn't so hard, was it?"

I reached a hand down to my favourite part of his anatomy. "Well, actually…"

A moment later, I was in his arms, and half an hour after that, I was in his bed. My bed. Our bed. What was mine was his, what was his was mine. We were each other's.

And that's the way I always wanted it to be.

27

SARA

> My last meeting got cancelled. I want you naked, blindfolded, and waiting.

*H*e was flying back right now? Tonight? This week without Garrett had felt like the longest of my life, even though I'd had fun working at the Craft Cabin each day and spent the evenings hanging out with Brooke and Romi. He'd become such a big piece of my life so quickly, and I couldn't imagine a future without him. Didn't want to. We'd talked on the phone every night he was away, and yesterday, we agreed that it was finally time for him to meet the Baldwins. Sneaking around had been fun at first, but rain was forecast next week and he didn't need to be squelching through wet undergrowth to get to the pool house.

Kayleigh's and Lillian's boyfriends visited—a whole string of them because none ever lasted long—and Easton had always brought women home before he went to prison. I was perfectly entitled to have Garrett stay with me. And maybe in the future, I'd spend more time in Roseburg too? Garrett wanted to wait a little longer before we went fully public with our relationship—to protect me, he said. As his official girlfriend, I'd be expected to be by his side at gala dinners and fundraisers and the kind of events I was more used to coordinating than attending.

The adjustment period was welcome. The thought of being thrust into the spotlight was a daunting one, and I was no social butterfly. Plus my wardrobe needed an overhaul. Brie and Romi had begun funnelling clothes and accessories in my direction, and Darla had offered to help with alterations when she was back in town, but would that be enough? I didn't know how to twist my hair into an artful chignon, and every time I tried to use eyeliner, it looked as if a toddler had gotten loose with a crayon.

But that was a problem for tomorrow. Tonight, I just had to take a shower, shave everywhere, dry my hair, and do whatever Garrett told me to do.

How long until you get here?

If I were making the trip back from Los Angeles, I'd have to find my way to LAX, spend an hour checking in and being groped by a TSA agent, fly to Portland, and then drive for nearly five hours until I reached Baldwin's Shore. Total journey time: at least eight hours.

GARRETT

Three hours x

But being wealthy bought you the one thing nobody had enough of: time. Garrett would take a private jet to Medford, then transfer to a helicopter for the trip to North Bend, where his Porsche was waiting. He'd explained the travel arrangements as if that were totally normal, and in his world, it was. I still felt like an interloper. At some point, I'd get a tap on the shoulder and a reminder to return to normality.

That was a journey I didn't want to make.

And tonight, I didn't have to.

The air changed when Garrett walked in. It wasn't just his cologne or the underlying smell of man; it was the energy. Every molecule became charged when he was around. I'd done as I was told, and the grey satin blindfold meant I couldn't see him, but I heard the soft *thunk* as he dropped his overnight bag, the quiet rustle of fabric as he shed clothing. Losing one sense meant the others were heightened, and soft footsteps told me he was barefoot as he approached the bed. He trailed something down my stomach. A feather? The vase of ostrich plumage was a new addition to my bedroom.

"You look beautiful, Saralisa."

The feather got lower, lower, and I squirmed as it tickled.

"Keep still."

"I can't."

"Which is why I brought you a gift." Tissue paper crinkled, and he took hold of one of my wrists. Cool metal encircled it, and he kissed my palm before he secured the other wrist into a cuff as well. Chain clinked, and then I was attached to my bed frame with my hands stretched over my head. "Don't fidget, or it'll hurt."

The handcuffs weren't the only thing he'd picked up in LA. I found my ankles buckled into leather restraints, and there was something between them. Something solid. When he pressed a kiss to my pussy and followed up with a flick of his tongue, I tried to squeeze my legs together, but I couldn't.

"It's a spreader bar. It keeps you exactly where I want you."

A *snick*, and I caught the scent of white jasmine and sandalwood—he'd lit the soy candles that had been last week's gift. A dozen of them in different colours, because he couldn't possibly buy just one. The overhead light turned off, making the setting so much more intimate. Drops fell on my skin, oil or lotion, and he massaged it in, paying particular attention to my breasts and my feet.

"I've been thinking about this all week," he rasped, his voice low and throaty. "You glistening and bare for me, my beautiful Cinderella."

If he wasn't careful, I'd come from his words alone. "I missed you."

"How do you feel about travelling?"

"With you?"

"No, princess, I thought I'd send you on an all-expenses paid trip to the Maldives while I jack off in the shower." He ran his tongue along the seam of my lips, and they parted with a soft gasp. "Of course with me. I don't think I can stand another week without you."

"I'll come."

"Eager, I like that." He ran one of those magic fingers over my clit. "But not yet."

"Please."

"Good things come to those who wait."

"Sometimes, I hate you."

"No, you don't."

He trailed his tongue down my stomach annoyingly slowly and finally, finally gave me his mouth. It didn't take much, just a few flicks, and I was gone. I screamed his name, at the same time sending silent thanks to whoever built the pool so far from the main house.

"Okay, fine, I love you."

"I love you too, Cinderella. Turn over."

He rotated the bar, and I didn't have a choice. A metallic *click*, and the cuffs around my wrists disappeared, clanking against the bed frame. More drops of oil. He started on my shoulders, my back, my ass, and I could swear he'd worked as a masseur at some point in his life because this was divine. And then...

"Shit! What was that?"

"Candle wax. It won't burn."

"What the hell are you doing with it?"

"Embracing my creativity. You're my canvas, Cinderella."

The wax dripped across my back and off my sides. It ran over my ass and trickled down my thighs before it cooled and solidified. If I moved, it cracked, leading to a whole new set of sensations. The heat, the cool air, the touch of Charming's fingers as he ran them through the mess.

Click.

I went rigid at the sound of a camera. "Are you taking pictures?"

"You're a masterpiece."

"You'd better not be planning to put them in a gallery."

"They're for my viewing pleasure only. And yours. You can delete them later, but I want you to see what you look like."

A zipper undid, and Charming's belt buckle clunked as he shucked his pants. A moment later, his cock nudged at my folds, open and bared to him. Ready. Waiting. He entered with one smooth thrust, and how had I ever thought I didn't have a G-spot? It had just taken the right man to find it. He raked my back with his nails as he fucked me, breaking off the wax and leaving heavenly tendrils of pain in his wake. Early on in our relationship, I'd wondered if there was something wrong with me that I got off on this, but then I'd come to the conclusion that it didn't matter what we did in the privacy of our own bedroom as long as we were both enjoying it. What was normal, anyway?

I arched my back, sending him deeper, and he leaned forward, fisting my hair and twisting my neck as he captured my mouth with his. Tongues, teeth... That little shard of pain as he nipped my lip... I fucking loved this man, and I loved fucking him too. I even liked my new dirty mouth.

Another orgasm surged through me, and Charming was on the edge too, I could tell. He came with a barely restrained cry, and it seemed he'd found religion. We panted there for a moment, me on my knees and him wrapped around me, and then sweet Charming returned and he nibbled on my ear.

"I love you." Another nip, and then the blindfold was gone. "I need to get rid of the condom."

"I should start taking birth control."

"Yeah, you should."

He unbuckled my ankles and padded across the room, leaving me to survey the wreckage of my bed. I'd changed the sheets this morning, but now they were a mess of oil and candle wax, the evidence of our filthy, wonderful voyage of discovery.

"What are you thinking?" he asked.

"I'm wondering if my laundry soap is up to the job. I should do something with"—I picked at a piece of wax—"with this."

"We'll deal with it in the morning. I'll buy you new linen, another mattress, whatever."

I was too tired to argue. Instead, I let him wrap me up in

his arms and snuggle me on a bed of slightly slippery wax pieces. There wasn't a thing I'd change about this moment. About our life together. I was living the twisted fairy tale, and I didn't want to wake up.

But I did wake up.

An hour later, my phone pinged on the nightstand, and I was conditioned to react to that sound like Pavlov's dog. It was an alert from the motion sensors outside, and that meant Charming was on his way. Except...except Charming was right here. His arms were wrapped around me. His breath was hot on my neck.

It had to be a false alarm, right?

"What is it?" he murmured as I reached for the phone.

"The motion sensors."

"What about them?"

"There must be a deer or something."

He got to the phone before I did, and another *ping* sounded. Whatever was out there, it was still moving around, and suddenly Garrett wasn't sleepy anymore. Gone was my filthy prince. He was all business as he lifted me out of bed.

"In the bathroom."

"Why? What's happening?"

"Hopefully nothing, but I need to check it out."

Garrett was already pulling on a pair of pants and a sweater, sneakers too.

"Bathroom, Saralisa."

"You're leaving me here?"

"It's the safest place."

"Then you should stay with me."

Another *ping*.

"You're probably right and it's just a deer."

Now he was rooting through his overnight bag, and holy fuck, was that a *gun*? It was, a black pistol, and he checked the magazine before he tucked it into his waistband.

"W-w-why do you have that?"

"Just a precaution." He pressed an urgent kiss to my lips. "Bathroom."

"But—"

He checked my phone one last time before he curled my fingers around it.

"Relax. I'll be back in a few minutes."

I backed into the bathroom while Garrett slipped out of the rear door, the one that led to the pump room and then the little grove of trees that Great-Grandma Agnes had planted. Should I call Luca? He'd said that if the motion sensors activated, I should let him know right away, but that was before Garrett came onto the scene. No, I'd wait. The sensors were set too high to pick up a rabbit or a hedgehog, and they had some fancy technology that meant they discounted birds. But a large deer would set them off, or a mountain lion. Not that we got many mountain lions around here, but Annie from the hair salon's brother swore he saw one in the parking lot outside Applejack's one night. Of course, Annie's brother also liked beer, which meant that nobody really believed him. Skip, who'd run the bar before Taya Swann, had sworn that extraterrestrials visited regularly, but nobody had believed him either. And Skip was gone now, in jail for robbing an armoured car, which had come as a surprise to everyone because Skip was a kind old guy who—

The first gunshot sent the phone tumbling out of my hand, and the second nearly gave me a coronary. Glass shattered. Every muscle froze. Three more shots came in quick succession, *bang-bang-bang*, and I couldn't even breathe.

The silence was worse.

Why was it so quiet?

Where was Garrett?

What was out there?

The monster.

The monster was out there.

A sob burst from my throat, and I fumbled blindly for the phone. *Call Luca, call Luca, call Luca.*

He was coming for me. He was here. He was in my home. The nightmares, they were all true. I could barely breathe, and the blood whooshed so loudly in my ears that I could hardly hear either. My fingers trembled as I dialled.

"Sara? You okay?"

"L-L-Luca? Somebody's sh-sh-shooting."

"Where?"

"At The Lookout. Near the pool house."

"Are you safe? Stay inside. Is there someplace you can hide?"

"I'm in the b-b-bathroom. Garrett went outside, and now...now it's quiet. Everything's so quiet."

"I'm on my way, okay? I'm on my way. Do you have a gun?"

"Of course I don't have a freaking gun!"

"Stay on the line."

I heard him talking to Brooke in the background, telling her to call Colt, then the slap of feet on concrete because instead of stairs or an elevator, the wide old ramp that had once been used by cars led up to his apartment on the second floor.

"Help, please help. I can't lose him. I can't."

"Any further alerts from the motion detectors?"

I fumbled with the phone again. "I— No, I don't think so. One of them has an error. What does that mean? *What does that mean?*"

"I'm getting into the car. Can you hear anything else?"

"No." Yes. Oh hell, yes. "There are footsteps."

I shrank into the shower stall and made myself as small as I could go. Suddenly, I was back in that car, hiding from the bad man, waiting for him to kill me too, waiting for a bullet to the head because I wasn't allowed to live. *I wasn't allowed to live.*

A siren sounded through the phone, but it would be too late. Luca wouldn't be here for five minutes at least, even if he drove like a madman, and I'd be dead. Dead like my mom, dead like my dad, dead like...like...

"Saralisa?"

My heart lurched. "G-G-Garrett?"

"I'm here, princess."

Then I was in his arms, sobbing uncontrollably because somehow I was still alive and I shouldn't be. My prince was still alive and murmuring soothing words like *it's okay* and *it's over* and *he's dead, don't worry.*

Dead?

Dead?

What the hell?

28

SARA

This couldn't be happening.

There was a dead guy on my portico. My boyfriend had just shot him. And then Parker had shown up waving a pistol and nearly shot Garrett because he thought he was an intruder. I'd had to jump between them and scream at my stupid dumb cousin to drop the gun, and honestly, they should ban those things because they were freaking dangerous.

Luca and Colt had arrived along with every single other deputy from the Coos Bay Sheriff's Department and the sheriff himself, who didn't know much about policing but who knew plenty about press coverage. We had lawyers, we had reporters, and we had nosy neighbours, but luckily, they were all being held beyond the cordon set up around the estate. Angela had texted me twice, and I'd ignored her both times.

The worst part was that now they'd separated us. Garrett had been taken somewhere for questioning, Parker too, and I'd been told to stay in the living room at the big house while the deputies searched the grounds, just in case there were any other psychos lurking outside. At least they'd let Brooke stay with me.

"Was it him?" she whispered.

"Who?"

"The guy from the Peninsula? The one you were worried about?"

I shook my head. I'd caught sight of the body after the drama with Parker, and although part of the head was missing, the one remaining eye had stared unseeing at the night sky. It hadn't been the monster. Or at least, not *that* monster.

"I didn't recognise him."

Neither did Garrett; he'd told me that much before he was taken away.

"Do you want me to make you a drink? Coffee? Hot chocolate? Water?"

"Just water."

I'd gotten dressed in a hurry, and there were still pieces of candle wax flaking off from under my sweater. Earlier, going to sleep covered in the stuff had seemed sexy, but now it was just more evidence of how truly screwed up my life was. I nudged a few red fragments under the table with a foot.

"How long do you think this will take? Garrett didn't do anything wrong. He was only protecting me."

"There's a bunch of procedures they need to follow. Luca said we're not meant to talk about what happened."

"We were asleep. Garrett didn't start this."

Brooke gave my hand a squeeze. "I know, sweetie."

An age passed before Colt came back with a deputy I didn't recognise in tow. I'd thought Sheriff Newman might put in an appearance, but he was probably outside courting the media and making sure the photographers got his good side.

"Are you up to answering some questions, Sara?"

Did I have much choice? "I'll do my best."

"Can you start by talking us through what happened?"

I took a deep breath and started from the beginning. The motion alerts, Garrett's concern, the shots. Parker's ill-timed appearance. I suppose at least he'd shown up. Either EJ slept like the dead, or he hadn't cared two hoots about my welfare. As for the twins, they'd run onto the scene in pyjamas after the cops arrived, gone slack-jawed when they realised Garrett Dorsey was there, disappeared, and come back ten minutes later wearing make-up and designer clothing.

"The intruder didn't enter the pool house at all?" Colt asked.

"No. I mean, I didn't hear him come in."

"I only ask because there appear to be some kind of restraints attached to the bed?"

My cheeks burned, and Colt wouldn't meet my gaze. "Those are mine."

"Right, uh, okey-dokey. So, moving on... Over the past several weeks, have you received any other alerts at night from the motion detection system?"

"Like an intruder? No. But I knew the sensors worked because they always picked up Garrett when he arrived."

"Does he make a habit of coming over late at night?"

"Yes. We're both adults. We don't have a curfew."

"I understand that. Any specific threats against either yourself or Mr. Dorsey?"

"Beyond the one you're already aware of? No. But after that...that incident at the Peninsula, Blue was asking questions about my parents. What if she pushed someone's buttons?"

"Rest assured, we'll be speaking with Ms. Carver."

"Do you know who the man was? The man Garrett shot? Where he came from?"

"We're still working on that."

"Out of all those deputies, nobody recognised him?"

"He most probably came from out of town."

"He was there to kill me, wasn't he?"

"We're still processing—"

"The evidence, I know. Well, process this—a stranger arrives at an estate in the middle of nowhere and instead of heading for the main house where all the valuables are, he somehow navigates his way to the pool house, which is usually devoid of both life and accoutrements, *with a gun.* Next you're gonna tell me he was just looking for a place to lay his poor, weary head."

"I understand your concerns."

"Do you? Do you really? Because right now, it seems like I'm the only one who's worried!"

I shoved the chair back and stalked across the kitchen, looking for something to throw. Damn Parker and his obsessive tidiness. In the end, I yanked open the refrigerator, found an apple, and hurled it toward the door. Right as Luca appeared.

"Whoa." He sidestepped, then peered around the doorjamb. "Is it safe now?"

"Sorry."

"I was going to ask how you're feeling, but I guess I already know the answer."

"Where's Garrett?"

"He's fine. His lawyer's with him now."

"Why does he need a lawyer? He acted in self-defence.

There was a man outside with a freaking gun, and it wasn't a social call."

"We just have a few issues to get straightened out. Sara, have you ever seen the man who came to your house before tonight?"

"Doesn't anyone in the sheriff's department talk to each other? No, I've never seen him before, same as I never saw the person who killed my mom and dad before he showed up either."

Luca beckoned Colt out of the room, and I was tempted to throw another apple. Why couldn't anyone be straight with me?

29

GARRETT

My phone vibrated on the table in front of me, and I ignored Angela for the seventeenth time. At least Luca hadn't decided to cuff me, and he didn't seem too worried about me checking my messages either. Probably because the situation was a clear-cut case of self-defence.

An intruder had shown up at Saralisa's home and set off the alarms. I'd flanked him, and while he was fiddling with the lock, I'd instructed him to raise his hands. He'd turned and fired at me, but he clearly hadn't spent much time on the range because both shots went wide. I'd shot him in the chest twice and the head once. The end.

Our family lawyer was far more excited about this than I was, no doubt because he was getting paid eight hundred bucks an hour plus whatever expenses he charged for driving to this godforsaken part of Oregon outside of business hours. Now he was pacing the study at The Lookout in two-thousand-dollar brogues and a custom-made suit.

"Burford, it's simple. The man had no business creeping

around the Baldwin estate at midnight, not unless you count committing a felony as a valid reason. I shot him in the fucking face with a legally registered firearm while he was in the process of trying to kill me."

"Your father's currently campaigning for tighter gun controls."

"Fantastic, let him. They can start by taking the guns away from the criminals."

"You know what the press is going to say."

"Have you been speaking with Angela?"

The door opened, and Sheriff Newman walked in. The guy had to be at least eighty, and his rumpled attire suggested he'd never been near a tailor or even an iron in his life.

"How are you holdin' up, son?"

"That's the question I should be asking my girlfriend. How much longer are you going to keep me here?"

"We need to make sure we cross all the i's and dot all the t's. I spoke with your father a few minutes ago—great guy— and he's sendin' a car for you."

"I already have a car."

"Just repeatin' what he said. Do you know a young lady called Angela? She called 911 and told the dispatcher she was concerned for your welfare."

For the love of fuck. "I'll deal with it."

"Women." The sheriff rolled his eyes. "Can't live with 'em, can't shoot 'em."

"Do you really think that's an appropriate joke to be making tonight?"

He held up his hands and backed out of the room. "Just sit tight, son."

The door closed, and Burford snorted. "I'm sure this

investigation is going to be handled in an entirely thorough and professional manner."

"Call Angela," I ordered, heading for the door myself. "Tell her to stop wasting police time."

"Where are you going?"

"To find Saralisa."

Except I didn't get far. When I pulled the door open, Luca and Colt were on the other side of it.

"We need to talk," Luca said.

"Don't you have enough information already? What would you have done in that situation? Invited the asshole in for coffee?"

"It was a righteous kill, but that isn't the issue. You'll walk on the shooting. The first problem is that he was wearing a backpack, and in that backpack was a pair of handcuffs, zip ties, duct tape, a knife, condoms, and what we believe might be a type of sedative. The lab will need to confirm."

He'd come to Saralisa's home with a fucking rape kit? My hands balled at my sides, and I wanted to put a fist through something, preferably what was left of that motherfucker's face.

"I wish I could go back and kill him again. Slower this time."

"I'm gonna pretend I didn't hear that."

"What's the second problem? You said 'the first problem,' which means there must be another."

"The second problem is more of a question: why was he there?"

"I thought you just answered that."

"That's merely logistics. I'm asking—and so is Sara, incidentally—why a stranger to this town ended up at the pool house on the Baldwin estate in the middle of the night. It's not the kind of place a rapist would head to by chance."

I'd been so busy thinking of the "what" I hadn't stopped to consider the "why." But now that the adrenaline was dissipating and the threat of jail had receded, I saw that Luca was absolutely right. Saralisa had been deliberately targeted.

"They knew she was there."

"The question is how? I can tell you that the fact she's been staying in the pool house isn't common knowledge in Baldwin's Shore. She only told me and Brooke two weeks ago. Until then, we thought she was staying in the big house the same as always. And before you ask, Brooke didn't tell anyone and neither did I."

It got worse.

"I wasn't supposed to be here tonight." The words were like sandpaper in my throat. "A meeting got cancelled at the last minute, and I flew back early to see her."

If Mandy Caukwell hadn't tripped over her Maltese terrier and ended up in the hospital getting her ankle pinned, I'd still have been in Los Angeles. And Saralisa would have gone through hell. She'd be in the damn morgue, not freaking out somewhere in this fucking house.

"So who knew the details of your schedule? The perp clearly wasn't expecting you, and he wasn't aware of the motion sensors either, which means we can probably rule out the Baldwin family hiring someone. When Brie's team was fitting the system, EJ complained that the drilling was too loud, and one of the twins had a hissy fit about privacy because she thought we were installing cameras and she likes to sunbathe topless by the pool."

Thanks for the warning.

Hold on a second... "You think her family would be capable of hiring that psycho? To rape and kill her?"

"We have to consider every possibility. What did Sherlock Holmes say? That once you eliminate the impossible, whatever remains, no matter how improbable, must be the truth."

"It was Arthur Conan Doyle, actually. But I see your point." And if we were going to philosophise, then another quote sprang to mind, this time from Arthur Schopenhauer: *All truth passes through three stages. First, it is ridiculed. Second, it is violently opposed. Third, it is accepted as being self-evident.*

I'd done the ridiculing, not openly, but in my own mind. And we'd sure had the violence tonight. I was heading toward stage three, but I wasn't certain I wanted to arrive at the destination.

"I used to think the Baldwins were irritating yet harmless," Colt said. "But one of them is in jail for murder and another for attempted murder, so I'm open to the idea that they could do something as fucked up as trying to have Sara killed. But the pieces don't fit. Which leaves us with the possibility that someone fixated on Sara. I don't think that happened here because the dead guy isn't familiar, but I hear she's been spending time in Roseburg lately. Did you see anyone following her? Get the prickly feeling that something was wrong?"

"We barely went out. Saralisa isn't a party girl, and I don't enjoy my every move being posted on the internet."

But the pieces... Those jagged, illogical, unconscionable pieces...

"The perp's prints aren't in AFIS. Either he's a first-timer, or he's been too smart to get caught."

Or he had connections.

"I need to make a call."

"We haven't finished here."

"Are you going to arrest me?"

After a moment's hesitation, Colt shook his head.

I found an unoccupied music room and dialled my brother. I had to know. I had to know whether the horror story I was writing in my head was fact or fiction. Two minutes later, my worst fears had been confirmed, and predictably, Trey didn't see what the big deal was.

"Lighten up. Elina probably forgot already. Hey, is it true that you emptied a clip at a guy with a machete?"

"Where did you hear that?"

"Facebook. Angela's hyperventilating. Mom made her breathe into a paper bag."

"I used reasonable force to stop a man from killing me."

"But was it, like, a whole clip?"

"It's called a magazine, you fuckwit."

I hung up and sank onto the piano stool, trying to collect my thoughts. This could all be my fault. I'd almost lost the woman I wanted to spend the rest of my life with, my soulmate, and it was my fault for brushing away her concerns. For hearing but not listening. For thinking I knew best when she'd lived this nightmare for sixteen years.

Grabbing Saralisa and moving to a desert island was tempting, but I had to face the music. In the Marines, I'd parachuted into hostile territory with less trepidation than this, my heart hammering and adrenaline coursing through my veins. Colt and Luca were waiting expectantly when I returned.

"I have..." The lump in my throat was almost too big to swallow, and it was fear. Fear that I'd fucked up. Fear for the woman I loved. Fear that I was about to tear two families apart. "I have a theory."

"Let's hear it," Luca said, arms folded.

The lawyer was still standing to the side, drinking in the conversation. I didn't want him to hear this part.

"Burford, please leave us."

"But your father said—"

"I don't care what my father said. This is my business, not his."

"He won't be happy."

"I've spent my whole damn life trying to make my father happy. Just leave me alone. Go and give Angela a Xanax or something."

He closed the door harder than usual on his way out, and it bounced back on its hinges and hit the wall. I was absolutely certain that Burford was dialling my father already. Let him. The old man would have to accept that not every decision was his to make.

Colt perched on the edge of the desk, and Luca leaned against the wall by the window, arms folded.

"So, what's your theory?" Luca asked.

"I met Saralisa at an ill-fated birthday celebration at the Peninsula just under two months ago."

"I'm aware of that."

"There was a slight hiccup with timings, and she ended up fleeing the hotel shortly before midnight. Later, I found out that she'd bumped into a man on the terrace and he triggered a wave of bad memories."

"She told you about that?"

"She told me a lot of things. We might have only known each other for a short time, but that time has been...intense."

"We followed up on the guy, but it was a dead end."

"I..." *Breathe, you coward.* "I also followed up on him."

Curiosity gleamed in Luca's eyes. "Did you get any farther than Delaware?"

"I didn't need to go via Delaware." I paused. Forced myself to inhale. "I recognised him. I was right behind her at the hotel, and when she told me the story, I realised I knew who she was talking about."

"So instead of telling her that, you what? Went rogue?"

"I have an investigator on retainer, and I asked him to make some discreet enquiries. Understand this: if I'd thought for a moment that Seth was the man who ran Saralisa's parents off the road, I'd have taken a different approach."

"Seth? His name is Seth?"

"He oversees security for a friend of my father's. They weren't at the Peninsula following Saralisa as she feared; they were there to pick up Graham's daughter from the party. That's another reason I thought the story sounded farfetched. I just wanted to get enough evidence to prove to Saralisa that Seth wasn't the man she thought he was, so she could relax and stop looking over her shoulder."

"But now you think he might be involved?"

"I think it's a possibility that can't be discounted."

"What changed your mind?"

"I only told one person in Roseburg that we were sleeping in the pool house, and that was my brother." The conversation had been so monumentally stupid. I'd introduced Saralisa to the family formally as Saralisa Baldwin-Forlani, and Trey had put two and two together—a miracle because he'd cheated in every high school math exam—and realised she was one of *the* Baldwins. After dinner, he'd begun ribbing me for hanging out with Kayleigh and Lillian, who were far beneath us in whatever social pecking order my brother and his cronies used, and I'd snapped back that we never saw the twins because Saralisa lived in the pool house. He'd made a comment about slumming it, I'd threatened to break his teeth, and we'd been ready to wrestle on the floor when Marlie defused the situation by asking for ice cream. "Trey just confirmed that he mentioned that fact to his girlfriend, who happens to be Graham's daughter."

Plus there was a reasonable chance that Dad had mentioned his son's new girlfriend to his old buddy. I'd never brought a partner to a family dinner before. It had been a memorable event.

Luca let out a long breath. "That's thin."

"Do you have anything thicker?"

"Not at this time. What has your investigator found so far?"

"Unfortunately, not a whole lot. Seth was working for Graham in the same role sixteen years ago, and I know he always travels when Graham does. Graham was in DC in the week before the accident—he voted on several bills in that period—although we're struggling to find confirmation of his whereabouts for the date itself. It seems likely that Seth was in the vicinity of northern Virginia during the time in question."

"Voted on bills?"

"He's a congressman. Graham Mandell."

Colt muttered a few choice curses under his breath, which summed up my feelings on the matter too. This was a can of worms nobody had wanted to open, and I'd inadvertently popped the top.

"We also have a photo of the doctor who performed the second autopsy at a fundraiser with Mandell," I continued.

"What about the doctor who performed the first autopsy?"

"He died in a hunting accident three months after the

crash. One detective working at the time recalls an order coming from the top to wrap up the case quickly."

"Sara was right?"

I nodded. "She was right."

Too late, I realised we weren't alone in the room. Too late, I realised I'd screwed up again.

"And I was also wrong."

The shaky voice came from the doorway, and when I spun, there she was, tears already rolling down her cheeks.

"I trusted you. I trusted you with my secrets, and this is what you did? You went behind my back and started digging into things that didn't concern you? I could have *died* tonight."

Fuck. *Fuck, fuck, fuck.*

"How much did you hear?"

"Does it matter? I heard enough. This whole time, you knew who the monster was and you didn't tell me."

"It *did* concern me. The Mandells are family friends, and the idea that Seth could have committed a cold-blooded murder... Let's sit down and talk about this calmly."

"We could have talked about it a month ago. Now? Now, it's too late. Way too late."

"Princess, I'm so sorry, I—"

"Get out. Get out of my house."

How the hell was I meant to fix this mess? I'd never had to stop a woman kicking me out of her house before. We were in new territory.

Hostile territory.

"We're in the middle of an investigation," Colt tried. "We still have questions for Mr. Dorsey."

"Fine, then I'll leave."

Saralisa stepped backward and bumped into Brooke, whose eyes widened at the scene unfolding in front of her.

"What happened? I only went to the bathroom."

"This asshole nearly got me killed, that's what happened. Can you give me a ride? My keys...my keys are still in the pool house."

The sobs got louder, and more than anything, I wanted to wrap Saralisa up in my arms and tell her everything would be okay. But that would be a lie. And I also didn't want to get kneed in the balls.

"Uh, sure." Brooke looked to Luca. "Should I take her to our place?"

"I'm coming with you," he said. "If Garrett's right, the intruder might not have been working alone."

I opened my mouth to protest, but what was I meant to say? Words couldn't make this better. Time couldn't be rewound. My girl turned around and walked out of my life, leaving me with the realisation that money could buy a lot of things in life, but it couldn't buy love.

SARA

"I can't believe he did that. Why? Why did he ignore everything I said and start asking questions?"

Brooke and Blue watched from the table as I paced the kitchen. Brooke had made waffles for breakfast, but how could I eat? I just felt sick, sick, sick.

"Because sometimes, men can be real assholes," she said.

Last night had been terrifying and devastating and utterly humiliating. After I'd nearly died and then broken up with the man I'd loved with my whole heart, I'd been forced to ask Brooke for help with the wax because the stupid stuff was still stuck all over me, and she'd ended up scraping it off with a library card while I sobbed in the shower.

Aaron had kept watch with a gun while we grabbed a few hours' sleep, but now he'd gone to The Lookout to help Deck board up the broken windows at the pool house and collect some of my clothes. Luca was on guard duty now, keeping a wary eye from the other side of the kitchen as he chopped fruit.

"I loved him. I thought he loved me."

Blue shrugged. "Maybe he does love you and he's just an idiot?"

"Thanks, that's really helping."

"Look on the bright side; he kept you alive."

"Can you *please* stop talking? I have a headache, and if he loved me, he wouldn't have put my life at risk in the first place."

"Playing devil's advocate, you don't know for certain that he was the root cause for last night's incident."

"Even he thinks he started it, and the only other person who was raking through my past was you. Are you saying *you* did something?"

She considered the question for a moment. "I don't think so. I only spoke with one guy, and I've known him for years. He's careful. Let the cops identify the dead guy, and then we might get a clearer picture of what happened."

"Why are you taking Garrett's side in this?"

"I'm not. I'm just saying that you finally found a guy you actually liked, and it seems dumb to throw away what you had if last night's incident was totally unrelated. But he has a hell of a lot of grovelling to do. I'm talking down on his knees, kissing-your-feet begging."

"He still lied to me."

"By omission."

"That doesn't make it better."

"Okay, then look at it this way. Say Garrett's heavy-handed investigator did set the chain of events into motion. That means we at least know who's behind the attempt to kill you, and possibly your parents' murder too. Garrett wasn't the one who tried to break in last night, sweetie. You can be upset with him for breaking your trust, but the blame for your attempted murder lies squarely with the guy in the morgue and whoever was pulling his strings."

"How can you be so...so..."

"Rational? Objective? Because it's my job. I'll still kick Garrett in the nuts for you if you want. He deserves that much."

"Thanks?"

I actually felt kind of numb. Years ago, I'd made the decision to keep my secrets to myself, both out of fear I'd die and fear I wouldn't be believed. I'd been right on both counts, but I took no pleasure in it. For two months, I'd learned what it was like to live, really live, and now... Now, I had no idea. I couldn't simply hide from the light again. The monster knew I'd talked.

"Blue's right," Luca said. "We've gotten nowhere with the Delaware connection, but the dead guy gives us a whole new avenue of investigation to work with."

The dead guy. I shuddered. "Don't you understand? They're always three steps ahead. If you go after these people, someone else is going to wind up in a casket."

Probably me.

Until last night, I'd assumed—well, hoped—that the monster was working alone. His was the only face I'd seen when I was nine. But now it had become clear there were more of them—two monsters at least, plus somebody directing them. And if Garrett's tenuous theory was correct, the puppet master was a powerful politician, insulated from justice by wealth and privilege. We stood no hope of bringing him down.

Of course, Blue ignored all the obvious issues.

"You know what's bugging me?" she asked.

I groaned and buried my head in my arms. "No, and I don't want to."

"This started when your parents died. But why them? What had they done that meant running them off the road was the only option?"

"How should I know? I was a child. My life consisted of school, dance classes, and play dates."

"It's something to do with your mom, I bet. Politics. It has to be. Your dad was just collateral damage."

"Don't talk about him that way."

"What can you remember about the weeks leading up to the crash? Specifically the period after your mom's boss died? Was she away from home more than usual? Did any strangers come to the house?"

"She always worked late. Sometimes Dad would complain about it, but he knew she loved her job. He painted, and I spent half my time at Marcin's place because we were practising for a big competition and they had more space. His mom and my dad used to take it in turns to drive us to dance classes."

Now Luca joined in. "We need to find out who else worked in Colvin's office with Claire. How many staff does a senator have?"

"I'll look into it," Blue said.

"This is a police matter now."

"How are you going to stop me?"

"If you interfere in an ongoing investigation..."

Brooke threw up her hands. "Stop! Just stop fighting. Sara's traumatised, and you're not helping." She took a seat next to me. "Sara, we need to get to the bottom of this. Burying it worked for years, but I don't think that's an option anymore. The best chance we have of preventing someone else from getting hurt is to stop these people, and we really, really need your help for that."

"But I don't know anything."

"There might be some little snippet of information that you don't even realise is important. Just talk Luca and Blue through your life. That's all you need to do."

That's all you need to do. Did she understand what she was asking? That digging the slivers of my past out of the grave I'd buried them in would leave damage I couldn't repair? A scar was better than an open wound. But I had to do it, didn't I? It was the only way to get out of this mess.

"What if they come after more people?" I asked.

"They can't kill all of us," Luca said.

"Are you sure about that? I don't want blood on my hands."

"We're doing this with or without your help, Sara."

"Fine." I heaved out a sigh. "Fine, I'll do it, but I need to find somewhere safe to stay first." Maybe Poland. "I can't go back to the pool house."

"Stay here with me and Brooke until we get this cleared up."

"That could take months. Years. What if we never—"

The buzz of the intercom interrupted, and the others looked at each other.

"You expecting anyone?" Luca asked Brooke, pulling out his phone. They had cameras here, alarms on every door and window, and there was an app that controlled them all.

"Paulo said he'd bring cookies at lunchtime, but it's only eleven o'clock."

"It's a guy I don't recognise," Luca said, tapping at the screen. "Stay here."

At least he hadn't told me to hide in the bathroom. That had to be a good sign. And there were no gunshots. Five long minutes went by, five minutes where Blue wouldn't let me leave the room and Brooke tried to make small talk that did nothing to calm my nerves. Finally, Luca came back with a stocky man in tow.

"Sara, this is Jack Morrow. He's heading up your personal protection team."

My what?

Jack Morrow held out a hand. "Pleased to meet you, ma'am."

I just stared at him. "I didn't... I don't know you."

"Mr. Dorsey hired us."

Oh, no, no, no. He did *not* get to stalk me by proxy. "Well, I'm sure you're a perfectly nice man, but I'm un-hiring you."

"I'm afraid that's not possible under the terms of our contract."

Somehow, this nightmare got worse with every passing hour.

"Can't you get rid of them?" I begged Luca.

"There's nothing I can do as long as they stay off private property and don't cause a public nuisance. I just spoke with Garrett, and he's standing firm."

Rich, powerful, privileged. This was what I was up against.

"Well, if you speak with him again, tell him I want to introduce his genitals to a chainsaw."

Both men winced.

"And you..." I turned back to Jack Morrow. "You're currently on private property, and you're not welcome here."

"Understood, ma'am. We'll be outside if you need us."

Once he'd retreated down the ramp, I took a bracing breath and parked my behind back on a stool. I couldn't live like this.

"Ask the questions. Ask me anything you want. Just end this, one way or another."

We started at the beginning. Before the beginning even, the way Blue had a month and a half ago. How I wished I could turn back the clock. Luca deferred to Blue on the questions, which was probably against police rules, but I felt much more comfortable talking with another woman. She got me to lie on the couch and close my eyes, and when I did that, I could almost imagine we were having a private conversation, just me and her.

"The accident happened in February, right? So let's go back a little farther. Let's think about Thanksgiving. Everyone remembers Thanksgiving, right?"

I did. We'd celebrated in Texas with the Colvins, over thirty of us seated at tables set out in a U-shape in Mike Colvin's vast dining room. While we were waiting for dinner to cook, his daughter had taken us kids out to the barn to see the animals, and I'd sat on a big brown-and-white Quarter Horse while she led me around the riding arena. Madison had been there with Scooter running around her feet as usual. It had been a good day. The best day.

We'd flown back to Virginia soon after, and normal life resumed. Dancing for me, painting for Dad, and work, work, work for Mom. Yoga too. She used to get up early and go to yoga classes three mornings a week. Marcin had a birthday, and I'd been both excited for the party—his parents had hired acrobats—and nervous because now that he was ten, we'd have to move up an age category and all those couples were so much more experienced than we were. Mom and Dad had date night once a week, but sometimes in those final months, I recalled them skipping it. Dad had been...not angry, more disappointed.

But Mom had made up for the missed evenings after Christmas. In January, she was home almost every night. At the time, I'd been happy to see her, but now that I picked through memories I'd kept shuttered for years, I didn't think she'd been happy. Mom and Dad didn't yell or throw things, not the way Marcin's parents had, but there was a weird tension.

"Your mom was upset, and yet she was spending more time at home?" Blue asked.

"Yes."

"And that was before Senator Colvin passed away?"

"Before and after. He died in the middle of January, didn't he? But I don't recall her working late at all after Christmas."

"Which suggests the problem was with work rather than your dad."

"I guess. I only ever heard them have one proper shouting match, and that was after Mike Colvin's funeral. Don't ask me what it was about—all I could hear was muffled yelling coming from the kitchen."

"Your mom went to pay her respects to Colvin?"

"Of course. Both of my parents went, and Marcin's parents too. We stayed at his place with a babysitter."

His babysitter had been nicer than mine. His babysitter helped us to make cookies and didn't hump her boyfriend on the couch.

"How did your mom seem after Colvin died? Sad? Scared? Angry?"

"None of those. I think...I think...relieved? There was a phone call one evening, as I was about to go upstairs to bed. Mom slumped into an armchair and stared at the wall for a full minute. Just stared. Then Dad came in and asked what the matter was, and she said, 'It's over.' That's all. *It's over*."

"What was over?"

"His life, I guess. Her job. She wanted to move back to Texas, but Dad's paintings were in a bunch of galleries in Virginia, and he wanted to stay. That was one of the things they fought about in our final month together."

"One of the things? What were the others?"

"The Baldwins, mainly. After the funeral, we had to fly to Oregon for Grandpa's eightieth birthday celebration. Dad didn't want to go, so Mom said fine, let's not go then, but he said they were still family, and they bickered all the way to the airport. We made it through two days in Oregon before Dad had a fight with EJ and we flew home again."

"He and EJ didn't get along?"

"They hated each other."

"Do you know why?"

"Probably because EJ's an asshole. He acts all meek and nice, but he has a mean streak. He and Marianna were perfect for each other in that respect."

"When you got home, what happened?"

"Well, obviously Mom was around more." I remembered her putting on lipstick in front of the hall mirror before she went to job interviews, dressed in a suit and high-heeled pumps. "Dad said she'd find a new position in no time, that she had connections, but Mom was being picky. She didn't want to make the same mistake again, she said."

"What mistake?"

"I...I don't know. Until now, I'd forgotten she even said that."

But she had. The memory returned with perfect clarity. My parents had been talking in the kitchen over coffee, and Dad was worrying about the mortgage payment. And that's when Mom made the comment. She didn't want to rush into a new role and make the same mistake again. Better to wait until the right boss came along. Someone with…with integrity. I repeated what I'd recalled.

"And I'm not sure she was looking for another job on the Hill, not right then. I think…I think she mentioned working in a ski resort."

Wouldn't it be fun, kiddo? We could make snowmen every weekend in winter.

Blue sounded just a tiny bit triumphant. "Told you there was something hinky going on with Colvin. Did she accept a new job?"

"Not that I know of. There would have been some kind of celebration, wouldn't there?"

"I'll look into it."

The words sent a chill through me. "Please, be careful."

"I will, cross my heart. Let's move on to the day of the crash. Can you talk me through what happened?"

I told her everything. About the babysitter, about me stowing away, about the headlights behind us. Being punched along the road, the screaming, the *crunch* of metal on wood. Mom being silenced by the monster. The cold that had seeped into my bones and the smell of death that hung heavy in the air in my crumpled prison.

Until I tasted salt, I didn't realise that tears were running down my cheeks. I felt a tissue being pressed into my hand and opened my eyes to see a blurry Brooke.

"Thank you."

"You're doing so well."

Was I? Really? I hadn't remembered anything useful at all.

"Your mom said to burn something," Blue prompted. "Burn them?"

"I don't know who or what 'them' was."

"Can you remember the rest of her words?"

"They made no sense. She told me that she loved me, and then it was just random words and numbers."

"Tell me."

I screwed my eyes shut again. "Third-floor window. Pipes. Fires. Dust. Eight sixteen. Burn them."

She'd repeated the first part twice, the words punctuated by her rasping breath, by my sobs and the creaking and ticking of the car. By rain pounding on the roof. By the ominous rumbles of thunder.

"How many floors did your house in Virginia have?" Blue asked.

"Only one."

It had been a pretty blue ranch-style home with a cosy kitchen and a yard full of flowers. Dad used to sit on the deck and paint them in the summer. In watercolour, mainly, but sometimes he used oils.

"What about her office?"

"At the Capitol? I don't know. I went there maybe twice? There was an elevator, so I'd guess more than two."

"Blue, you can't get into a congressional office," Luca warned.

"Why would we need to do that?" I asked.

"A woman isn't going to waste her last words. When you were under attack this morning, what was going through your head?"

"How does that freaking help?"

"Just take a deep breath, stop, and think. In and out, that's it."

I did as she instructed and tried to put myself back in the bathroom. The last place I wanted to be.

"I was...I was scared for Garrett." That traitorous

bastard. "And then I heard footsteps, soft ones coming across the portico and into the living room, and I hoped with every atom in me that Luca would catch whoever was out there and make them pay."

"Your mom probably had the same thoughts. She told you that she loved you, and she wanted justice. So she gave you a message."

"A message? But it was gibberish."

"I bet it means something; we just need to work out what. How many floors at The Lookout?"

"Two. Unless you count the attic, but nobody ever goes up there." My eyes flew open. "Wait, you don't think...?"

"Does it have windows?"

"Small ones."

Blue grinned. "Who wants to drive?"

31

SARA

"Haven't you caused enough trouble for one day?"

EJ blocked the hallway, hands on his hips. When you'd spent your whole life backing down, standing up was hard to do, even when you had Luca, Brooke, and Blue at your back. For one wild moment, I considered inviting Jack Morrow and his crew inside, but we'd left them at the far end of the driveway where they belonged.

"I just need to get some things."

Uncle EJ nodded at the key in my hand. "From the attic?"

"I—"

Parker appeared behind him. "Let her take what she wants, Dad. It's only a bunch of old junk up there."

"She can't walk in here with a group of people and expect to start rifling through family possessions."

"Actually, she can."

"Says who?"

"Says Grandpa's trust deed."

"Thank you," I whispered to Parker as EJ turned on his heel and stomped off toward the kitchen.

He shrugged. "You okay after last night?"

"Of course I'm not."

"Watch out for the twins. You have the right to remain silent, and anything you say may be used against you on Instagram."

"Where are they?"

"Some local news show wants to interview them this afternoon, so they went to get their hair and nails done. I'd say you have"—he checked his watch—"around five hours."

"Thanks for the warning."

"Do me a favour and try to keep the noise down. I already have a headache today."

Parker disappeared toward his home office, leaving us a clear run to the attic. To the third floor. Could Blue really be right? Had Mom hidden something among the old books and toys all those years ago?

Opening the door to the attic was like stepping into a time warp. Dust motes danced in the shafts of light illuminating dusty treasures that had belonged to my grandpa and probably his parents before him. Old pictures stacked in gilded frames, steamer trunks filled with clothes long since outgrown, an age-spotted cheval mirror in one corner. Grandpa hadn't liked to throw anything away, and EJ was too lazy to sort through the mess.

"I remember that rocking horse," I whispered, stepping closer to stroke the rough mane. "It belonged to the twins. They wouldn't let me sit on it."

Even though they'd only used it to drape clothes over.

It was all there—old dollhouses, model cars, a veritable museum of old computers. Mismatched dinnerware, Christmas decorations, suitcases, some of it broken. And windows. So many windows, small and grimy, and they probably hadn't been cleaned in my lifetime. I counted eight from where I stood, and there were more hidden behind the junk. It was a big attic.

"Where do we start?" Brooke asked.

"I guess with the closest window and move on from there."

It was a daunting task.

Everything was filthy. We needed gloves and dust masks too. Coughing, we cleared a space in the middle of the room and used it to stack the detritus of the Baldwin family's previous lives while we checked each item for a mystery object that didn't belong. The problem was, we had no idea what we were looking for. It could have been anything. Anything that could lead one person to murder another. What were the motives for murder? Money? Revenge? Love? My mom wouldn't have gotten involved in any of that, not unless she was trying to protect a person she cared about. Or what if...what if someone else had transgressed and my mom witnessed it? The monster could have eliminated her the way he was trying to eliminate me now. Or what if there'd been a mistake? Could the monster have killed the wrong person? And now he had to clean up the evidence?

So many questions, and absolutely no answers.

The four of us searched through every box and bag and stack and pile, starting near the windows and working our way back. Six hours later, we were all filthy, and we'd found nothing useful. Blue had packed six old pipes into a box for further examination just in case, but they appeared to contain nothing but desiccated tobacco. Either our prize had been moved years ago, or it had never existed in the first place.

And worse, now I heard Kayleigh and Lillian moving

around below. Could I squeeze out of one of those windows? It was really tempting to try.

After a quick stop in the bathroom to wipe off as much dirt as we could, the four of us tiptoed down the stairs. Blue in particular looked dejected. Me? I was used to losing hope. The living room door was open, and I could hear the twins griping as we snuck past.

"Who are the men at the end of the driveway? Why are they there?" That was Kayleigh. Nobody could whine as well as she did.

"How should I know?" Parker said. "They're probably something to do with the police."

Poor Parker. I should send him a bottle of Tylenol.

"Can't you find out?"

"Why don't you ask them?"

"It's cold outside."

"Maybe you could take them coffee?"

"Are you going to go and talk to them or not?"

"Not. Leave me alone."

At least by getting on the twins' nerves, Garrett's goons had served some purpose. While they were distracted, we made it to the back door and escaped around the side of the house before Kayleigh and Lillian realised we were home, but I still wasn't going to thank him for sending his spies after me.

We were almost back at Brooke's apartment when Luca's phone rang. I could only hear one side of the conversation, but it made my ears prick up.

"Last night? You're certain it was the same man?" ... "How long was he there for?" ... "Did you speak to him?" ... "Okay, okay." ... "Thanks, I appreciate it. I'll swing by to collect it in the next hour."

"Well?" Blue asked the second he hung up.

"That was Nico. Our man showed up at the Peninsula again last night."

"Do you mean Seth Harless?"

"Nico believes so. He took a better picture, and he kept a water glass with fingerprints."

"Nice."

"He got curious and spoke with him," Luca said. "It was late, almost midnight, and Harless claimed he was taking a break on the way to pick up a friend from PDX."

"While also establishing an alibi for the shooting. Convenient. I bet he was waiting around to collect his buddy after he'd done the deed." Blue leaned back in the seat. "Damn, this case is frustrating. I can see a picture emerging, but it's all circumstantial. There's no actual evidence, nothing that'll stand up in court. Sara's parents went off the road: accident. Case closed. A guy tried to break into Sara's house: burglary gone wrong. Case closed. The only thing that links them is Sara's memories."

It's all in my head.

Which meant they were going to try and kill me again. They had no other choice.

32

GARRETT

"*D*o you want to talk about it?"

"No, I want to drink myself into oblivion."

And I'd done a pretty good job so far. The bottle of top-shelf liquor I'd picked up on the way from the airport was respectably empty.

"Suit yourself." But Gracie sat down beside me anyway. "You look like shit."

"I love you too. Want some?" I held out the Scotch.

"No, I do not. Did you really tackle a burglar with your bare hands and shoot him with his own gun?"

"Where did you hear that?"

"TikTok."

"It's bullshit. It wasn't nearly that dramatic."

"Then why are you so upset? Is it the girl? The one you asked me to make the dance shoes for? They're almost finished."

I couldn't stay in Oregon any longer, not when Saralisa refused to have anything to do with me, not when I wanted to punch my brother in the mouth every time I saw him, and not when I wanted to line Seth Harless up in my sights and pull the trigger. If I'd stayed at home, I would have ended up doing something I regretted. There were only two people I trusted to have my back in this situation, and the idea of flying to Europe to hang out with Johannes and half a dozen naked debutantes filled me with as much joy as a root canal, so I'd hired the best personal protection team money could buy, told them not to let Saralisa out of their sight, and headed to New York.

Gracie lived in Tribeca, in a loft that she'd decorated in an eclectic mix of antique and modern. An ornate glass lamp cast a glow over a wooden rocking chair. A MacBook sat on a leather-topped writing desk. The only bed occupied a low platform at the far end of the cavernous room, beside a bathroom with glass-brick walls. Kind of awkward when one of us was showering. Usually, it didn't matter to Gracie because she hated houseguests. This was her personal space, hers and hers alone. I'd be sleeping on the couch tonight.

"Yeah, it's the girl."

Despite claiming I didn't want to discuss it, I found myself spilling the details. Not the intimate ones, just the bare facts. Gracie was no Trey. She wouldn't go broadcasting our conversation to the enemy, and I hoped that by talking to her, she'd be able to offer a woman's perspective on how I could win Saralisa back.

"So let me get this straight... You fell in love with a girl and she trusted you with her darkest secrets. And rather than respecting her privacy, you went behind her back and hired an investigator to delve into her past?"

"It sounds so much worse when you say it out loud."

"Brother, it's going to take more than flowers or chocolates to dig yourself out of this hole. Or shoes. Why didn't you just talk to her?"

"Because...uh."

"Because you knew she'd say no to your dumb idea?"

Ouch. I swallowed what remained in the glass and poured myself another three fingers. Who cared about ice? I chugged that too and lay back on the couch with an arm over my face because the lights were hurting my eyes.

"Maybe," I mumbled. "But what was I meant to do? She said Seth Harless murdered her parents and tried to suffocate her. You know Seth? Graham's security guy? Don't you think that sounds crazy? I certainly did at the time, although now I'm not so sure. Would you honestly have believed her?"

Silence followed, and I hoped to hell that Gracie had painkillers in her bathroom cabinet. That was one advantage of staying with Johannes. He came with a whole selection of drugs—some of them were even legal—and if he didn't have it, he could get it.

"Yes, I absolutely would have believed her."

Something in Gracie's tone sent a chill through me. No, not a chill. It felt as if somebody had poured liquid nitrogen into my spinal column. I tried to sit up, but it took me two attempts because the room kept spinning.

"Why? You've never even met her."

"But I've met Harless."

The way Gracie bit her lip reminded me of Saralisa, and her eyes...fuck, her eyes.

"What did he do to you, Gracie? What did he do?"

"It wasn't him; it was Mandell." Her voice was hollow. Despite how close we used to be, despite the years we'd spent growing up together, I'd never heard her speak that way before. "Harless is just there to clean up afterward."

"That doesn't answer my question."

"Put it this way—if Satan ever needed to adopt a human

form, Mandell would make the perfect vessel. I know. Trust me, I know. He preys on women, and he thinks he's untouchable. Maybe he is? He's an expert in turning fear to his advantage. Garrett, if you put an innocent woman into his crosshairs, then I'm not sure *I* can forgive you either."

Cold dread mixed with alcohol, and the effect was nauseating.

"What. Did. He. Do?"

"I'm in the same position as Saralisa. Talk and regret it. I'd love to meet her someday, seeing as we're members of a reasonably exclusive club. We've both been fucked over by Graham Mandell, although in my case, it was more literal than figurative."

It took a while for the meaning of her words to penetrate my addled brain, but when they did, I grabbed the bowl full of glass baubles on the coffee table and puked most of the Scotch into it. That son of a bitch. I'd kill him.

"He..." I couldn't even bring myself to say the word. "He raped you."

"If you ask him, he'll say it was consensual. That I came onto him, *threw* myself at him, and he'd had a few drinks so what was he meant to do? He regrets it, of course. It was a moment of weakness. Really, he's a fine, upstanding citizen while I'm the good-time girl, always falling out of some club or another. The slut with a penchant for older men. The dirty bitch who called him Daddy and begged him to fuck me. Who would have believed my story, Garrett? Nobody, that's who."

And that same man had sat across the dinner table once a month for the last ten years, laughing and joking with my father as they complimented Letti's cooking and sampled bottles from the wine cellar.

That motherfucker.

"How long ago?" I asked, but I had a nasty feeling I already knew.

"I was twenty-one. Why do you think I can't look at my daughter, Garrett? Why do you think I moved to another state?"

Gracie dissolved into tears, and I wrapped her up in my arms. Just held her. Held her for long enough that the red-hot anger in my gut solidified into a cold resolve. Mandell was going down if I had to strangle him with my bare hands. Harless too. If I had to do time, I didn't care. Someone needed to get justice for Saralisa and Gracie, and if the legal system wouldn't—couldn't—act, then I would.

"We can bring a civil case. The burden of proof is lower, and if Mandell is Marlie's father, then we have evidence he can't refute."

"Do you think he hasn't considered that? Whatever you're thinking, he's already a hundred steps ahead." Gracie sagged back onto the couch. "I confronted him after I found out I was pregnant. Well, first I tried to get a termination, but there were so many people outside the clinic, yelling and screaming. And then I saw the cameras and I couldn't... I couldn't walk in there, not through the crowd. Not when I knew I'd be recognised. So I confided in Letti, and Grandma Margaret overheard, and then I didn't have a choice anymore."

"What happened when you confronted him?"

"It went about as well as you might expect. Worse, actually. He promised that if I told anyone about Marlie's parentage, he'd ruin our family. He had a video. You know, on second thought..." Gracie grabbed the Scotch and took a long swallow straight from the bottle. "He had a video of Dad. Grainy, but it was definitely him, with a younger...with a younger woman. Maybe even younger than me. He was whipping her, Garrett. She was tied to a cross, and he was whipping her. He was *hurting* her. It's not only Graham Mandell who likes to damage women; our own father does too. At home, he pretends to be this loving dad and husband, and then he goes out and...it's just sick."

Gracie had lost all colour now, and it seemed the cans of worms were on buy one, get one free today. How could I even start to explain this?

"A part of me wanted to say 'to hell with it' and tell Mandell to release the damn video," she continued, "but we're meant to protect the family at all costs, right? Well, I wanted to protect Letti. She didn't deserve for her name to be dragged through the mud, and neither did you, but even now I'm not sure I did the right thing because what if Dad lost his mind and used that whip on her?"

"He does. She enjoys it."

"What? Don't make stupid jokes, Garrett. It's not funny. Nothing about this is funny."

"I'm not joking, I swear. Look, Mandell might be a monster, but everything Dad does is consensual. Still not the sort of thing any of us would want to become public knowledge, but he isn't doing anything to women that isn't agreed upon in advance."

"How do you know? How do you know that?"

I shrugged. "Like father, like son."

She stared at me, open-mouthed. "What?"

"Sex isn't always about sunshine and rose petals. People have varied tastes."

"Are you serious? What did you do, bond over handcuffs on your fishing weekends?"

"Hell no." The mere thought was horrifying. "We got into it separately, and then I started noticing little things in the way Letti acted. She's his sub as well as his wife.

Eventually, I told him that I knew, but it's not exactly something we discuss over coffee. Go easy on the Scotch, sis."

"I can't believe this."

"Just set your mind at rest about Dad and Letti. Whatever they're doing in the bedroom, they're both happy with the arrangement."

But the video... The video was a problem. Dad was always careful, we both were, but too many people were willing to sell out for money. Things were easier now—my "welcome back to civilian life" gift from him had been membership of an exclusive club that more or less guaranteed privacy. The members of Nyx were carefully vetted, and applications were only accepted from those with something to lose. Politicians, actors, rock stars, even royalty. Electronics were banned from any sensitive areas, and non-members who visited were required to wear blindfolds at all times. Until I met Saralisa, that was how I'd gotten my kicks. Dad and Letti were members too, I knew that much, but we studiously arranged our visits so he and I weren't there at the same time. There was being close to your family, and there was being *close*. I definitely didn't need to see my stepmother on a spanking bench.

"This is a lot to take in."

"You're telling me. Did you get a DNA test done for Marlie?"

"I didn't have to. Despite my reputation, I never made a habit of sleeping around. When I went to see the OB-GYN, I was four months pregnant—denial's a wonderful thing, huh?—and I hadn't been with anyone for at least three months before the night with Mandell. Or after. Do you know what he told me? He said that if I claimed I had no idea who the father was, everyone would believe me because I'd probably fucked every inbred millionaire with a title while I was in Europe." She gave a hollow laugh. "And they did believe me."

"Gracie, I'm so sorry."

"Don't be. You're the only one who doesn't treat me as an outcast. And thank you..." She wiped away more tears. "Thank you for looking out for Marlie. She deserves so much more than I can give her."

"You deserve more too. You deserve your life back."

"I miss Oregon," she sniffed. "I miss Letti, and you, and I even miss Trey. Dad too, I guess, now that I know he's not the freak I thought he was. Do women really like that stuff?"

"Not all of them, but some do. It's just a case of finding a willing partner whose desires align with yours."

"Saralisa?"

"She's perfect in every way. We slotted so neatly into each other's lives, and I can't imagine a future without her. I don't want to."

"You screwed up epically. You and Dad might get off on tying women up, but Mandell gets off on control. He's a manipulative psychopath who enjoys toying with people. It's like a game to him."

"We're going to beat him."

"How?" Her eyes widened as she read my mind. "Oh, shit. Garrett, promise me you won't do anything stupid."

"I'll do whatever it takes."

"I've already lost my freedom; I don't want to lose my brother too."

"Somebody has to stop him."

"Not like that. Not the way you're thinking of doing it."

"He deserves a shallow grave."

"There has to be another way. And if you're in jail, how will you win Saralisa back?"

Those two women were the only thing that stopped me from grabbing a gun right now. I lumbered to my feet and began pacing—wonkily—because Gracie was right. If Mandell was playing a game, then sacrificing my freedom would be another victory for him. That had to be a last resort.

When I put my anger aside and looked at the problem objectively, there were a few points we might be able to turn to our advantage. Firstly, I'd put a dent in Mandell's plans last night when I took out his man. Secondly, the corpse at the pool house was yet to be identified, and it was possible the cops would find a link to the congressman. Or Harless, seeing as he was the man who liked to get his hands dirty. And thirdly, Mandell didn't know how much we already knew. He had come after Saralisa, probably because whomever Carson Broad foolishly delegated the DC investigation to had screwed up, but he had no idea she'd fingered Harless as the man who'd killed her parents. He was just tying up loose ends.

"Will you come to Oregon with me?" I asked Gracie. "I don't mean stay at home or even in Roseburg, but I could really do with someone in my corner."

"I'll come," she said softly. "But if I see Mandell, I'm the one who's gonna end up in jail."

33

SARA

Day three post-Garrett, and my heart ached every bit as much as when he'd torn it in half in the early hours of Sunday morning. I'd spent yesterday with Brooke, alternately crying and cuddling her dog, but today, I'd come to the craft store. Mindlessly stacking yarn on the shelves was better than being alone with my thoughts, and it wasn't as if anyone could shoot me now, not with the three stooges sitting outside in their shiny black SUV.

Darla had flown back from Virginia yesterday, and I was grateful she was working today's shift rather than Paulo. I adored him, but I'd had enough drama for one week. Darla's quiet calm was exactly what I needed. Nothing seemed to faze her.

"Should we take those gentlemen in the car some coffee, hun?" she asked. "Or do they bring their own?"

"Honestly, I have no idea."

"I'd better go ask. It's only polite."

"Darla, when you were living at The Lookout, do you remember anybody moving things out of the attic?"

"Can't say I recall. Why do you ask?"

"I think my mom left something there for me, but I didn't realise until now, and we couldn't find it when we went to look."

"What did she leave?"

"That's the problem; I have no idea."

"I'm sure if there was anything valuable up there, Marianna would have found it and sold it after your grandpa died."

"That's what I'm afraid of."

Darla headed out to the parking lot to offer drinks, and the stooges would probably get snacks as well because she'd brought several bags of treats back from the airport. I went to the break room to put the kettle on.

"Three coffees, two with milk, one without, and the black coffee needs sugar," she announced when she came back. "We should plate up some of those cookies too."

See?

"How was Virginia?"

"The new store is looking wonderful. It's big enough for a proper coffee bar at the front, so I'm hoping that'll lead to additional passing trade."

"Come for the cappuccino, stay for the crochet class?"

"Something like that. We'll have a lovely work area too. Paulo wants to add a couch, but I'm not so sure about that."

Darla stacked half a dozen cookies onto a plate, then added some wrapped candies for good measure. I felt slightly guilty for ignoring Jack Morrow, but at the same time, I hated being followed constantly. Although I did feel safer with the team around. My head was just such a mess right now, and after Garrett, there was no way I'd ever get tangled up with another rich, handsome, sexy, strong, commanding man again. Especially one with a tongue like a lizard who— Gah. I *had* to stop thinking about him.

"I think a couch would be nice, especially if you want people to treat the place as a social hub as well as a store. People could sit there and knit."

"Or read. We're planning to put in a bookshelf, more of a little free library, where people can leave their old books and take home a new one."

Brooke appeared behind me. "Speaking of 'we,' did you go on a date with Alex?"

Darla turned coy. "I did."

"And?"

"A lady never kisses and tells."

"Oh, so there was kissing?"

"I really should take these cookies out."

"She's definitely getting kissed," Brooke whispered as Darla snatched up the plate and marched off. "Did you see her blush?"

"At least someone's happy."

"I'm so sorry. Did you hear anything from Garrett?"

"No, and I don't want to."

"What he did was wrong, but he didn't deliberately set out to hurt you."

"Please, can we not talk about this?"

"I'm just saying that he clearly still cares. The evidence is sitting in the parking lot." Brooke stood on tiptoes and looked past me through the break room window. "And leaning against the wall out there."

I turned to look, and stooge number three raised a hand to wave.

"When will this ever end?"

"Luca and Colt are both working on it, and a bunch of other deputies too. I mean, violent crime is rare around here."

Apart from when it was committed by the Baldwins,

obviously. Plus there was a vigilante who showed up occasionally, although he seemed to be on the side of good rather than evil. Last year, he'd rescued Brooke from a horrible situation, and rumour said he was responsible for saving Colt from impending doom as well.

"Have they ever tackled a case where they knew who was responsible, but they just couldn't prove it?"

"I'm not sure about that. But I bet you Garrett has a team working on it as well."

"Because he didn't learn from his mistakes?"

Brooke grimaced.

The bell over the front door jangled as I finished making the coffee, and I arranged three mugs on a tray for Darla to take out to the parking lot. I wasn't officially working today, but I was grateful to have a safe place to hide out while the sheriff's department tried to work a miracle. If I'd been stuck on my own at The Lookout, this situation would have felt a hundred times worse. Perhaps I'd get out my paints later? Dad always said that art was just emotions on paper, and that was another reason I knew he and Mom had been happy. His paintings had been filled with bright colours, a hug in a frame. No stormy skies or moody colours. He'd painted Mom often, but he hadn't sold those pictures. No, they were tucked away in a safe deposit box, and the key lived around my neck.

Close to my heart.

I was in there too, plus a few self-portraits, sketches of our home, and several watercolours of Mom's pet bearded dragon. Sir Duster of Dessau had been a gift from her mom for her fifteenth birthday, and I remembered him sitting on my arm when I was four or five years old. He was buried in our old yard in Virginia. Dusty had outlived Grandma Susan by three years, which I thought was why Mom had cried so much when he died. It was like losing another piece of her mother. Maybe someday, if I ever found a place I felt settled enough to stay, I'd adopt a pet of my own.

Darla poked her head into the break room. "It's for you, hun."

Tell me Garrett hadn't... Oh, he hadn't. Parker appeared, and Brooke picked up the tray.

"I'll leave you two to talk."

Great.

Parker leaned against the wall next to the door, hands in his pockets. "How are you doing?"

"Badly." Why was he here? This conversation could have been an email. "Did you want something? I'm not planning on coming back to The Lookout any time soon, so you'll have to do your own laundry."

"I just wanted to see how you were."

"Did the twins send you?"

They'd messaged me incessantly over the past few days, mostly with questions about Garrett. Not once had they enquired about my welfare.

"Nope."

"Can you tell them if they text me one more time, I'm going to block their numbers?"

"I'll pass on the message. Do you need anything from the house?"

"I could do with some more clothes," I admitted, although I didn't love the idea of Parker going through my underwear drawer. Yes, he'd been surprisingly nice to me lately, but there were certain boundaries I wasn't about to cross.

"Write me a list, and I'll bring them. Did you find whatever you were looking for the other day?"

I shook my head.

"Need any more help with the search?"

"No offence, but I don't trust anyone with the surname 'Baldwin.'"

"Can't blame you for that. If I did, I'd be a hypocrite."

Really? Had he forgotten his own last name?

"Oh, please. You're one of them."

"Am I?"

I ticked off the very valid points on my fingers. "You learned business from Grandpa. You work at Baldwin Estates with EJ, and you worked with Marianna too, before she went to prison. You hung out with Easton all the time. You go to parties with the twins."

"Ever heard the phrase 'keep your friends close, but your enemies closer'?"

"So are you saying they're your enemies now?"

He paused for a moment, then kicked the door shut. "Yes."

"And you expect me to believe it?"

"I can't control what you believe, but I'm telling you I'm not the enemy. It's up to you what you do with that information." He sighed. "Living in that house is a mindfuck."

"Then why don't you leave? I bet you've already met your stupid inheritance goal."

"Because I like to win. One down, two on the ropes, one to go."

Was he talking about the inheritance? I did the math. The one down must be Easton—he couldn't make money from prison. Were the two on the ropes the twins? If they got sued over the peanut allergy, then LKB's reputation would be in the toilet. Who was the one to go?

"Don't you mean two to go?"

He shook his head. "You'll be fine."

Now I knew he was talking crap.

"How? How will I be fine? Grandpa added a codicil to his will, did you know that? It gave me better terms, and somebody stole it. It might even have been you, seeing as you 'like to win.'"

"I didn't realise you knew about that."

"So you also know it existed? *Did* you take it?"

Not that I expected him to admit it if he did. Parker had always held his cards close to his chest. At best, he was confusing, at worst, a duplicitous snake.

"That was EJ."

"*What?* I mean, how do you know?"

And, more importantly, how did I know whether Parker was telling the truth? *Never trust a Baldwin.*

"Because I saw him put it through the shredder. It took me hours to piece it back together."

Alert, alert, alert. Information overload. Parker's quick-fire revelations left my brain so befuddled that all I wanted to do was sit in the corner and rock.

"So you...you have the remains of the codicil?"

"If anyone else ever asks me, I'll deny it."

"Then you *are* screwing me over, just like the others. Thanks. Thanks a lot."

"No, I'm not. Over the past six years, Saralisa Baldwin-Forlani has made some *very* shrewd investments. Going forward, she'll continue to collect interest on the $280,000 sitting in her brokerage account until it's time to play show-and-tell with the executive trustee."

Had I somehow fallen into the Upside Down and just not noticed? Was I in Wonderland? Had the roller coaster dumped me into an alternate universe where nothing made sense?

"I don't have a brokerage account."

I didn't even know what a brokerage account was.

"Yes, you do."

"Wait, *you* set up a brokerage account in my name?"

"Yes."

"And you made $280,000?"

"Yes."

"Why? Why would you do that?"

"Because you're not like the others. Because EJ tried to cheat you. Because Grandpa always intended for you to inherit a portion of his estate. Take your pick."

"I don't buy it. You say you wanted Easton to lose out, so why wouldn't you let the codicil stand? It would have increased his target."

Nothing made sense today. Not my cousin's words, not the nightmare I was living through, not that stupid little bud of hope that kept trying to blossom in the darkness.

"I couldn't let the codicil stand," Parker said.

"But why not? It doesn't affect you. You're not even mentioned."

"How closely did you read it?"

"I...I've never actually read it. I just heard about it."

"From who?"

Without thinking, I glanced toward the store, and Parker nodded.

"Ah, from Darla?"

Great, now I'd dragged her into the mess.

"She's always been kind to me, unlike everyone else in that house."

He ignored the dig. "In the final paragraph, East refers to me as his grandson. *The conditions for my remaining son, Easton Baldwin II, my grandson Parker Baldwin, and my granddaughters Kayleigh Baldwin and Lillian Baldwin remain as stated in my original will.*" Parker's tone turned bitter. "Only it turns out I'm not actually his grandson. EJ informed me of that little fact when I confronted him with the codicil. If I'd called in a lawyer as I threatened, he would have fought to get me thrown out of the will completely."

What? I sank onto the couch, reeling, because if that was true, then...my so-called family had been lying my entire life. Was there *anything* they'd been honest about?

No.

No, of course there wasn't.

"I can't believe this."

"You don't believe much, do you?" Parker gave a quiet snort. "But I did a DNA test, and for once, EJ was telling the truth."

"Then who's your father?"

"That's the big mystery, isn't it? I've never discussed the matter with Mom." A shrug. "Which means that if necessary, I can deny the conversation with EJ ever took place, just like I'll deny this one. I still don't trust him not to try and screw me over in two years."

I had so many questions... "Did Grandpa know? Why didn't EJ say something sooner? Why did he take the codicil if it didn't benefit him? Was he protecting Easton?"

"I have no idea if Grandpa knew, and I can't be sure when EJ found out, but I do know that he needs me right now. He can't run Baldwin Estates alone, and Marianna didn't have the right skill set either." Parker raised his gaze to the ceiling. "Damn, I was hoping he'd go down with her, but it wasn't to be. As for taking the codicil, I'm not sure if he was protecting Easton, or he just hated your father enough to screw over his descendants. Either way, I have two years left to work out a way to fuck EJ over, and I intend to make the most of them."

"This whole time...you've been feeling the same way as

me? As if you didn't belong, but you were trapped? Like you've been pushed into a family you didn't want to be a part of?"

"Yes."

"Why didn't you tell me?"

"Because I was never sure whose side you were on."

"I was on my own side."

"So was I. I won't pretend to be a good guy, Sara, but I'm not the man you think I am."

I wasn't entirely sure that I believed that, but I did find myself wanting to. Having an ally, an ally who understood a little of what I'd been through over the past sixteen years, let a petal on that bud of hope unfurl.

"Saralisa," I corrected. "I want that part of my old life back."

"Saralisa." Parker nodded. "For what it's worth, I'm sorry things didn't work out with Dorsey. I only met him a couple of times, but he seemed like an okay guy."

"For a while, I thought so too." I chewed at my lip, considering. "Parker, do you want to get lunch with me?"

"Not in Baldwin's Shore. If EJ suspects we're cooking up a plan together, my job becomes a whole lot harder."

"In Coos Bay? Or North Bend?"

After a moment's hesitation, Parker offered the merest hint of a smile. "Sure. Why not?"

34

SARA

*P*arker and I met at La Cantina, and I was tempted to ask Jack Morrow if he could give me a ride home so I could order a margarita. If ever a day called for alcohol, it was this one. Parker opted for sparkling water.

"Not hungry?" he asked, gesturing toward my barely touched nachos. Usually I loved the nachos at La Cantina. They were the perfect mix of crunch and dip, and they didn't skimp on the cheese.

"I lost my appetite three days ago."

"You were the one who wanted lunch."

"I know. I guess I just wanted to talk. We've never really spoken before, not properly."

"Two ships, passing in the night. Who are the guys in the SUV? Cops?"

"Garrett sent them."

He raised an eyebrow. "So he *is* still on the scene?"

"No, he isn't."

"I see. Is that something to do with the handcuffs?"

My cheeks burned. "You know about those?"

"Somebody had to clean up the pool house."

Why had I thought having lunch with Parker would be a good idea?

"I wish you'd just burned the place to the ground. But no, the handcuffs weren't the issue—it was something else."

"Then the twins still stand a chance? They'll be thrilled to hear that."

"Sorry to burst their bubble, but Garrett detests them. He only goes to parties to stop his brother from doing anything dumb."

"I can identify with that. I lost count of the number of times I stopped Easton from trashing the family's reputation, but he still managed it in the end. His one success in life."

"Then Marianna said, 'Hold my beer.'"

We stared at each other for a beat, and for perhaps the first time ever, I heard Parker laugh. Not a sarcastic chuckle, but a proper belly laugh, eyes crinkled. And I realised that although I'd lost so much in the past week—my boyfriend, my heart, my nerve—I'd gained a new co-conspirator.

"You can run from karma, but you can't hide," he said.

"Speaking of karma, I heard a rumour the twins might get sued over a peanut allergy?"

"Only a matter of time. The complaint letter arrived yesterday, and it was glorious. Almost as glorious as Easton investing ninety-five percent of his money in crypto right before the market crashed."

Amazing what schadenfreude could do for a girl's appetite. I scooped up a blob of guac and chewed slowly. If Parker was telling the truth about the brokerage account— and Parker was all about subtlety, I didn't think he'd tell such an outrageous lie—then I might inherit a third of

Grandpa's estate. Four million dollars. I could run far, far away from the monster, away from Garrett, and never worry about money again. Was it feasible to live in a beach shack? I could sit on the sand and paint sunsets for the rest of my life.

"Were you serious?" I whispered. "About the brokerage account?"

Wordlessly, he pulled out his phone and opened an app. A moment later, he slid it across the table. The screen showed some sort of investment account, and my name was at the top. And there was the money. $280,413.57. I began shaking.

"Promise me you'll keep this quiet," he said. "I need those two years."

"I promise."

"If you want control of the funds, I'll turn it over, but you can't spend the money. Do you have enough cash to live on until Judgment Day?"

Even if I had to pay rent, I could manage. "Yes."

"Then just keep your head down and hold on."

And survive. A part of me wanted to tell Parker about the monster, about Harless and Mandell, but I wasn't ready to have that conversation, not yet. I'd jumped in so fast with Garrett, and it had backfired. With Parker, I'd be more cautious.

"I will. Can I ask you a question?"

"I reserve the right not to answer."

"Do you remember EJ or Marianna taking anything out of the attic during the time I was at the house? I know it's a long shot."

"What kind of thing? They fetched the Christmas decorations every year."

"I don't know. Before Mom died, she said a few words that made me think she'd maybe left something at the house for me, probably when we visited for Grandpa's eightieth birthday."

"Why would she have done that? You hardly ever came to Oregon."

"I have no idea. As I said, it's a long shot. She just said it was on the third floor."

"That was it?"

"All I remember is 'Third-floor window. Pipes. Fires. Dust. Eight sixteen.' Does that mean anything to you?"

As usual, he took his time thinking about it. Parker never acted in a hurry. If I'd had to describe him in three words, they would have been "cold," "deliberate," and "boring." Actually, that was yesterday. Today, I'd switch out "boring" for "sneaky." I ate a couple more nachos. They were room temperature now, but my appetite was finally returning.

"Sorry, it means nothing at all. You checked around the attic windows?"

"Every single one."

"The pipe repairs were on the second floor, not the third, and I don't recall any fires at that time. Easton burned down the old gazebo, but that was the year after."

I remembered that. He thought it would be fun to play with matches and because it hadn't rained for weeks, the whole of the back lawn caught fire. He'd been grounded for a month. But pipe repairs? I didn't recall any pipe repairs.

"What happened with the pipes?"

"The copper corroded, and we had a new leak every month. In the end, Grandpa said to hell with it and hired a plumber to replace the whole lot. We had to play musical bedrooms while he pulled up the floors."

I didn't remember any of that, but...but we'd been staying in the pool house. That was another reason I'd moved out there—because of the good memories. Now the monster had ruined those too.

"When was the work done? Can you remember? Was it around the time of Grandpa's party?"

"EJ was meant to be overseeing the project, but it overran, and I remember him and Grandpa fighting in the kitchen while Mom iced the birthday cake."

Could Parker's memory be the key? I didn't want to get my hopes up, not again, but at the same time, I had to check out the possibility.

"Uh, I might need to look under the floor."

"I had a horrible feeling you were going to say that."

"EJ's going to have a conniption, isn't he?"

Another long pause. "Only if he knows."

"Oh, you think he won't notice if I sneak in and start dismantling the house?"

"Apply some logic, Saralisa. Your mom said 'third floor window.' If we're talking about the second floor and not the attic, then the 'third' is a separate part of the riddle. Split it up: third, floor, window. Consider the layout—two wings, each with a central hallway—and start with the third door on each side. We know the floor part, so we just need to trace the pipes and check each point where they pass under a window. You have friends that can help? Luca and Brooke?"

"Yes." Hell, I'd even drag Jack Morrow in with a claw hammer if I needed to.

"If I can get EJ and the twins out of the house tomorrow, would that work for you?"

"I know we haven't been close, and technically we're not even family now, but I love you."

The corners of his lips quirked. It wasn't a whole smile, but maybe a quarter of one.

"I'll text you with a time."

35

SARA

*P*hase two of the search felt like a military operation. Thankfully, Luca was a former Army Ranger, and he'd taken over the organising, so I was free to drink copious amounts of coffee while quietly freaking out. I hadn't told the others every detail of my conversation with Parker as some parts were family business—or rather, non-family business as it had turned out—but I'd divulged his theory about Mom's words.

We had a time slot from two until four this afternoon, and I just hoped it would be long enough. Luca was coming, and Colt, plus they'd roped in Deck, who'd promised to bring the necessary tools for dismantling a floor. Blue would be there too—she was practically champing at the bit—and Everly had offered to cover the afternoon for Brooke at the Craft Cabin so she could join us. Plus we had Aaron, who advised that there could be no legal ramifications for attempting DIY in a house I part-owned as long as we put everything back in its rightful place afterward.

Last night, I'd lain awake wondering whether Mom might

have said "door" instead of "floor." Those final moments had been so rushed, so terrifying, that I could easily have misheard. I only hoped I'd remembered the rest right.

"Channelling Goya today?" Darla asked, setting a coffee beside me. The mug was one of Paulo's and decorated with a rainbow entirely too cheerful for my mood. I'd picked up a paintbrush to keep my hands from tearing my hair out, but now the monster stared back at me from the paper. A ghoul with pale eyes.

"I don't need to channel anyone when it comes to painting darkness."

"I think I'd better bring you a donut, hun."

"Oh, I'm really not—"

Never mind. She was already heading out the door to the bakery.

I was about to wad up my work and toss it in the trash when the front door opened with a cheerful jingle. Over the past year, I'd spent enough time at the Craft Cabin to know the newcomer didn't quite fit in. I'd never seen her in town before, and tourists tended to arrive in twos and threes, relaxed and chatting as they browsed the shelves. This polished, beautiful blonde looked around the store, but she didn't seem interested in the craft materials.

"Can I help, ma'am?" Brooke asked.

She shook her head, and then her gaze settled on me. Uh-oh. A moment later, she slid into the empty seat beside mine.

A week ago, my first thought wouldn't have been *Do assassins wear four-inch heels?* but boy, had things changed. Surely Jack Morrow would have stopped her if she was dangerous? Which meant she was probably a reporter.

"No comment."

"Huh?" Her frown relaxed, and she offered a hesitant smile. "Oh, I'm not with the media."

"Then who are you?"

"My name is Gracelynn Dorsey. Gracie."

No way. "Seriously? He sent his *sister* to do his dirty work?"

"Garrett knows I'm here, but he didn't ask me to come. Believe me, I'm as annoyed with him as you are." She studied my painting for a moment, then tapped the monster with one manicured fingernail. "That's him, isn't it? Harless?"

"Is there anyone Garrett didn't tell about my private business? Literally anyone at all?"

"He didn't need to tell me. I see Seth in my own nightmares. Can we talk? I really need to speak with you."

Her voice turned my blood to ice, not so much the words but the tone. And her eyes... They were haunted.

I found myself both morbidly curious and nodding. "Okay. Okay, we can talk."

Gracie perched on the edge of the couch in the break room, twisting her hands. She didn't want coffee. She didn't want a cookie. It was clear she didn't want to be there, period, and yet she'd come.

"I hadn't told this story to a soul until Garrett flew to New York the day before yesterday. And I never intended to, but then I found out what they'd done to you, and I couldn't stay silent any longer. For so long, I thought it was just me."

Cold dread pooled in my stomach. "Seth Harless did something to you as well?"

"He helped."

If ever I'd doubted my capacity for tears, I found out the truth that day. My ability to sob was limitless. Gracie told her story from the beginning, starting with the carefree young woman she'd once been and ending up with a daughter she couldn't bear to touch. Seth Harless had guarded the door while his boss raped her, and the senator's lapdog couldn't plead ignorance because he'd cleaned her up with a washcloth afterward. And that sweet child, that sweet, beautiful child whom Garrett and I had taken to Fall Creek Falls, was the product of an act every bit as heinous as the one I'd experienced. Gracie and I held each other and wept. Harless and Mandell had ruined both of our lives, and who knew how many other women they'd hurt along the way?

"I'm so sorry," I whispered.

"Garrett won't give up. Now it's not only you that he's fighting for, it's me as well."

"But they're so careful. Every lead is a dead end."

"Yesterday, he was ready to fly to DC and send them to meet their friend from the pool house, consequences be damned."

My heart lurched. "Did you stop him? Tell me you stopped him? He'd end up in prison."

"I talked him out of it, temporarily at least. But I don't think he cares about prison. Right now, he doesn't think he has much to live for."

"He has everything. People the world over envy him."

"They envy his money, and money isn't all that important to my brother. He was always happier living in barracks with twenty other men than in a mansion. He only quit the Marines because Dad put pressure on him to step up and do what was best for the family, i.e. for Dad."

"I understand about family pressure."

"People see the glitz and the glamour, but they rarely check under the hood." Gracie grabbed another tissue from the nearly empty box. "What Garrett did to you was the most egregious breach of trust, and in your position, I'm not sure I'd forgive him either. But he really is devastated. I've never seen him like this before."

"Contrite?"

"In love."

"Oh."

"Yup. He's head over heels, and he's also terrified you'll never speak to him again."

"I need time."

"Absolutely. You know, I can understand why he doubted you, and it's not a slight on your character. Graham Mandell is just so, so good at hiding the darkness within. I used to think of him as an uncle."

"Before that night on the terrace, I don't remember ever meeting him."

"He's caused so much hurt. Maybe someday, would you consider speaking with Garrett?"

"Maybe someday. I do miss him. I miss everything we had, but I'm not sure I'd be able to trust him again."

"Can I ask a really personal question?"

I could always refuse to answer, couldn't I?

"Okay."

"So during my talk with Garrett, some things came up about my family that...well, they shocked me, and I'm just not sure... Can being tied up truly feel pleasurable? And, uh, spanking?"

Wow. That must have been a heck of a conversation. If I'd looked in the mirror, a ripe tomato would have stared back at me.

"Uh, yes?" *Please, couch, swallow me now.* "Yes, with the right man, those things can be very pleasurable indeed. That's where the trust comes in."

"Good to know. So, uh, we'll never speak of this again, okay?"

"Agreed. Can I interest you in a coffee?"

"I'd love a coffee. And I understand there's a guy here who customises shoes? Paulo? I have a friend who'd like his number."

"He's gay, and he also has a boyfriend."

Gracie giggled. "Oh, this isn't a romantic proposition. She made the shoes you ran away from my brother in, and she wants to speak with Paulo about collaborating on a limited edition. I also design shoes, by the way. If he can't agree on terms with Riya, I'd be interested in poaching him myself."

"He doesn't work Wednesdays, but he'll be here tomorrow. Are you planning to fly back to New York right away?"

"We're staying at the Peninsula."

We? The rush of heat was unexpected and unwelcome. "Garrett's here too?"

"I made him promise to stay out of your way. Tell me if he screws up, won't you? I'll kick his ass."

Out of darkness is born the light. This week, I'd found not one but two new allies. Parker and Gracie, an old acquaintance and a new one.

"We should swap numbers."

"Definitely. Do you want to get lunch? Not at the Peninsula, obviously. Garrett said the Coffee House serves good food?"

"It does. And lunch sounds great, but I have to be back here by one o'clock. There's something I need to do this afternoon."

"Why do they get power tools while we only get pencils and duct tape?" Gracie asked.

Parker had come through, and the house was empty of Baldwins. An "intermittent electrical fault" at one of the properties rented out by Baldwin Estates meant EJ needed to go investigate, and the twins had driven to Eugene to meet with a friend of Parker's who'd agreed to pretend she was planning a party. Yes, *she*. Until today, I didn't even realise Parker *had* female friends.

Luca put a hand on each of our shoulders. "Because you'll do an excellent job of writing numbers on floorboards, and none of us Neanderthals can count."

By one o'clock, it had felt as if I'd known Gracie for months rather than hours, and I'd come to another realisation. For over a decade, we'd both been trapped in the same limbo, unable to move on with our lives and afraid of our pasts. This story was as much hers as it was mine, which was why I'd invited her to The Lookout. Whatever my mom had hidden, it could impact both of us. With Gracie's blessing, I'd explained the barest bones of the situation to the others, and they'd agreed she could come along.

While we were talking, the men had been planning, and I had to admit that despite my organisational expertise, they'd done a better job of it than I would have. Based on Parker's "third door" theory, we had four rooms to search, six if you counted the en-suites—an empty guest room, Easton the Third's man cave, a smaller space Marianna had turned into a closet-slash-dressing room, and her old home office. Where to start? Unfortunately, Parker's recollections didn't include exactly which rooms had been sans floors at the time of the party.

"Why don't we tackle the easier rooms first and hope we get lucky?" Deck suggested, and by "easier" he meant "emptier." Easton didn't understand the concept of tidying, and Marianna had owned more clothes than one woman could ever need. Too bad she was stuck in an orange jumpsuit now. "You're sure we don't know what we're looking for?"

"Anything that doesn't belong," Blue told him. "We'll know it if we see it."

In the guest room, the men turned the bed on end and pulled back the carpet, and Gracie and I got to work. She numbered the boards in the order they had to be replaced once we'd checked the cavities, while I taped each set of screws so we didn't lose any. Blue and Brooke went on ahead and began moving the lighter furniture away from the windows in the old office. I'd made use of Jack Morrow, and he'd call if anyone turned into the driveway. As for Parker, he said he'd rather not know the details—there was that plausible deniability thing again—but he'd stick around to monitor EJ and the twins and warn us if they were going to arrive home early.

Even with all of us working together, it took twenty minutes to remove the boards in front of the windows. There was nothing down there but dust bunnies, dead spiders, and an empty bag that had once contained potato chips. Then we had to put everything back again. Forty minutes gone. We had to be faster.

We shaved off five minutes in the office, but that still left the two untidiest rooms.

"Maybe we should come back another day?" Deck suggested, surveying the dressing room. "Why do all the women in the house share the same closet? Is that normal?"

"These are just Marianna's clothes," I told him.

"Sheesh."

"I'll make a start on Easton's room with Gracie."

A decision I quickly regretted. To call Easton lazy was an insult to slobs everywhere. The Baldwins had a cleaner, but either someone had told her not to bother with the room of doom, or she'd taken one look inside and suffered a nervous breakdown.

"How does a person live like this?" Gracie asked. "How long have those plates been in here?"

"Six months, give or take." It was hard to tell whether they were covered in mould or just dust. "We should have brought respirators."

Easton hadn't heard of a laundry hamper either, and mountains of dirty clothes had been abandoned by the windows. We were meant to put everything back exactly as we'd found it, but in this hovel, that would be impossible. I nudged one pile with my foot. Damn Seth Harless for forcing me into this position.

"Why are there so many wadded-up tissues on the floor? Did your cousin have hay fever or something?"

"Trust me—you don't want to know. I'm gonna owe the guys so much beer after this."

"I'll buy them a whole brewery."

They'd deserve it. I couldn't wait for the day when I never had to set foot in this house of horrors again. We shifted the detritus of Easton the Third's life in lumpy piles, and the men came to do their thing.

Then my phone rang. Parker.

"The good news is that the twins are still tied up discussing table decorations. The bad news is that EJ's a better electrician than he is a father, and he's on his way back from North Bend. You have thirty minutes."

"Shit!"

My time with Garrett had changed me in many ways— my language had certainly gotten fouler.

"What's up?" Luca asked.

"EJ will be back in a half hour."

He stood, screwdriver in hand. "That'll be cutting things mighty fine. Stay or go?"

Why did I have to choose? Each decision I'd made lately turned out to be a bad one. But everyone was staring at me. And the clock was ticking.

"Stay. If we leave this room a mess, nobody will notice."

Practice makes perfect. The men went to work with a vengeance, Luca and Aaron lifting floorboards, Colt and Deck replacing them. They'd made it almost as far as the en-suite when Luca stilled.

"Hey, what's this?"

I practically climbed onto his back in an attempt to look. It was a hard drive. A small, portable hard drive, definitely not something that should have been lurking under the floor in my dumbass cousin's room. Luca handed it to me, then slotted the board back into place and grabbed an electric screwdriver. If speed carpentry ever became a thing, my money would be on this team. They were a well-oiled machine.

"Easton the Turd should get another ten years for the state of this room," Blue muttered. "It's a crime scene."

My phone rang again, and this time, it was Jack Morrow. "A black Toyota just turned into the driveway, ma'am. Looks like a middle-aged gentleman behind the wheel."

I threw the last pile of clothing in the direction of the nearest window. "EJ's home. Run."

"Head for Sara's old room," Blue ordered. "We're helping her to pack the last of her belongings, understand?"

EJ opened the front door as I reached the bottom of the stairs with an armful of books. The others followed carrying clothes, knick-knacks, a nightstand, and the comfy little overstuffed armchair that I loved to curl up in and read.

My darling uncle just scowled. "Don't take anything that doesn't belong to you."

"I won't."

That hard drive had absolutely been meant for me.

Parker meandered past as I crossed the hallway. "Any luck?" he murmured.

"Yes, and thank you."

"Don't be a stranger."

Then he was gone, and so were we.

36

———

SARA

"At least she didn't use a flash drive," Blue said. "The data would be degraded for sure. How close was the hard drive to the hot water pipe?"

Luca considered the question. "A couple of feet away? There were two joists in between."

"So we stand a chance. One time, I did a job for an old guy in Reedsport, and I remember him bitching and moaning because he wanted to show me a document on his portable hard drive and it wouldn't work. They just don't make things like they used to, he said. So I asked how old the drive was, and he said he'd bought it the day after his granddaughter's twelfth birthday. When I asked how old she was now, he said she'd be thirty next month." Blue rolled her eyes. "Of course, even if the drive opens, we might need technical help to read the actual files. It depends on what format Claire used."

We'd regrouped in Aaron's apartment, all eight of us. When I'd quietly questioned whether it was appropriate for Deck to stay, Luca had shrugged and said Deck wasn't a gossip. Even so, his presence left me uncomfortable.

"So what do we do next?" I asked.

"We find the oldest laptop we have that still works, plug the drive in, and pray."

And curse, it turned out. Because when we loaded up the drive, we got our miracle as it whirred slowly into life. The disc held only one folder, called "Claire," just in case there was any doubt over who had put it there, and when Aaron clicked on it, a box popped up, asking for a password.

Blue huffed. "Well, shit."

Seven heads swivelled to look at me.

"Any ideas?" Aaron asked.

"Absolutely none."

"We could try the usual suspects? Password123?"

Oh, please. "My mom was smart, and she went to all the trouble of hiding a hard drive under the floor. She wouldn't have used a dumb password like that."

"So come up with a better idea."

"How? I don't even recall her owning this hard drive, and I barely used the computer. I was nine years old, remember? Mom and Dad thought it was better for me to dance and read and spend time outdoors."

"Let's just try it," Aaron said, typing.

Incorrect password. Two attempts remaining.

Luca smacked him on the shoulder. "You asshole."

"Maybe we should call Parker," I joked.

Blue shook her head. "We don't need to. Don't you see—your mom gave you the password. Third floor window. Pipes. Fires. Dust. Eight sixteen. We've already used the first four words."

"So the password is 'fires dust eight sixteen'?"

"Probably."

"Probably? We only have two tries left."

"Is 'eight sixteen' numbers or letters?" Aaron asked.

"I'd assume numbers," Blue said. "August sixteenth is Sara's mom and dad's anniversary."

It was? When you were a kid, you never thought of those things, only birthdays and Christmas, basically the occasions when you got gifts. And Thanksgiving, because who didn't love food?

"So, 'firesdust816'? Any capital letters?"

"Maybe one at the beginning? Isn't that what normal people do when they get one of those stupid password prompts that says you have to include a capital letter? And if you need a special character as well, it's just an exclamation point at the end."

"I'm pretty sure these files were created before passwords began demanding a hieroglyph, a gang sign, and the soul of your firstborn," Luca pointed out.

"So are we trying lower case?" Aaron asked.

Blue made a decision. "Yes."

Password incorrect. One attempt remaining.

Dammit.

Once again, everyone turned in my direction. Why were they looking at me? Didn't they realise how little I knew about anything?

"Why couldn't she have picked a normal password?" Brooke asked. "Regular people use the name of their pet and their birthday, don't they?" A pause. "Or is that just me?"

Luca snorted. "Better change your passwords, sweetheart."

Fires... Dust... Oh my gosh. The pieces began to click

together. If I'd gotten the "third floor" part confused, then perhaps I'd misunderstood "fires" too? Because what did we have in front of us? *Files.*

"Can I try?" I asked, and Aaron angled the laptop toward me.

My fingers trembled as I entered *Duster816.*

Password accepted.

I'd never felt relief like it, not even on the day a semi swerved into my lane and missed me by inches. When the driver got arrested—he landed in a tree—he'd claimed he was avoiding Bigfoot, and then he blew double the limit in a breath test after a deputy took him back to the station.

Thank goodness.

"Told you that you knew it," Blue said, sounding smug. "You should trust your instincts more."

No way. I'd just used up my entire quota of luck for the next decade.

The drive contained seven files—a plain text document and six videos. Aaron tried opening the document first, and we all leaned closer when several paragraphs popped up on the screen.

If you're reading this, then I'm dead. And the person responsible is one of the six men in these videos. Scum rises to the top. Those in power protect themselves.

But I should start at the beginning...

Eight weeks ago, a young woman approached me after my yoga class and said a friend needed to speak with me. Usually, I'd have brushed her off, but she was persistent. She talked the whole way to my car. Her friend was in trouble, she claimed. She'd seen things she shouldn't, and she believed her revelations would rock Capitol Hill to its core. She had to speak with me because Mike Colvin was the one man who she thought might be able to help. What can I say? I got curious. Pete drove me, and we met at a diner in Maryland.

She introduced herself as Samantha, but I have no idea if that was her real name. It probably wasn't.

Samantha claimed she'd been recruited two years ago to work as a high-end escort. The money was good, she said, and the work sure beat waitressing. But after six months, she started to recognise some of her clients. Rich men, powerful men, politicians. And she began to overhear things. She realised that her clients weren't the men she was servicing, but instead were the men who watched. Who recorded the interactions. They called themselves Compass, and she was a tiny cog in a vast machine. Honestly, I thought she was a fantasist when she talked about a new world order, about a small but mighty movement slowly aligning governments to its own way of thinking. But then she showed me the videos. Just a sample, she said. There are hundreds more, thousands even, blackmail material against those in positions of influence.

She was terrified, that much was obvious. She'd come to realise that women like her didn't have a long life expectancy. If they learned too much or if they outlived their usefulness, they disappeared. Her time was coming, she feared, and if the worst happened, she didn't want her death to be in vain. I asked why she didn't just run. She told me they'd always find her.

Samantha came to me because Mike was one of the few targets Compass hadn't been able to catch in a compromising position. Squeaky clean, she said. She wanted him to see the videos, to set wheels in motion to investigate what sounded like a huge conspiracy theory.

A conspiracy theory that I think might be real.

Watch the videos and read Mike's obituary, mine too. You'll see.

I took copies of the videos, and I went to Mike. I truly thought he would do the right thing, the honourable thing. But that was my biggest mistake. I came to realise that when you mix men with politics, greed trumps everything. Instead of starting an investigation, Mike tried to use the videos to his own advantage. The opportunity was too good to pass up, he said. Margins in the House were razor thin, and if he could swing a vote or two our way... Our way. I no longer wanted to be a part of this, and I told him so. We fought about it. He promised to reconsider, but by then, the damage was already done. This morning, I attended his funeral. A heart attack, the powers that be said. A simple yet unfortunate medical issue.

Samantha said professionals were good at that. At making death look like an accident or pinning the blame on somebody else.

It's not only money that makes the world go round; it's blackmail and murder too.

So, now you know.

Do with this information what you will, but do it very, very carefully.

Claire Baldwin-Forlani.

There was absolute silence in Aaron's study as we all digested the contents of the letter. Now I knew why my mom had died, and the reason was worse than anything I could possibly have imagined. She'd stumbled across a den of vipers, and then someone she cared about had betrayed her. I'd experienced betrayal myself, but for Mom, it had been a hundred times worse. Not knowing who to trust, not knowing who to turn to... At least I had my friends.

Luca was the first to speak. "Well, fuck."

Blue was next. "Come on, let's watch the videos."

Gracie gripped my hand as Aaron clicked on the first file, but truthfully, it was a bit of a let-down. Two men eating in a restaurant, and one passed an envelope across the table to the other. I didn't recognise either of them.

"Any ideas?" Blue asked.

It was Deck who answered. "The man on the left is Senator Presley, and he's an asshole. No idea about the other guy."

"Let's move on."

Video number two showed a grey-haired man kissing a woman young enough to be his granddaughter. Not his wife, I was guessing.

"Anyone?"

"Garrett might know," Gracie said softly. "If the man is in politics, I mean. My brother goes to a lot of fundraisers."

"Why don't we look at the third video?" Brooke asked brightly.

Whoa. We all recognised the subject of that one, although I had to squint to believe it.

"Is that...is that President Harrison?"

Also not with his wife. The First Lady had dark brown hair, and this was a blonde. How long ago had the president gotten married? I wasn't sure. He opened the car door for the blonde to climb out, tucked an arm around her waist, and the two of them set off along the street. But they didn't get far before he pushed her up against a dark storefront and kissed her passionately. Another shot showed them in a restaurant, looking cosy as they ate dinner.

Whoever Samantha was, she'd been right. These people, this Compass, they were watching everyone. Had James Harrison even been a senator sixteen years ago? Or had they been smart enough to preempt his rise to power?

"Claire said one of the men in these videos was responsible for her death," Blue reminded us. "If the President of the United States was involved, we might have bitten off a little more than we can chew."

And I'd always thought Harrison was one of the good guys. Yet more evidence that I was a poor judge of character.

"Play the next video," Colt said.

Oh, yikes, too much boobs. The man in question was sucking them, pressing them together, sliding his dick between them as their owner moaned dramatically underneath him.

"Are those real?" I asked without thinking.

Blue snorted. "I doubt it. But that's former Congressman Bull. You remember him? He's the jackass who went viral when his ex-wife cut the ass out of his pants, and he didn't realise before he set out to open a new mini-mall."

I did remember. And now that I'd seen this video, I honestly couldn't blame her.

Number five had been filmed in a bathroom, and judging by the attire—a tuxedo and a ballgown—the couple featured had been attending a gala or an awards show or a fancy dinner. The man was fucking his companion from behind, one hand over her mouth to muffle her cries. I thought I might have seen the face on TV sometime, but I couldn't put a name to it.

"Well, hello, Governor DeVaio," Colt said. "I met that guy at some dinner with Brie. The woman on the tape isn't his current wife."

We had one video left, and even before Aaron pressed play, I had a good idea of who we'd see in it. Five bucks said movie star number six was a politician, he was a sleaze, and he never went anywhere without a human pit bull at his side.

And I was right.

In the grainy footage, Congressman Mandell ground away on top of a pretty young blonde. Although her eyes were open, she seemed frozen, and light glistened off her cheek. She was crying. The camera was high up and to the side, and I'd bet my inheritance neither of the pair knew they were being filmed.

"Fuck."

Deck caught Gracie a second before she hit the floor, and too late, I realised that we'd opened old wounds. Nine years ago, this had been her. We'd just taken a box cutter to suppressed memories, and pain was spilling out.

"Get off, get off, get off!"

She came to and began to struggle as Deck carried her to the couch on the other side of the room, and he nearly dropped her. I crouched at her side and tried to take her hand, but she smacked me away. She was shaking now, and she drew her knees up to her chest and squashed herself into the cushions, cheeks red, breathing hard.

Brooke knelt beside me. "I think it's a panic attack."

"What should we do?" I asked.

"I don't freaking know!"

Okay, not helping. "Relax. Just relax and stay calm."

I wasn't sure whether I was addressing Gracie or Brooke or myself, but Gracie didn't relax. No, she trembled harder.

"I could ask Dr. Google," Aaron offered. "Unless anyone knows a real doctor? Should we take her to the hospital?"

I knew who to ask. I also didn't want to ask him, but I had to. Quaking myself, I dialled Garrett Dorsey.

"Saralisa? Thank fuck. I mean, it's great to hear from you. I was terrified you'd—"

"Has Gracie ever had a panic attack before?"

"Not for years. Why?" Hope turned to concern. "Is she having one now?"

"I think so? What do I do? I don't know what to do."

"Okay." I heard him suck in a breath. "Okay, do *not* tell her to relax. It only makes her more agitated." Oops. "Reassure her that you're there and you're not going anywhere. Then make her do multiplication."

"Multiplication?"

"Like the times tables. It makes her focus."

"Really? That's...." Weird, but nothing about this situation was normal. "Okay, I'll do it."

"I'm on my way."

He hung up, and I took a bracing breath of my own. I could do this; I could.

"Gracie, I'm here, and I'm not going anywhere. What's three times three?"

Blank stare.

"Three times three, Gracie. Can you help me with the answer?"

Finally, a small voice. "Nine."

"That's great, you're doing great. What's two times six?"

"Twelve."

Instead of staring into the distance, she began to focus on me.

"How about four times eight?"

"Thirty-two."

"Somebody needs to let Garrett in," I whispered. "Gracie, what's five times three?"

My math game was rusty, but I carried on for what seemed like forever, the rest of the room and the people fading away so it was just the two of us. Gracie let me take her hand, and her breathing gradually returned to normal. Then *he* was beside me. I felt Garrett before I saw him, that change of energy, and although he was careful not to touch me, my skin prickled with goosebumps.

"Gracie, I'm here. Hey, what's sixty-seven times nineteen?"

She managed a teary smile. "I'm not a calculator."

"But you're better at math than me." He tucked her hair behind her ears. "How are you feeling?"

"Tired."

"Me too, me too. Do you want something to drink?"

"A glass of water?"

"I'll get it." Aaron slipped out of the room.

"Can you remember what worried you? Is there anything you want to talk about?"

Her face crumpled, and Garrett wrapped her up in a hug until the tears stopped. If Congressman Mandell had been in the room at that moment, I would have taken a blowtorch to his balls and enjoyed every second of it.

"There was a video," I whispered. "We'll show you later."

"I need to get her back to the hotel. Can I call you tomorrow?"

"Okay."

That night, I lay awake, turning over the latest horrors in my mind. The revelations. *Compass.* I knew now why my parents had died, and it was all so...so pointless. Mom had been trapped between a rock and a hard place, between Compass and Congressman Mandell, and it hadn't even been her fault. And as for Mike Colvin... What a snake. Sure, he might not have cheated on his wife or accepted bribes or raped a helpless young woman, but he'd turned the other cheek to the abuse and exploited the situation instead of trying to fix it. No wonder Mom had wanted to leave politics.

A car drove past on the road outside, and I tensed.

Harless was still out there. But the engine faded away in the distance, the building remained silent, and I relaxed again. Thought of my own mistakes.

Because I'd messed up too. By bringing Gracie to help in the search at The Lookout, I'd invited consequences I hadn't foreseen. I'd hurt her, and it wasn't lost on me how mad I'd been at Garrett for doing the same thing to me. We'd both done what we thought was right.

We'd both been wrong.

37

SARA

"How's Gracie?" I asked Garrett.

Thursday morning, and he'd arrived at the old car dealership bearing pastries I didn't deserve and coffee I couldn't stomach. His sister wasn't with him.

"She's doing better."

"Is she mad at me for putting her in that situation?"

"She's mad at Mandell. She mentioned something about a flamethrower."

"I'm so sorry. I'm so sorry for everything. For stirring up her pain, for bringing both of you into my mess, for shutting you out these past few days. I was scared—no, terrified—after everything that happened, and losing control of my secrets and the circumstances meant I couldn't think rationally."

He opened his arms and I stepped into them, borrowing a little of his strength as I tried not to cry.

"Can you forgive me?" I asked. "Can Gracie?"

"There's nothing to forgive. Gracie's resting, but she asked me to give you a hug. As for me, I love you, and that isn't going to change. You're mine, Saralisa, and I'll destroy any man who tries to harm you. Can you forgive me?"

Garrett shouldn't have gone behind my back, but he'd been trapped too, trapped between a man he thought was a family friend and my hazy memories. If I threw away our relationship, Mandell would win yet again.

"I already have."

I kissed him. It was only meant to be a quick peck, but he tunnelled his hands through my hair and suddenly, the atmosphere got a whole lot hotter. I finally felt whole again, complete, back where I was meant to be. At least, I did until Blue made a gagging noise behind us.

"Okay, we get it, you're back together. Congratulations. But we have work to do, hotshot, so put her down. Is that coffee?"

"Help yourself."

"And you brought Danishes too? Fine, you can stay."

Garrett kept an arm around my waist as we followed Blue back to Aaron's study, the scene of so much drama last night. Brooke and Deck were both working today, so there were only six of us present, and Aaron opened up the files one at a time for Garrett to view, first the letter and then the videos. With each clip, Garrett's fingers dug harder into my hip. By the time we got to Mandell, I had bruises and Garrett had a face like a thundercloud.

"Do we know who any of the women are?" he asked.

Blue shook her head. "No. But if we release the tape, they might come forward."

"I can see some of those girls being paid players as Samantha alleged, but not the woman with Mandell. She wasn't acting."

"I don't think so either."

"And if you release that tape, her picture's going to end

up all over the news. If she's been working through the trauma as Gracie has, seeing herself like that will set her recovery back years. Maybe even forever. We want revenge, but I don't want another woman to get hurt in the process. People will never look at her the same way again."

"So we blur out her face. This is how we get payback, Dorsey. Graham Mandell had three people killed to prevent this tape from seeing the light of day, and if it's out there in the public domain, he'll have no reason to come after Sara anymore. Plus everyone will know what kind of man he is."

"If you blur out her face, nobody will see the tears. And without a witness coming forward, he'll say it was consensual or some sort of role play. He'll twist it and play the victim. Someone recorded a private moment, he's the innocent party, yada yada yada."

"What about the voters?"

"Maybe they'll care, and maybe they won't. Politics has changed in the past sixteen years."

"Enough for rape not to matter?"

"Capitol Hill has more drama than a soap opera, and Congress, the Senate, and the White House are a three-ring circus. President Harrison's ass has its own TikTok account. A dead guy got elected to the state senate in Wisconsin. Folks in Texas chose an ex-gym teacher who got fired for spying on teenage girls in the shower as their mayor, and the polls barely moved when a congressman from Georgia took his mistress on a luxury vacation in Bermuda while his wife was having chemo. There are conspiracy theories about conspiracy theories, and if Mandell put out a statement saying the Deep State had faked the video, too many people would believe him."

I recalled the Bermuda scandal. The papers had been full of pictures of the congressman's pasty white pot belly as he frolicked in the ocean with a girl barely out of high school, and he'd still kept his seat. Unless the Mandell video was released a day before voters headed to the polls, I had a horrible fear that Garrett might be right. There was a scarily large cross-section of the population who would pat Congressman Mandell on the back for acting like a Real Man and vote for him anyway.

"And Seth Harless would get off scot-free," Aaron pointed out. "There's no evidence against him here."

"What's the penalty for homicide in Oregon?" Garrett asked Aaron. "Ballpark?"

Blue snorted. "Asking for a friend?"

"A premeditated double murder in the first degree? Even with your father's connections, you'd be lucky to see freedom again. Ditto if you're thinking of hiring someone."

I tensed because Garrett sounded alarmingly serious. "No, no, no. Don't even consider it. I just got you back, and I don't want to lose you again. And what about Gracie?"

Garrett sighed. "I'm frustrated, that's all."

"We all are."

"Someone hired the man at the pool house. Is there any news on his identity?"

"Not yet," Colt told him.

"We'll get Harless on something," Luca said. "He's committed two serious crimes that we're aware of, and with the way Mandell acts, there are bound to be more. If we're not trying to maintain the same degree of secrecy now, we can speak with the police in Roseburg and see what shakes loose."

"I can take a look too," Blue offered. "Speak with my guy in DC again."

Garrett's arm tightened around me. "I can hire any additional help you need. I don't care how much it costs or how long it takes—we need to make Mandell and Harless pay."

And I'd be nicer to the security team. Jack Morrow and his men were only doing their jobs, and I'd been rude because I was annoyed at Garrett. Tomorrow, I'd be the one to take them coffee and cookies.

"What if there was another way?" Aaron asked quietly.

Aaron, Luca, Colt, and Blue all looked at each other, and a silent communication passed between them. What did they know that we didn't?

"I'm in," Blue said.

Luca nodded. "Me too."

Colt was more hesitant. "I'd need to review every scrap of evidence we have. It isn't a decision to take lightly."

I couldn't stand it any longer. "What are you talking about?"

"Do you trust that guy?" Luca asked me, meaning Garrett.

We'd both learned from our mistakes. I thought of everything we'd been through together, from the crazy first dates to the magic in the bedroom to the way he'd risked his own life at the pool house, and I nodded. Our path had been rocky, but he was still here. Still fighting for me.

"Yes, I trust him."

Luca came to a decision. "Okay, who wants to do this?"

Aaron took over. "Sara's familiar with some of it already, but over the past year, an alternative justice system has emerged here in Baldwin's Shore. It started when a stranger rescued Brooke from a stalker who'd drugged and abducted her. We nicknamed him the Bad Samaritan, and we thought it was a one-off, but the same person saved Colt in the forest one day when a man turned a gun on him. Took the guy out with a shot to the head from...how far was it?"

"Eight hundred yards," Luca supplied.

Garrett gave a low whistle, so I assumed that meant it was an impressive feat.

"He also located a number of missing cats, although that was small potatoes for him," Aaron continued. "Plus there was one more matter he was involved in at the end of last year."

At the end of last year? That was when...oh! I gasped.

"Do you mean Marianna?"

"We're not exactly certain of what he said or did, but we believe there was some coercion."

"And you think he'd help with the Mandell situation?" Garrett asked. "Why would he do that? Money? You pay him?"

"No, there's no money involved. It's hard to explain. He likes to show off, and he seems almost...playful. When he led us to the cats, it was like a treasure hunt. He drew a map with clues. Plus he's fond of breaking in here and leaving us notes."

"Notes?"

"The last one came in February. The girls went salsa dancing in Coos Bay, and I headed out for beers with Luca. When we arrived home, there was a note on my kitchen counter congratulating us on passing our latest security audit." Aaron shrugged. "Seems nobody can sneak in but him."

"Doesn't that worry you?"

"It did at first, but he made valid points the first several times. And I don't think he means any harm, not to us anyway."

"But what about me?" I asked. "Why would he help me or Gracie when he doesn't even know us?"

"He does know you."

Icy claws needled at my spine. "What?"

"He mentioned you in a note one time."

Garrett didn't look happy about that in the slightest. "Should I beef up security again?"

"No need. It was in a positive light."

"So you're saying that this stranger, this cat-loving vigilante sniper, would somehow get justice for Saralisa and Gracie while the entire legal system fails?"

"I'm saying that I think it's exactly the type of challenge he'd enjoy."

Garrett still looked far from thrilled with the idea, but what choice did we have? I knew from experience that sometimes the wheels of justice didn't only turn slowly; they didn't turn at all.

"In the absence of other options, how do we contact this guy?"

"We don't contact him. If it happens, it happens."

"So we just wait? That's it? We wait?"

"Kind of."

"What does that mean?"

"It means that we've narrowed down his identity to a couple of possibilities, and last time..." Aaron glanced in my direction. "Last time, we planted a few seeds. Made suggestions."

That was insane. "So you're saying you suggested that Marianna wind up in jail, and then by a miracle, she did?"

"We didn't go into that level of detail."

"It was more of a 'we'd like to see justice' approach," Blue explained.

"So he could have given her a slap on the wrist or shot her or anything in between?"

"Pretty much, yeah. He did whatever he thought was appropriate."

Had sending Marianna to jail been appropriate? Undoubtedly yes. She'd deserved more, if I was honest, but the Bad Samaritan had shown restraint. Whoever he was, he wasn't a bloodthirsty lunatic.

"And if we planted these seeds, as Aaron puts it, there would be no way to stop him?" I asked.

"Not that we're aware of."

"I'm in," Garrett said. "Fuck it, I'm in. Let him do his worst. Mandell is a wolf in sheep's clothing. For years, he sat at our dinner table, *opposite his daughter*, and pretended he hadn't torn our family apart."

"Who are the possible candidates?" I whispered. "Who in this town would be capable?"

I thought they'd keep that to themselves, but Luca surprised me.

"Deck or Nico," he said, and then I understood. I understood why Deck had been with us at the house yesterday, why Luca had wanted him to stay while we opened those files. He'd been planting seeds already.

He'd known it would come to this.

Deck or Nico... I knew both of them, not well enough to call them friends, but well enough to be shocked by Luca's revelation. Deck had done work at The Lookout. He sold sculptures in the Craft Cabin. Sometimes I bumped into him running when I went for a walk along the beach. And Nico, he seemed so smooth, so polished. Over the past several years, I'd had a number of meetings with him about events at the Peninsula, and he'd never been anything but courteous.

Neither of them had given off any dangerous vibes, and until now, I would have quite happily spent time alone with either of them, for professional reasons only, of course. More wolves in sheep's clothing.

I thought of Congressman Mandell and the stories I'd heard, and then I thought of Seth Harless and his cold, dead eyes. I thought of Gracie's terror and Marlie's happiness, only possible because her mom had done her best to shelter her from the awful truth about her DNA.

And again, I nodded.

"I'm in too."

38

SARA

Three weeks passed. Colt and Luca reviewed the evidence, including an off-the-record interview with Gracie. Tiny seeds were planted in two separate plots, although I felt guilty that we might be asking Nico to get involved, seeing as he'd dealt with quite enough problems already in the past month. His new girlfriend had brought quite the shitstorm with her to Baldwin's Shore, which at least meant people had stopped gossiping about the pool house incident.

On the positive side, it seemed more likely than ever that the Bad Samaritan was either Nico or Deck. Even though Nico swore he'd had a conversation with the man on one drama-filled afternoon, Luca was convinced it was a cover story, that Nico was trying to throw people off the scent.

I incorporated SBF Events with the Oregon Business Registry, and on the days I wasn't filling in at the Craft Cabin, I plotted out my professional future. Oh, and Garrett bought a house in Baldwin's Shore, because apparently that was a normal thing that people did when their bank balance was bigger than a phone number.

It was only a small place, and it needed renovation—the roof leaked in the kitchen and a family of raccoons had made themselves at home under the porch—but it was cute, and the view over the ocean soothed my soul. I'd only been a tiny bit annoyed when I found out the deed was in my name. Garrett said he wanted me to have a home, one that didn't come with strings attached. Although there would be rope. And handcuffs. He didn't want to stay at the family estate in Roseburg right now, not when Graham Mandell might show up, not when he couldn't throat-punch that slimeball.

As part of our deadly pact, we'd agreed to stay silent about everything we knew, at least for a few weeks. Aaron had tucked the hard drive away in his safe. Garrett had called off his investigators. Jack Morrow and his team were still on my tail, but now I found their presence reassuring rather than exasperating.

And we waited.

Johannes had returned to Oregon, and I finally met him and his girlfriend, a statuesque blonde who spoke six languages and appeared to be allergic to underwear. Johannes offered to paint me. Garrett offered to break his nose.

Gracie sent me shoes, the most beautiful dance shoes, blue and sparkly and modelled on the pair I'd worn the night I met Charming. I wore them on a trip to Casa de Salsa, and while my toes survived two hours of dancing, in the battle of migraine versus mojito, the alcohol won. Charming carried me to the car, and a chauffeur drove us back to the Peninsula, which was where we were staying until our new home was ready to move into. Yes, the Peninsula. After some consideration, I'd decided that if Nico really was this Bad Samaritan, then we were probably safer there than anywhere else, especially since he knew what Seth Harless looked like. Brie was back in town too, and she had her own security. Jack Morrow was coordinating with Kasper, the head of her team, so we didn't end up with all the men in one place.

The day before yesterday, I'd met Parker for lunch in Coos Bay, Italian this time, and caught up on the latest gossip about the twins. Apparently, they'd been served with the lawsuit Parker was expecting, and both Aaron and Asa Phillips had declined to represent them. They were stuck with a guy from Coquille who kept asking difficult questions like *Did you read the email from March seventeenth that listed the dietary requirements and included details of the peanut allergy?* I could have answered that for them: of course they hadn't. Operation Inheritance was apparently on track apart from the tricky problem of EJ.

Today, I was at the Coffee House with Brooke for lunch when our phones pinged, first hers and then mine. The message was the same.

AARON

Dinner at my place tonight?

A moment later, I got another message.

GARRETT

Aaron wants us to go to dinner at Deals on Wheels.

Even though the car dealership had closed years ago, everyone still called the building by its old name, including Aaron and Brooke.

She grinned at me. "If Aaron's cooking, the answer is always yes."

"Maybe I shouldn't have had that third donut."

Having a social life instead of merely facilitating other people's was a novelty. I was still settling into this new normal, but I never wanted it to end.

"Before I take the lasagne out of the oven, I need to show you something." Aaron beckoned us toward his study. There were six of us there for dinner tonight—Aaron and Blue, Brooke and Luca, and Garrett and me. "It's good news and bad news."

"Can we just skip the bad part?" I asked.

"It's kind of the same thing."

He punched in the code to open the safe, and the first thing I saw was the empty space where the hard drive had once been. In its place was a note, a single folded piece of paper with a smiley face on the outside.

"Where is it? Where's the hard drive?"

"Gone."

"Gone? Gone where?"

He removed the note and unfolded it. There were only two words, written in neat black capital letters.

BE PATIENT

"The Bad Samaritan took it."

"Are you serious? Out of the safe?"

"Unfortunately. Blue copied the files into the cloud, but the drive itself is gone."

"How did he get in? I mean, he broke into the building and then the safe? What about the cameras? The alarm?"

"The log shows a remote deactivation for thirty minutes

yesterday afternoon. He hacked the system, then picked the lock on one of the doors and cracked the safe."

Garrett squeezed my hand so tight it hurt. "Are we in any danger here tonight?"

"No more than any other night. And the good news is that the Bad Samaritan is going to act. All we need to do is wait a little longer."

"Maybe we should wait somewhere other than Baldwin's Shore?" Garrett suggested. "Cinderella, how do you feel about taking a vacation?"

"I'm not going to say no."

"When we get back to the Peninsula, you're packing a bag."

Aaron chuckled. "Thought you might have that reaction, and in your position, I'd probably do the same. But before you flee the country, let's go eat. The dough balls are drying out in the oven. Can someone open a bottle of wine?"

"I'll do it," I offered.

And I'd probably drink most of it myself.

39

GARRETT

*S*aralisa wanted to visit her friend Marcin in Poland, so we went to visit her friend Marcin in Poland. I'd never been to Gdańsk, only to Drawsko Pomorskie for a period of training when I was in the Marines, and this trip was far more civilised. No dorms, no shared showers, no wet-behind-the-ears trainee mistaking a live grenade for a dummy and fuck, that had been a hair-raising moment.

At the beginning of June, temperatures were in the low sixties, pleasant for walking but not sunbathing weather. The firm that provided Jack Morrow and his team had an office in Poland, and I'd engaged them to find us a secure rental property. I didn't think Mandell would come after Saralisa overseas, especially since we'd mothballed the investigation, but I wasn't taking any chances.

"Home sweet temporary home."

I unlocked the door of our apartment and ushered Saralisa inside. The security team would base themselves in the unit next door, and I hoped to fuck the soundproofing was up to scratch.

"This is beautiful."

"No, you're beautiful. This is pleasant."

Three bedrooms, a large, open-plan living area, and a quiet office so we could both work remotely—it was everything we needed. And she was everything *I* needed.

Marcin had invited us to stay with him and his boyfriend, but since we weren't sure how long we'd be spending in Europe, we hadn't felt comfortable imposing. We'd see enough of them in the dance lessons Saralisa had signed us up for. Plus we were having dinner with them this evening—Marcin and Andriy, plus Marcin's father and his fourth wife. Saralisa was looking forward to it, and so was I, but first, I had to do something about my aching cock.

Convincing Saralisa to join the mile-high club would take a few more flights and possibly a private jet. I'd had to settle for getting her off in first class somewhere over the Atlantic, but she'd been too nervous to return the favour.

And now she was running around the apartment like a kid, opening all the doors and drawers. Four months ago, she wouldn't have done this. No, she'd have sat in the corner, quiet, and accepted whatever life threw at her.

"They left us a bottle of champagne. And chocolates! I love it here already."

The bed should also be covered in rose petals, and I waited for her to find them. It didn't take long.

"Oh my... Did you do this?"

"Do what?"

A moment passed. "You'll have to come and see."

My lips twitched with a smile as I headed for the master bedroom, pulling my shirt over my head as I went. Yeah, I'd see. And then I'd come. My belt was undone, my cock half-hard by the time I saw her naked on the bed, arms resting above her head.

"Turn over."

She did as she was told, stretching languidly like a cat. That was another way she'd changed—shyness took a back seat to confidence these days, although she'd happily cede control in the bedroom. My perfect woman. Right now, her ass was pretty as a picture, just waiting for my palm. I toed off my boots, dropped my jeans to the floor, and knelt on the bed behind her.

"Not fast enough."

"Sorry, sir." Saralisa turned her head and bit that lip, knowing exactly what it did to me. "Show me how bad I've been."

She wasn't even a tiny bit sorry, but I gave her what she wanted. Her ass turned deliciously pink, and those breathy gasps made me throb. This woman was mine in every way.

"I need you," she choked.

Her pink pussy lips gaped open, and she got me. Hard. Bare. She was on birth control now, not that I'd be unhappy if she ended up pregnant. I wanted kids someday, and I wanted them with her. She'd agreed to the "someday." When her new business was up and running, when Mandell was out of the picture and her inheritance was finalised, then we'd start thinking about a family.

For now, it was just the two of us, and I gave in to the urge and slammed into her, knowing she'd stop me if she was uncomfortable. So far, she'd only used her safe word once, and that was when I'd been tickling her feet with a feather and she was giggling uncontrollably. This rough, hard pounding was precisely what she liked.

I didn't need to ask whether she was close; I knew she was. Saralisa didn't hide her feelings in bed. I reached for her clit and circled that perfect nub with a fingertip, following her over the edge as she milked my cock.

"I love you," she told me, her voice weak from exertion.

"I love you too."

And someday, I was going to marry her. Not yet, but someday.

"It was our first competition. We were...seven?" Marcin said, and Saralisa nodded. "We were seven, and she borrowed a dress from the dance school, but—"

She buried her head in her hands. "Do you have to tell this story?"

"If you prefer, I could tell the one where you found a box of candy in your dad's closet and—"

"On second thought, tell the first one."

"So we were dancing a Viennese waltz, and I trod on the edge of the skirt, and *riiiiiiip*. She was standing there in her leotard, and I didn't know whether to carry on dancing, or pull the fabric back up, or just apologise profusely."

"What was the decision?" I asked.

"Saralisa dragged me away from the skirt, and her mouth was set in...you know, that little line, and she told me off for missing out the steps."

"I was competitive, okay? I still think we could have won if you'd just smiled through it."

The way she always had? "I'm curious what happened with the candy now."

Her cheeks reddened. "It was Mom's Valentine's gift. Cherry liquors. I ate nearly the whole box before Dad found me, and I ended up puking in the emergency room. Even now, I'm not fond of cherries. But since we're doing embarrassing stories, why don't we discuss the time Marcin took his mom's make-up to dance class and nearly blinded himself with a mascara wand in the bathroom?"

Marcin batted his eyelashes. "I've improved my skills, don't you think?"

"Only because I taught you," Andriy said.

The ribbing was good-natured, and Marcin was the only man I'd ever met who could carry off eyeliner. His father, Eryk, acted warmly toward Saralisa, and it was clear he'd once cared deeply for her and still did. Losing Marcin's friendship in childhood had been one more tragedy she'd suffered.

Before dessert, Eryk held up his glass in a toast. "To friendships old and new. I'm so glad we were finally able to reconnect, little Saralisa. We all missed you when you went to Oregon."

"I missed you too."

"Marcin begged us to bring you to live with us, and we did offer, but your grandfather wouldn't hear of it. He said you needed the fresh start. An authoritative man."

That was the first Saralisa had heard of any offer; I could tell by the way her spine stiffened. And if I had to guess, I'd have said she would have been a hell of a lot happier in the Baluch household.

"Authoritative? Yes, he was."

"We never stopped thinking of you. Until you turned eighteen, we sent the Christmas and birthday cards, but then... We thought you had moved on. Hoped you had moved on."

"I never received any cards."

"I always wondered if that might be the case. Maybe your grandfather threw them away, or your uncle? There was no love lost between him and your father."

"Dad told you that?"

"We were friends. Of course, we told each other many things." He chuckled, patting the fourth Mrs. Baluch's hand. She'd barely said a word during dinner. "All the secrets we didn't want our wives to know. Nothing bad," he added quickly. "Your mom used to worry about Pete's cholesterol constantly after her own mother's heart problems, and he used to appreciate a good medium-rare steak."

"Every time I mentioned Dad, EJ got annoyed, so I stopped talking about him. Do you know why they didn't get along?"

"As with so many feuds, it had to do with a woman. I don't know her name, but Pete found EJ in the back of a car with her when EJ was sixteen. The way I understand it, the woman had been drinking too much, far too much, and EJ was, how should I say...taking advantage?"

EJ had tried to rape an unconscious woman? That's what Eryk was saying? This was shades of Mandell all over again.

"Pete got her out of there?" I asked.

"He took her home, and he also told his father." Eryk sucked in a breath. "Who paid off the young lady and made EJ's life very difficult for the next six months. Pete called it slave labour, but your grandfather called it atonement. EJ never forgave Pete for telling tales."

Saralisa was looking green, and it had nothing to do with the lighting. "Dad did the right thing."

"I agree with you, but that wasn't the end of it. A year later, they were both going to the junior prom, and EJ's date declined to accompany him at the last moment because she heard what happened in that car. EJ blamed Pete for talking, but it wasn't him. For better or worse, he protected his family. It was probably the girl herself. Pete said she had a big mouth."

"Do you know who she was?" Saralisa asked, and her

voice had gone quiet, the way it tended to do when she was trying to cope with bad news.

Eryk shook his head. "I don't believe her name was ever mentioned. Anyhow, EJ had been drinking, and when Pete left with his date, EJ took his grandfather's car and tried to run them off the road. Ended up crashing the vehicle into a tree. After that, Pete decided to go travelling."

"The whole family is toxic," Saralisa whispered.

"Yes, that's exactly what Pete said, word for word. Saralisa, I'm so very sorry for your loss. When I initially heard about the crash, I'll admit my thoughts went straight to your uncle. I even contacted the police in case there was a link."

"But they didn't find one?"

"I assume they quickly ruled him out because they declared it a tragic accident just a few days later. The detective who came to see me said the weather conditions were poor that night."

Could there be a connection? No, that was farfetched. Pete Forlani had been out of EJ's life for over a decade by that point, Saralisa had recognised the culprit as Harless, and Claire had written a posthumous statement. Mandell was behind the incident. Wasn't he?

I'd always thought my family was fucked up, but the Baldwins were in a whole other league.

Eryk raised his glass again. "Enough talk of the past. Let's drink to the future. And eat! This is sernik, a traditional Polish dessert. It's said that the king brought the recipe back with him after victory against the Turks at the Battle of Vienna."

I leaned across to Saralisa. "You okay?" I asked softly.

"Perhaps more okay than I've ever been."

That was my girl. She was strong, stronger than she even

realised herself. I was in awe of both her and Gracie for not only surviving the lives they'd been forced to lead but also coming out on top.

In the future, they'd both have my support.

And maybe they'd have the Bad Samaritan fighting in their corner too.

40

SARA

Saralisa's to-do list:

- Visit the gardens at Versailles.

- Pick up gifts for the girls.

- Dance the night away at Le Balajo.

- Drink all the champagne.

- Live out another filthy fantasy.

The call came at four p.m., Paris time. Garrett and I were sitting outside a cute café in the Montmartre, watching the world go by. Okay, Garrett was replying to emails from Tawna, who was holding the fort admirably back in Roseburg, and I was watching the world go by.

We'd spent two weeks in Poland with Marcin, dancing and walking on the beach and exploring Gdańsk. Then we'd flown to Valetia to meet with Brie for a weekend since she was in town, and after that, we'd hopped on a plane to Milan, rented a car, and driven through Italy, Switzerland, and France. Because Garrett had made the arrangements, the car was a Ferrari, and our luggage was riding with the security team.

It had been the most amazing six weeks of my life, this period of limbo as we waited for the Bad Samaritan to do something, anything.

And now Parker wanted to speak with me.

"Isn't this a little early for a chat?" I asked. What was the time over there? Seven a.m.?

"Ding-dong, the warlock's dead."

"What? I don't understand."

"Five minutes ago, the cops took EJ away in handcuffs."

"*What?* I mean, why? Colt and Luca arrested him?" I asked, just to make sure.

"Not them. The state police. Homicide was mentioned, which is quite ironic because he keeps saying how much he misses Marianna. Maybe they could share a cell?"

Garrett was watching me now. "You okay?"

"Yes. No. I don't know. Parker, you're gonna have to start from the beginning."

"Sure, I would if I knew what that was. The cops knocked on the door just after six, I showed them through to EJ's room because I'm a helpful, law-abiding citizen, and they read him his rights. Do you think I should call a lawyer? I'd happily let him rot in jail, but appearances..."

Homicide? My brain was still catching up. And I agreed with Parker—after hearing from Eryk what EJ had done to my dad, how he'd driven him from Baldwin's Shore, I wanted him to stay in jail for as long as possible. I'd been wrong. Parker did give gifts after all, so many gifts.

"Could you call a really bad lawyer?"

Parker gave a rare chuckle. "I'll see what I can do."

"And I'll call Luca. Maybe he's heard something about

the arrest. Oh, wait—he's actually calling me. I'll get back to you, okay?"

"Who got arrested?" Garrett asked as I juggled calls.

"EJ. Shh. Hey, Luca."

Garrett waved down a passing waiter and asked for a bottle of champagne with two glasses. A knot of tension tightened in my stomach because what was this about?

"How's France?" Luca asked.

"It's wonderful. We went to the Moulin Rouge last night."

"Is that the thing with the windmill and the strippers?"

"The dancers are only topless, and it's very tasteful." But who cared at this moment? "Is it true? Did EJ get arrested?"

Luca barked out a laugh. "The state police let us know 'as a courtesy' after they took him away."

"What did he do?"

"Therein lies the question." Luca blew out a long breath. "They arrested him for arranging the murder of your parents."

All the air whooshed out of my lungs. "*What?*"

I was saying that a lot today.

"A week ago, a man walked into a police station in Roseburg and confessed to running your parents off the road sixteen and a half years ago. Said he'd recently found God, and he needed to get his sins off his chest. He claims EJ hired him for the job. Apparently, suspicions were raised at the time regarding EJ's involvement, but nobody followed up until now."

"And the man was…"

"Seth Harless," Luca finished. "They're both in jail."

"Oh my gosh."

"Harless claimed EJ and your dad had a fight a couple of weeks before the accident. Is that true?"

"Yes, at Grandpa's birthday party, but...but..."

"The Bad Samaritan moves in mysterious ways," Luca said. "I need to go, but I expect you'll get a call from the state police soon. I gave them your number."

Holy smokes.

I hung up in a daze, and Garrett reached across the table for my hand. "Tell me."

I repeated what Luca had said, and saying the words out loud didn't make it any more real. EJ had hired Seth Harless to kill my parents? But what about the videos? What about Mandell? What about the letter from my mom?

"Do you believe it?" Garrett asked.

"No. No, I don't think I do. What does this mean? Congressman Mandell gets away with everything?"

The waiter arrived with the champagne, looked at Garrett's frown and then my tight expression, and hesitated with his hand on the cork.

"Sir, do you still want this?"

"Ask the lady."

Harless was in jail. It *was* a victory, just a smaller one than I'd hoped for. And if ever there was news that called for alcohol, it was today's revelation.

"Pour away."

Once the waiter had departed, Garrett squeezed my hand and took a sip from his glass. "What does it mean? It means we have to be patient."

With Harless out of the picture, we decided to return to Baldwin's Shore. Parker had been left in the lurch at Baldwin Estates, and I agreed to help out in the office while he interviewed a handyman to replace EJ. The judge had deemed my uncle a flight risk, so he was still sitting in the county jail, awaiting trial on murder in the first degree for soliciting Harless to run my parents off the road.

Garrett and I moved into our little home overlooking the ocean, and I kept myself busy planning Kiki's birthday party and a handful of other events. I didn't need to worry about marketing. Plenty of people wanted to curry favour with the Dorsey family, and what better way to do that than to hire Garrett's new girlfriend to plan their next shindig? It all felt slightly nepotistic, but at the same time, I wasn't going to turn down work. Soon, I'd need to hire more staff, but for now, I was being picky over which clients I took on. No spoiled brats, no bridezillas, no frat boys. Today, I was working from the terrace at the Peninsula while I waited for Brooke, Addy, Blue, and Brie to arrive for lunch. Living the dream rather than the nightmare.

My phone pinged as I sifted through résumés and email enquiries.

PARKER

I found a replacement for EJ.

When is he starting?

PARKER

Next week. And he's a she.

Oh, really? I had a hundred questions.

Meet for lunch tomorrow?

PARKER

Coffee House at 1 p.m.

With EJ safely out of the way, there was no need for us to drive to Coos Bay anymore, and the twins were keeping a low profile. LKB Events was imploding thanks to Peanutgate —the victim's husband had told just about everyone in the county what happened to his wife.

> BRIE
>
> Running a few minutes late. Can you order me a house salad?

Brooke slid into the seat opposite, and Addy sat stiffly beside her. Thanks to the drama with Nico's girlfriend, she'd spent a while in the hospital, and although she was putting a brave face on things, the pain was obvious when she let her guard down. I didn't dare to give her a hug, so I offered a smile instead.

"How are you feeling?"

"Great!"

"Really?"

Brooke shook her head. "She's just saying that so her mom will let her move back home."

"At first, all the attention was nice. You know, having people make casseroles and bring me candy. But I've put on six pounds, and I'm sick of watching game show reruns."

"You can always come over to our place if you need a break." *Our place.* The words sounded weird, but a good weird.

"I just miss having my own space. Heck, I even miss going to work."

"There might be some shifts at the Craft Cabin available now that Saralisa's starting her own business," Brooke offered.

"After you spent the whole ride here telling me how crazy it was there this morning?"

Crazy? The Craft Cabin was usually an oasis of calm,

unless Paulo was tripping over the cat, anyway. "What happened?"

"A tour bus full of seniors broke down near Main Street, and most of them decided to visit the Craft Cabin while they waited for the engine to get fixed. We almost sold out of yarn. I called Everly in to help, and I thought she was gonna have a panic attack when they all headed to the register at the same time."

"Did they get on their way?"

"Not yet, but after Paulo gave them a quick lesson in arm-knitting, they went next door to the Coffee House, so they're Mary's problem now. What are you having for lunch?"

"Just a sandwich. Brie wants the house salad."

"But we're having dessert, right?"

"Oh, yes, of course."

Addy began fanning herself. "Don't look now, but hot guy alert."

"Where?"

"Okay, two hot guys. One of them is yours."

Garrett had left early for a business meeting, and now I turned to see him heading toward us with a dark-haired man in tow. Addy was right about the heat factor. If I hadn't been very much in love with the perfect partner already, I might have drooled into my soft drink.

Garrett bent to kiss me on the cheek. "Just passing through. This is Lewis—we went to school together. Lewis, meet Saralisa and her friends Brooke and Addy."

This was Lewis? Garrett had asked me if I minded his old friend coming to stay for a few weeks, and of course I'd said it was okay, but holy heck, he'd said nothing about him being so easy on the eye. Lewis shook hands with all three of us, and Brooke kept staring, even though she was nearly married. Being that handsome couldn't be healthy. What if he distracted a driver? Or caused someone to walk into a wall?

He stepped backward and landed squarely on Blue's foot, and it seemed one of us at least was immune to his charms.

"Watch where you're going, asshole."

Garrett's smile grew wider. "And this is Blue. She's a real ray of sunshine."

"Shut up," she growled as she took a seat.

"Bad day?" Brooke asked.

"I saw my ex outside court, and my stun gun was out of battery."

Lewis's eyes widened, and he took another step back. This time, he nearly took out a waitress, but fortunately, she was quick on her feet and hopped sideways.

"Damn, I do apologise." He steadied her, and she practically swooned. "Nice to meet you folks."

"He's so pretty," Addy said wistfully as the two men walked away. "I need to go to the bathroom."

Blue snorted. "Pretty clumsy. Do you really need to go to the bathroom, or do you just want to stare at his ass for a while longer?"

"I plead the Fifth."

Addy got up carefully and headed after Lewis as Blue snorted.

"She must be feeling better if she's hunting dick again. Anyone want to share a bottle of wine, or should I drink it all myself?"

"Isn't it a bit early for that?"

"Somewhere in the world, it's happy hour."

In New York, in fact. I'd barely taken a sip of my rosé when Gracie phoned.

"Did you see the news?" she asked.

"No, I'm in a restaurant."

"Find a TV. Then find a bottle of champagne." She gave a long exhale. "My gosh, I can't believe it's over."

"What's over? What do you mean?"

I found out two minutes later when Blue convinced the bartender to hand over the remote. It didn't take much channel-hopping to land on the news.

Police have released the name of the man killed in a fiery crash in northern Virginia last night. Graham Mandell, who served the people of Oregon in Congress for the past twenty years, left the road in what is understood to be a single-car accident. The late-model Lexus was found by a passing motorist, and although emergency services were fast to arrive on the scene, it was sadly too late for the occupant of the vehicle. During his time on Capitol Hill, Congressman Mandell put forward a number of bills to...

I tuned out the reporter. Mandell was dead? Really gone? Holy heck. Brooke looked as shocked as I felt, but Blue's expression was more admiration than anything else.

"That...is fucked up. And also damned impressive."

As the details began to sink in, I had to agree. Mandell had left the road in northern Virginia, the same way as my parents had, and the Bad Samaritan had made my mom's last wish come true. He'd burned. Was that a coincidence, or was the Bad Samaritan psychic as well as smart and deadly? I was shaking. I was actually shaking.

And relieved.

And free.

I waved the bartender across. "Please could you bring a bottle of your best champagne?"

Gracie was right. It was over.

And as usual, Blue's mind was racing ahead. "Did you know Deck's out of town? I wanted him to fix the railing on my stairs, but he said he wouldn't be back until later this week."

Brooke's mouth formed a perfect O. "So you think...?"

The bartender returned with a bottle. "Ms. Baldwin-Forlani?"

I hadn't realised he knew my name. "Yes?"

"The boss says this is on the house."

"What? Why?"

"He didn't give any details, ma'am."

Blue dug an elbow into my side. "You mean Nico? We should thank him in person. Is he here?"

"He's unavailable right now, but I'll be sure to pass on your appreciation. How many glasses do you need? Four? Are those gentlemen with you?"

I spun to see Garrett approaching with Lewis trailing behind, and Garrett's concerned expression said he'd seen the news. He took his place by my side and kissed my forehead.

"You okay?"

"Today, I'm better than okay." I turned back to the bartender. "Seven glasses. We'll need seven glasses."

I thought it was over.

I thought I was safe.

The Bad Samaritan had done my dirty work, but I should have known there'd be a catch. A price. I found out what it was when Garrett and I arrived at our little house by the sea and found an envelope on the kitchen table. We'd installed an alarm system. Garrett had insisted on it. But all the defences in the world meant nothing to the Bad Samaritan; I knew that far too well.

Lewis had come back with us—he was working on a research project for his boss, something to do with precious stones, and he needed to be near Coos Bay. We'd barely notice he was there, he'd promised. Unlikely.

"Is this yours?" Garrett asked him. They must have swung by the house earlier because Lewis had left his suitcase in the hallway.

"Is what mine?"

"This envelope."

There was no name on the front, just a smiley face. My chest seized. Even before Garrett opened it, I knew who had been in our house. Our *home*. The doodle matched the note in Aaron's safe.

Lewis shook his head. "No, it's not mine. Is everything okay?"

Garrett forced a smile, and I knew it took an effort because every other part of him was tense. "Yeah, it's fine. Probably a note from the builder."

"Give it to me," I said. "I'll open it."

The message was for me. It was my problem the Bad Samaritan had solved. My life he'd fixed. I slid out a single sheet of paper and read the single verse written in now-familiar handwriting.

I'VE BANISHED YOUR DEMONS
AND YOUR FUTURE IS BRIGHT
BUT ADDY'S STILL HURTING
YOU CAN HELP TO MAKE THINGS RIGHT

That was it? That was the price? The breath I'd been

holding rushed out of me in a *whoosh* because that really wasn't much of a cost at all. Of course I'd help Addy, and maybe I knew how to do it? She'd been working as a PA-slash-accounting assistant, and I'd need help to get SBF Events established. I already had one employee—Nico's girlfriend had a background in events and entertainment, and she'd offered to help out part-time. If Addy was interested, I could create a role for her.

"I can offer her a job," I said at the same time as Garrett said, "We can give her a job."

I loved that we always thought on the same wavelength.

"Weird note," Lewis said, reading over my shoulder. "Addy's the pretty blonde, right?"

"*No*," Garrett told him, his tone sharp.

Huh? "Yes, she *is* the pretty blonde."

Lewis laughed. "Garrett's just telling me she's off limits, but don't worry; I'll behave."

He sauntered off, whistling a quiet tune as he headed for the stairs. I didn't know much about Lewis other than the fact that he clearly had money, but he seemed polite enough.

Garrett watched him go, a dark look on his face. "Well, this should be interesting..."

A FEW WORDS FROM THE BAD SAMARITAN…

Curious about the Bad Samaritan's methods?
I've included a few of their thoughts in a bonus chapter,
FREE to members of my reader group.

You can join here:
www.elise-noble.com/b4rbecue

WHAT'S NEXT?

My next book will be a Blackwood Security vs. Baldwin's Shore crossover novel, *Secrets from the Past*...

Years have passed since Nico Belinsky last saw Kaylin La Rocca, but he can't forget the girl he once thought of as a sister. Or the fact that she's wanted for murder. When Emmy Black, a woman who lives up to her name by walking on the dark side, offers a favour, Nico tasks her with searching for his old friend.

He's playing with fire in more ways than one—not only does he risk stirring up a hornets' nest, but the last time he saw Kaylin, his feelings toward her were anything but brotherly.

Kaylin La Rocca fell for a man out of a romance novel, but it turned out to be more of a horror story. Now she's his prisoner, a pretty little princess trapped in a glittering tower. She dreams of rescue, but any potential prince will have to face not only the cops but the villain who's claimed her as his own. Can Nico and Emmy rescue her from the devil's clutches and prove that happily ever afters do exist?

For more details:
https://www.elise-noble.com/secrets-from-the-past

If you haven't read any of the Blackwood Security books yet, why not start for FREE with *Pitch Black*?

After the owner of a security company is murdered, his sharp-edged wife goes on the run. Forced to abandon everything she holds dear—her home, her friends, her job in special ops—assassin Diamond builds a new life for herself in England. As Ashlyn Hale, she meets Luke, a handsome local who makes her realise just how lonely she is.

Yet, even in the sleepy village of Lower Foxford, the dark side of life dogs Diamond's trail when the unthinkable strikes. Forced out of hiding, she races against time to save those she cares about.

For more details:
www.elise-noble.com/pitch-black

If you enjoyed *A Secret to Die For*, please consider leaving a review.

For an author, every review is incredibly important. Not only do they make us feel warm and fuzzy inside, readers consider them when making their decision whether or not to buy a book. Even a line saying you enjoyed the book or what your favourite part was helps a lot.

WANT TO STALK ME?

For updates on my new releases, giveaways, and other random stuff, you can sign up for my newsletter on my website:
www.elise-noble.com

If you're on Facebook, you might also like to join Team Blackwood for exclusive giveaways, sneak previews, and book-related chat. Be the first to find out about new stories, and you might even see your name or one of your suggestions make it into print!

And if you'd like to read my books for FREE, you can also find details of how to join my advance review team.

Would you like to join Team Blackwood?

www.elise-noble.com/team-blackwood

facebook.com/EliseNobleAuthor

x.com/EliseANoble

instagram.com/elise_noble

goodreads.com/elisenoble

bookbub.com/authors/elise-noble

tiktok.com/@EliseNobleWrites

Chimera

The Devil and the Deep Blue Sea (2024)

Blue Moon (2024)

Blackwood Elements

Oxygen

Lithium

Carbon

Rhodium

Platinum

Lead

Copper

Bronze

Nickel

Hydrogen

Out of Their Elements (novella)

Blackwood UK

Joker in the Pack

Cherry on Top

Roses are Dead

Shallow Graves

Indigo Rain

Pass the Parcel (TBA)

Blackwood Casefiles

Stolen Hearts

Burning Love (TBA)

Baldwin's Shore

Dirty Little Secrets

Secrets, Lies, and Family Ties

Buried Secrets

A Secret to Die For

Blackwood Security vs. Baldwin's Shore

Secret Weapon

Secrets from the Past (2023)

Blackstone House

Hard Lines

Blurred Lines (novella)

Hard Tide

Hard Limits

Hard Luck (TBA)

Hard Code (TBA)

The Electi

Cursed

Spooked

Possessed

Demented

Judged

The Planes

A Vampire in Vegas

A Devil in the Dark (TBA)

The Trouble Series

Trouble in Paradise

Nothing but Trouble

24 Hours of Trouble

The Happy Ever After Series

A Very Happy Christmas (novella)

A Very Happy Valentine (2024)

Standalone

Life

Coco du Ciel

Twisted (short stories)

Books with clean versions available (no swearing and no on-the-page sex)

Pitch Black

Into the Black

Forever Black

Gold Rush

Gray is My Heart

Audiobooks

Black is My Heart (Diamond & Snow - Prequel)

Pitch Black

Into the Black

Forever Black

Gold Rush

Gray is My Heart

Neon (novella)

Dirty Little Secrets (2023)

9 781912 888726